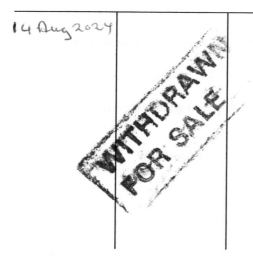

"Another masterpiece in the series. The DCI Ryan mysteries are superb, with very realistic characters and wonderful plots. They are a joy to read!"

OTHER BOOKS BY LJ ROSS

THE DCI RYAN MYSTERIES IN ORDER:

THE ALEXANDER GREGORY THRILLERS IN ORDER:

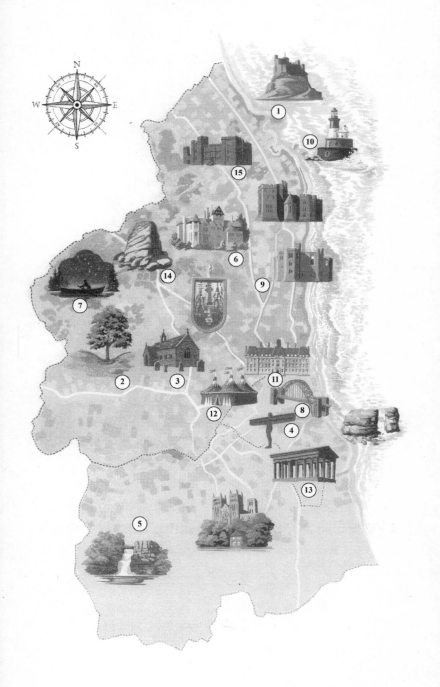

THE HERMITAGE

A DCI RYAN MYSTERY

LJ ROSS

ISBN: 978-1-912310-09-8

First published in 2018 by LJ Ross

This edition published in September 2020 by Dark Skies Publishing

Author photo by Gareth Iwan Jones

Cover layout by Stuart Bache

Cover artwork and map by Andrew Davidson

Typeset by Riverside Publishing Solutions Limited

Printed and bound by CPI Goup (UK) Limited

MIX
Paper | Supporting
responsible forestry
FSC
www.fsc.org   FSC® C171272

"Hatred is blind and anger deaf: the one who pours himself a cup of vengeance is likely to drink a bitter draught."

—*Le Comte de Monte-Cristo*, Alexandre Dumas

PROLOGUE

Wednesday, 21ˢᵗ February

Warkworth, Northumberland

The river was silent on the night Edward Charon died.

Barely a whisper of breeze stirred the long reeds brushing against its muddied banks and the water was eerily still; a glassy mirror broken only by the ripple of the ferryman's oars as he made his way towards the hermitage. The air was bitterly cold after a long northern winter and the old man tucked his chin further beneath his overcoat to stave off the chill.

His eyes darted here and there, searching the shadows of the trees and peering into the darkness that had fallen quickly since the tourists left. He'd watched them go, chattering and squawking like magpies, trampling along the worn path back towards the ruined castle that dwarfed the landscape from its craggy hilltop. He glanced up at it now, tracing its murky silhouette against the ink-blue sky and his movements became jerky, sending waves across the moonlit water as he laboured.

The sooner he finished, the sooner he could go home.

When he clocked off, he'd make his way back to the cottage he'd bought a few months before. Maybe he'd even wander down to the pub at the end of the road and have a pint. He could almost taste the sweet, amber liquid and his throat ran dry at the prospect of oblivion; of the joy of not having to think.

Or to remember.

He cast his eyes across to the other side of the River Coquet, where a dim light shone through the undergrowth. He frowned, wondering how the light had come to be there. The hermitage had not been equipped with solar-powered lighting, the trappings of modern life seeming too much of an anachronism. The old priest's dwelling had been carved into the cliff-face on the river's northern bank hundreds of years ago and was accessible only by boat, to preserve the sanctuary of its surroundings.

Once, a hermit had lived there, but nobody occupied it now unless he counted the thousands of people who visited each year to catch a glimpse of another world through the scattered remnants of the past. He rowed them across the water and they peered at the worn carvings on the walls, *ummed* and *ahhed* and shuffled their feet before he ushered them out and back across the river again, to their ordinary lives.

That was the sum of his existence now.

His jaw clenched as he thought of the cottage with its bare walls and freezer full of microwave meals. Once, there had been fine dining and wine tasting; there had been tailored suits and expensive holidays. He had been *somebody*.

It didn't matter now. He wouldn't think of it.

He turned back to the light glinting across the water and felt uneasy. His hands gripped the oars, the boat slowing to a glide as he warred with himself.

Turn back, his mind whispered.

And yet, it was barely four-thirty. In the distance, he could hear faint sounds of life in the village beyond the river bend. It was foolish to imagine spectres lurking in the darkness, roaming the riverbank.

He let out a short, nervous laugh.

"Soft bastard," he muttered, and picked up his oars with renewed vigour.

He would not be ruled by fear. He might lock and bar the doors of his cottage but that was good sense and nothing more. You could never be too careful, could you? And if he liked a drink to help him sleep at night, where was the harm? He deserved to unwind after a day spent chugging visitors back and forth across the river.

No, he decided. There was nothing to fear. Certainly not here on the tranquil river. The setting might have been a postcard for all that was safe and beautiful. As for the light across the water, it was probably just kids messing around, that was all. He'd give them a good telling off and a lecture about trespassing when he got his hands on them.

Kids had no respect these days.

With righteous indignation flowing through his veins, Edward Charon ferried himself towards the light flickering in the gloom. From the undergrowth, another soul watched him approach; eyes burning with unshed tears and hands clenched tightly, waiting for the gaunt old man to complete his final voyage from one world into the next.

There would be no going back.

CHAPTER 1

Thursday, 22nd February

"Matthew! Can you give us a hand, pet?"

The young man looked up at the sound of his supervisor's voice and then wistfully back at the fresh cup of tea he held in his hand.

Doreen's head popped around the door.

"Sorry, love, I need you to run down to the ferry and see if you can find Eddie. Apparently, he hasn't turned up for work and I've just had an earful from one of the package tour guides telling me there's a crowd starting to gather."

Matthew pulled a face.

"It's only just gone ten o'clock," he grumbled. "How come there are so many people with a burning desire to see the hermitage on a Thursday morning anyway?"

Doreen gave him a stern look.

"Matt—"

He set the cup back down on the counter with a bit of a slosh and held his hands up.

"I'm going, I'm going."

"Good lad," she said, eyeing the tea covetously. "If you see Eddie, tell him I want a word with him."

Matthew grinned as he shrugged into a green jacket emblazoned with the castle's logo and thought that the ferryman would be the one getting an earful, if Doreen had her way. He hurried out of the castle keep and towards the public footpath leading down to the river. As he stepped outside, his eyes watered as the wind slapped him hard in the face, stinging his cheeks as it whipped through the tumbled walls and crenellations of the old fortress.

"Bloody freezing," he muttered.

Frost-coated leaves crunched beneath his feet as Matthew covered the half-mile between the castle and the boat landing, rubbing his hands together briskly as he followed the river path. The toes of his boots kicked at stones and sent them hurtling down the path ahead as he battled to relieve his general discontent at having to spend another month volunteering, when he'd rather be working as a club promoter or something else that held the vague promise of female attention. With the memorable exception of a Spanish exchange student he'd met the previous summer, his job at the castle was hardly a draw for the ladies.

It was with such melancholy thoughts that Matthew eventually reached the small jetty advertising boat trips to the hermitage. As Doreen had warned him, a crowd of perhaps ten people had gathered and were clearly disgruntled about the cold weather and lack of a ferryman. Their ringleader spotted him and peeled away from the rest.

"Do you work for the castle?" he demanded.

Matthew drew himself up to his full height.

"Aye, sorry to keep you all waiting. What's the trouble?"

"Well, there's nobody here, is there? Now, look, our package included a visit to see the hermitage and that's what we're getting—"

"I'll just see where the ferryman's got to. He's probably just running a bit late today."

To forestall a tirade about the virtues of punctuality, Matthew hastily pulled out his mobile and dialled the office number.

"Doreen? Any word from Eddie?"

"Not a peep," she replied, taking a sip of hot tea. "He's still not arrived, then? I've tried his landline and he's not picking up his mobile. I wonder if he's poorly."

Matthew sighed and glanced over his shoulder at the baying crowd.

"Probably just hungover," he said, a bit unkindly. "He left the boat tied up, but the oars are just lying on the jetty."

At the other end of the line, Doreen sighed.

"We can't have that," she said. "Eddie knows he's supposed to lock the oars away at the end of the day. What if somebody decided to jump in the boat? The kids in the village could have found those oars and played havoc during the night. It's an accident waiting to happen."

Matthew murmured his agreement, but it still brought them no closer to solving the immediate problem.

"So, should I tell the visitors to come back up to the castle? No point in them hanging around if we don't know where Eddie is, or when he's likely to come back."

"What?" Doreen let out a tinkling laugh that grated on his nerves. "No, love, I'm sure a strapping young lad like you can manage to row them across. Just take it slow, a few at a time."

"Ah—"

"Thanks, flower!"

The line went dead, and Matthew glared at the offending piece of plastic in his hand, gripping it tightly and wishing it was Doreen's throat instead.

Despite his misgivings, Matthew managed to ferry a heaving boatload of tourists the short distance across the river to the hermitage. By the time they reached the wooden landing, he was sweating profusely, and his ears were ringing with a litany of historical questions he'd been expected to answer whilst keeping them afloat.

"Here we are," he panted.

Matthew's legs wobbled as he stepped onto the jetty to anchor the ropes but, as he tied them off, he noticed a set of keys lying discarded in the undergrowth nearby. Automatically, he bent to retrieve them. He held their weight in his hand for a moment or two while he wondered who might have lost them, then he gave a slight shrug and pocketed them to hand in at the office later. As he did, there came a sudden gust of wind and Matthew spun around, searching the trees lining the river path.

But there was no sign or sound of life other than nesting birds and the people who waited impatiently on the jetty for him to begin their tour.

"Ah, right," he said, with one final look towards the trees. "The hermitage was probably built as a private chapel for the first Earl of Northumberland in about 1400. If you'll follow me up the stone steps to the main entrance, I'll show you around. Please be careful on the stairs, they're slippery at this time of year."

Matthew led them towards a set of stone steps and gripped the metal handrail that had been added for safety. When his skin promptly stuck to the iced metal, he wished he'd remembered to wear gloves. But as he climbed up to the hollowed-out entranceway and stepped inside its cavernous interior, all thoughts of winter clothing were shoved forcibly from his mind.

The body of what had once been Edward Charon lay prostrate on the cold stone floor, dimly lit by the sun which shone weakly through the gaps in the stone. A pool of blood had formed around his head and was beginning to congeal against his skin, which was sickly grey and discoloured in parts. Matthew felt his stomach revolt as it sought to reject the sight and smell of violent death, and he began to see dark spots in his peripheral vision.

"Oh, God," somebody whispered.

The animals had found him first, was all he could think.

During the long hours of the night, scavengers had feasted, leaving the old man's face ripped and torn. There was a ringing in Matthew's head as he struggled to take it all in; a long, buzzing sound that seemed to come from far away as his body fought valiantly against the effects of shock.

A piercing scream from one of the tourists penetrated his foggy mind and he was galvanised into action, stumbling over uneven paving stones and throwing out his arms to urge the small crowd back to the boat.

"Hurry. *Hurry,*" he repeated. "We need to call the police."

CHAPTER 2

"Oh, for the love of Alan Shearer!"

Detective Inspector Denise MacKenzie turned from her inspection of the road ahead to cast patient eyes over her sergeant and soon-to-be husband.

"What on Earth's the matter?" she asked him.

Frank Phillips grunted from his position in the passenger seat beside her.

"It's the ceilidh band," he said. "They've cancelled on us. Double-booked, *apparently*."

He said it with such an air of suspicion, MacKenzie almost laughed.

"That's a pity but what does Alan Shearer have to do with it?"

"Nothing," he muttered. "But in times of crisis, we all need a hero to look up to."

MacKenzie chuckled and flicked on the windscreen wipers to clear the film of drizzle that was beginning to settle against the glass.

"It's hardly a crisis, Frank. We'll find another band."

Phillips tucked his smartphone back into his pocket and glanced across to study her profile as she manoeuvred the car. He admired the fall of glossy red hair framing her face and the capable way she handled the vehicle, just as she handled every other challenge that presented itself. Denise MacKenzie was a pragmatic, hardworking woman with a generous heart. In their line of work, she faced the worst of what one person could inflict upon another with grace and compassion and never complained. He knew she could look after herself but, to the best of his knowledge, she'd never in forty-four years been spoiled or pampered. He wanted to be the one to spoil her now; not just for a day but for the rest of their lives. A ceilidh band wasn't much, but it would have been a good start.

"Aye, you're probably right," was all he said.

"I usually am," she winked at him, then was serious as a thought struck her. "Besides, there are more important things to worry about at the moment."

Phillips made a low, rumbling sound of agreement.

"That's a fact," he said, and then heaved a sigh. "I *told* the lad, if he'd only wait a few months, some new evidence might crop up. He wouldn't listen, never does," he grumbled, with a trace of pride. "He says he can't live with knowing how many people might get hurt while he sits around waiting for something to happen."

The 'lad' in question was, in fact, his superior officer and a grown man of thirty-seven. But, regardless of age and title, Detective Chief Inspector Maxwell Finley-Ryan would always be a 'lad' to Phillips, who was more than merely his sergeant; he was like family.

"I told him, I said, 'Mark my words, it's dangerous to go flying around the world—'"

"To Italy," MacKenzie interjected.

"It might as well be bleedin' Borneo!" Phillips burst out, and folded his arms across his stocky chest. "He's chasing a killer who's already wriggled off the hook once before. Does Ryan think the bloke'll hold his hands up this time and say, 'Fair cop, guv'?"

He shook his head as if to answer his own question, then turned to stare out the window at the passing scenery.

"Nathan Armstrong won't come quietly—it's not in his nature. The man's like a cockroach, bloody untouchable. It'd take a nuclear bomb to get rid of his type."

"Nobody's untouchable," MacKenzie murmured, echoing what Ryan might have said if he had been with them.

She slowed the car to take the winding coastal road signposted for Warkworth and then reached across to give Phillips' knee a quick, supportive squeeze. For all his bluster, genuine concern lay beneath it.

"Ryan will be back soon," she said. "He'd never miss your stag do, for one thing. In the meantime, we'll keep the home fires burning."

Having been distracted momentarily by the knee-squeeze, it took a second or two for Phillips to remember what they had been talking about.

Ryan.

"Oh, aye. Well, just so long as he doesn't decide to up sticks and buy some fancy villa while he's over there. That's all we need."

"Right enough, I can think of nothing worse than a friend with a villa in Tuscany. Imagine our embarrassment if he asked us to visit," MacKenzie drawled.

Phillips was momentarily lost for words.

"Here we are," she said, as they entered the village of Warkworth a few minutes later.

The sun had risen higher in the sky, burning away the misty fret that had rolled in from the North Sea to shroud the village, leaving a clear, crisp morning in its wake. Stone-built cottages and shops lined the main village square and the castle towered proudly above it all in the wintry landscape, its pale gold walls sprinkled with a layer of frost that shimmered like diamonds as it melted in the gathering heat.

"Pretty place," Phillips said. "What did you say the old feller's name was?"

"Charon," MacKenzie told him. "Edward Charon."

"Why would anybody hurt some old codger who manned a rowing boat?"

MacKenzie frowned as she pulled into the castle's car park.

"That's what we'll have to find out, Frank."

CHAPTER 3

A thousand miles away, Detective Chief Inspector Ryan stepped outside the main terminal building of the *Aeroporto di Firenze-Peretola* and into a wall of heat. Unlike the conditions back home, Florence was experiencing unseasonably warm weather and he closed his eyes, allowing himself the briefest of moments to enjoy it.

"Shall we find a taxi?"

His eyes flickered open again at the sound of his wife's voice. He turned and swept his gaze over the woman by his side and thought, as he always did, that he was a very fortunate man. She stood tall and elegant, the morning sun burnishing her dark hair to a rich mahogany. If circumstances had been different, he might have smiled and slung a casual arm around her shoulders, drawing her in for a lingering kiss before spending the rest of the day sightseeing in one of the world's most beautiful cities.

But circumstances were not different.

This was no holiday and neither of them harboured any illusions about the dangers they faced in travelling to Italy. Ryan dropped his leather holdall and reached across to take her hands, which were cold despite the weather.

"You don't need to be here," he said, urgently. "I told you before, I'd rather you stayed at home, safe and sound—"

"How do you know I'd be safe?" she interrupted him. "While that monster is out there roaming the streets, none of us are safe."

Honesty compelled him to agree. Nathan Armstrong was a killer without conscience, a man who had taken a life at least twice that they knew of, but probably more. Despite his best efforts, Ryan had been forced to let him walk free months earlier and each day since then had been a physical wrench; a constant ache in his gut as he thought of how many others might fall prey while the dangerous man remained at large.

But the person who mattered most was standing right in front of him.

"Anna, if anything happened to you, I don't know what I would do."

She tried to reassure him.

"I won't be a burden," she said. "But I can't wait around at home, worrying, never knowing…" She shook her head. "It would drive me mad."

The pads of his thumbs rubbed absent circles against the soft skin of her hands.

"You're never a burden to me," he said quietly, and meant it. "But that won't make a difference to Armstrong. He doesn't care about 'right' and 'wrong', or about the destruction he might leave behind. He cares about one thing, and one thing only: himself. He's a dangerous predator and, if it means hurting you to save himself, he'll do it, make no mistake about that."

The words, spoken aloud, were both chilling and oddly prosaic.

Anna shivered, the tiny hairs on the back of her neck standing on end as she thought of the man they had come to find and, she hoped, to bring to justice.

God help them, if they didn't.

"It was my choice to come here," she reminded him. "I know the risks and so do you. I don't believe I'm a target for Armstrong because he's careful. He doesn't act without thought or planning. It would be too much of a leap for him to hurt me, the wife of the detective who wants him behind bars. He has a reputation to uphold and he won't want to draw the wrong kind of attention to himself, not so soon after his arrest last year."

Ryan searched her face for a long moment and then silently drew her towards him, into the warmth of his body to hold her close. Her reasoning was sound, he thought, but she hadn't considered the other possibility: that killers sometimes change their MO.

"We could turn back," he said softly.

The top of her head brushed the underside of his chin as she shook it.

"He sent postcards to our home, Ryan. He knows where we live. Until he's behind bars, we'll never be able to rest because he could come for us at any time, any day he chooses. He could murder us while we slept, and we'd never see it coming."

Ryan's arms tightened around her as they stood there, surrounded by the hustle and bustle of the airport as people came and went. He thought of the sinister cards that had been mailed to him from around the world, blank except for the DNA they'd found on each of the stamps—a different profile every time. As far as he was concerned, Armstrong had sent them as a calling card; an arrogant, taunting message to the detective who had failed to lock him up.

"It'll never be over until I bring him in," Ryan agreed. "But it won't be easy. Armstrong's spent a lifetime hiding behind the persona he's created for himself."

His eyes fell on a newsstand carousel bearing a selection of glossy Italian paperbacks, including several copies of a book entitled, *Il Mostro*. The shiny sales copy declared it the twentieth-anniversary edition of the worldwide bestseller and there, in bold red typeface, was the name of its author.

Nathan Armstrong.

Before they could seek out a taxi, Anna and Ryan were met by a smart-looking man of around forty. He wore a tailored grey suit with considerable panache and a pair of wraparound sunglasses which he propped atop his dark head, revealing eyes that were quietly assessing. Ryan recognised the look as being one he often employed himself and knew instantly that the stranger belonged to the same profession.

Police.

"DCI Ryan? I am Alessandro Ricci, an inspector with the *Gruppo Investigativo Delitti Seriali*. I have spoken with the *Direttore Generale della Polizia Criminale* in Rome, who tells me you are here to assist with one of their enquiries, yes?"

When Ryan said nothing, Ricci clucked his tongue and produced an identification card from his inner breast pocket.

"*Scusi, signore.* I am well known in Florence, so I forget."

Ryan scrutinised the identification card, which appeared to be in order, before extending a hand. Although he was fluent in Italian, he addressed the other man in English for Anna's benefit.

"Ricci?" he enquired. "DCI Ryan, Northumbria CID. Thanks for coming down to meet us. May I introduce my wife, Doctor Anna Taylor-Ryan."

True to stereotype, the other man's demeanour altered dramatically as he focused his attention on the striking, dark-haired woman at Ryan's side.

"*Signora,*" he breathed, and snatched up her hand before Anna had a chance to utter a token protest. As he bent his head to kiss it, she threw a look of surprise in Ryan's direction and received a broad grin and distinctly continental shrug in response.

"I am honoured to welcome you both to my city," Ricci said, straightening up again. "Please, come this way."

As he turned and walked in the direction of a sleek black Mercedes, Anna raised an eyebrow.

"Looks like the police lead a more glamorous lifestyle out here," she observed. "Maybe you should raise it with the Chief Constable and see if you can get a few perks for the office back home."

Ryan huffed out a laugh.

"Chance would be a fine thing," he said. "We're lucky the Department sprang for a plumber to fix the blocked drain in the gents toilets, let alone budgeting for luxury cars and silk suits."

Anna wrinkled her nose. "In that case, maybe you should budget for a few extra cans of air freshener, instead."

"Either that or put an embargo on baked beans in the staff canteen," Ryan replied.

Anna laughed, just as he'd hoped she would, and he drank in the sound of it until they reached the car where Ricci held the door open in readiness for them.

"Where are you staying, Chief Inspector? We can drop your wife there, before going on to the office—?"

But Ryan gave a small, firm shake of his head.

"We prefer to travel together, for the time being," he said, in a voice that brooked no argument. "Let's go straight to the office."

Ricci glanced between the pair of them with troubled eyes but dipped his head, raising an arm to indicate that they should step inside the car.

"*Prego*."

CHAPTER 4

The headquarters of *Gruppo Investigativo Delitti Seriali (GIDES)*, the elite Florentine police team dedicated to investigating serial crimes, was based out of the *Commissariato San Giovanni* on the Via Pietrapiana. It was a stone's throw from the famous Basilica of Santa Croce, containing the tombs of such luminaries as Michelangelo, Machiavelli and Galileo inside its neo-Gothic walls, but the interior of the police building was a far cry from the white-marbled grandeur of its neighbour. It boasted the same level of amenities to be found in any government building across the globe and, consequently, Ryan and Anna were met with a familiar scent of stale sweat and cooked meat as they stepped inside its glass-fronted double doors.

"Some things never change," Ryan muttered. "It's like a home away from home."

Before long, they reached a door at the end of the hallway. A tarnished brass name plaque declared it to be

Ricci's office and he swung open the door, gesturing for Ryan to enter.

"Please, make yourself comfortable," he said, then turned to Anna. "With your permission, *signora*, I will show you to our break room, where you can relax while your husband and I discuss certain confidential aspects of our case."

Anna and Ryan exchanged a meaningful look.

"I won't be far away," he murmured.

She nodded, and he waited to see which room she was taken to before stepping inside Ricci's office.

"You are protective," the other man said, when he returned a moment later. "But you are in one of our police headquarters, my friend. There is no safer place to be."

Ryan made no comment and Ricci indicated one of the over-stuffed chairs on the other side of his desk.

"Can I offer you a drink? Some coffee, perhaps?"

When two steaming cups of fragrant brown liquid arrived shortly after, Ryan was forced to question whether there might be a God, after all.

Ricci leaned back in his desk chair and smiled genially.

"Let us speak frankly to one another," he began. "When I heard from my colleague at the directorate in Rome, I was confused. Why would an English detective travel to Italy to assist an investigation which, forgive me, is far outside his jurisdiction?"

He lifted his hand, then let it fall away again.

"And to bring your wife? It is irregular, to say the least."

Ryan finished his coffee in two strong gulps, then faced Ricci squarely.

"I agree, it's highly irregular," he said, and watched surprise flit over the other man's face. "But we have very little choice. I assume your colleague, Director Romano, informed you of the postcards my wife and I received at our home address over the past few months. Most recently, from Vienna, and from Paris before that."

"Yes, but I don't see—"

"The cards contained no message," Ryan continued. "But our forensic team was able to extract a DNA profile from the saliva found on each of the stamps. The profiles weren't the same," he added. "We ran numerous searches of our domestic databases, as well as European and International databases, to see if we could match the DNA to a missing person. Nothing turned up, until we heard from Director General Jacopo Romano last week."

"*Si*, he tells me the DNA on one of those cards matches a missing Italian national," Ricci said. "I cannot see how it is possible, *signore*. It is more likely that your forensic team made an error."

Ryan smiled, but it failed to reach his eyes.

"The missing Italian national is a man called Ricardo Spatuzzi," he said, and watched recognition flare in Ricci's eyes. "I understand Spatuzzi is a lawyer attached to the United Nations Office on Drugs and Crime, based out of Vienna. He's worked there for three years, according to his employer, and went missing after a gala dinner. You recognise his name?"

Ricci visibly squirmed.

"Spatuzzi...It's a common name in our country," he said, affecting a thicker accent than before. "There are countless missing persons reported each year."

"But not so many with as high a profile," Ryan argued. "I wonder why Spatuzzi's name hasn't been reported more widely in the national press?"

Ricci made a dismissive gesture with his hand.

"The press is notoriously unreliable," he scoffed. "Isn't it an English saying, that we should not believe everything we read?"

Now it was Ryan's turn to be dismissive.

"The fact remains that Spatuzzi's DNA ended up on the back of a stamp which was sent to me. Romano tells me that the Austrian police enquiry threw up a guest list of people who attended the gala in Vienna and, aside from Riccardo Spatuzzi, there is another name on that list we recognise."

Inspector Ricci scrubbed a tired hand over his face.

"I have heard it already," he muttered.

"Nathan Armstrong," Ryan said, very clearly.

The name seemed to drift on the stuffy air inside Ricci's office for a moment or two, until he broke the silence that followed Ryan's bald statement.

"Signor Armstrong is a very famous man," Ricci said. "Especially in this city, Chief Inspector. His most famous book was based on the real-life crimes of *Il Mostro di Firenze* and is still very well regarded. *Mio Dio,* a Hollywood movie was made of his book years ago!" He held up both hands as if to ward off any arguments. "No, my friend. I cannot believe that a man of Armstrong's calibre would have anything to do with Spatuzzi's disappearance."

"Believe it or not, the facts speak for themselves," Ryan ground out. "Armstrong attended the same gala whilst he was in Vienna as part of his world book tour."

"Coincidence."

"That's what Armstrong will say," Ryan agreed. "So, let's consider another postcard, this time the one sent to me from Paris."

He leaned forward, demanding Ricci's attention.

"Listen. The Parisian police have identified a list of missing persons whose DNA could match the saliva we recovered from the back of the stamp," he explained. "On that list is a young waiter named Luc Bernard, who was reported missing by his family a month ago, shortly after he attended Nathan Armstrong's book signing at *Shakespeare's* bookshop, in Paris."

This time, Ricci did not suggest the timing was coincidental. Once he could excuse, but twice was curious, to say the least.

"Is there any evidence—?"

"Nothing," Ryan told him. "The police haven't found a scrap of physical evidence that would implicate Armstrong in either disappearance."

Murder was a word that remained unspoken but neither man was naïve enough to imagine that either Spatuzzi or Bernard would turn up alive and well any time soon.

"There must be camera footage of their movements," Ricci said. "GPS tracking linked to their mobile phones?"

"It's in the process of being recovered," Ryan replied.

"Still, I cannot believe—"

"You don't have to believe anything," Ryan interrupted him. "All you have to do is question Armstrong about his movements. It's already been cleared by Director General Romano, who agrees that the circumstantial evidence provides reasonable grounds to interview Armstrong when he lands in Florence."

Ricci ran agitated fingers through his hair.

"And what part do you play in all this?"

Ryan smiled grimly.

"I'm here in an unofficial capacity," he replied, although the words stuck in his throat. "My superiors have liaised with the Director General and have come to an understanding: I will assist in any way I can, but this is your baby, Alessandro."

The other man studied Ryan for a long moment while the sound of blaring horns and traffic filtered in through the window overlooking the road outside.

Eventually, Ricci came to a decision.

"When does Armstrong land?"

This time, when Ryan smiled, it reached his eyes.

"Tonight."

CHAPTER 5

In Warkworth, MacKenzie stood on the banks of the River Coquet dressed in polypropylene coveralls, ready to perform an initial walk-through of the crime scene awaiting her across the narrow stretch of water. She was joined by Phillips and an assortment of first responders, including two local police constables, a couple of castle employees and representatives of the local RNLI, who had been called in from the nearby fishing village of Amble to supply a dinghy for the duration of their investigation.

After transporting a pair of sombre-faced paramedics back across the water, the bottle-green rowing boat belonging to the castle had been impounded for forensic analysis on the orders of the Senior Crime Scene Investigator attached to Northumbria CID, Tom Faulkner. His team had already begun to protect the scene at the hermitage with the addition of a forensic tent and metres of plastic sheeting while they awaited the arrival of their Senior Investigating Officer.

It was hardly the first time MacKenzie had acted as SIO in the case of a suspicious death, but she was feeling nervous all the same. No matter how experienced she was, nor how confident of the steps and procedures she needed to follow, there was no getting away from the fact that she was responsible for keeping things on an even keel for the short time that Ryan was absent on special leave. The Chief Constable had told her, in no uncertain terms, that the Department needed a safe pair of hands to steer the ship while its captain was abroad and MacKenzie was the woman for the job.

Without any false modesty, MacKenzie knew herself to be a highly competent person and a damn good murder detective. But the thought of managing a disparate group of detectives, all of whom she knew and respected, was enough to bring her out in a cold sweat. It wasn't all nerves, she acknowledged. Her leg still ached badly following the severe injuries she'd sustained at the hands of a madman, so much so that even an hour's drive from Newcastle to Warkworth had taken its toll. Almost a year had passed since the horror of that encounter, but the scars remained, serving to remind her that she was not fully recovered, nor quite as invincible as she would like to imagine. Just lately, she'd begun to worry she may no longer be up to the physical demands of the job.

And, if that were the case, she didn't know what she would do with herself.

"Alright, guv?"

It took a moment before she realised Frank was speaking to her.

"I—yes, thanks. Just running things through my head."

Phillips pursed his lips. He recognised the tired look on MacKenzie's face and, in the ordinary way of things, would have offered her a shoulder to lean on. But they lived by a hard-and-fast rule that, no matter what their personal relationship, when they were at work he would treat her as he would any other senior officer. That meant no canoodling in the stationery room and no cuddling on the riverbank.

More's the pity.

"I had a word with the lad who found the body," he said, getting down to business. "Matthew Finch is one of the volunteers at the castle."

"Oh yes?"

"Aye. He says the rowing boat was moored on this side of the river with the oars lying on the jetty beside it when he came down around ten this morning."

"Is that usual?"

Phillips shook his head.

"Nope. The ferryman always stows the oars in a locked shed and secures the boat to make it safe overnight."

MacKenzie was a quick study.

"Well, since our man is still lying dead inside the hermitage, I'll take a wild guess that it wasn't Edward Charon's ghost who rowed back over here and left the oars lying about."

"Aye. Which means he—or *she*—fled the scene from this side of the river. Question is, which way did they go next?"

MacKenzie murmured her agreement and took a wide, sweeping survey of the vicinity. To reach the landing point where they now stood, they had followed a public footpath from the castle in a westerly direction for half a mile running parallel to the river on its southern side. Across the river, on the northern side, there was an identical landing point where they could see a pathway leading to the hermitage and a large sign which read, 'NO PLEASURE BOATS ALLOWED TO LAND HERE.' Turning to look behind, she noticed a single-track country lane leading up through the trees.

"Where does that lead?" she asked. "Is it a farm access road?"

"That's Watershaugh Road, leading to Coquet Crescent," one of the castle volunteers chimed in. "It circles back up to the outskirts of the village."

MacKenzie nodded her thanks and turned again to Phillips, speaking in an undertone. "Frank, when we're finished here, I want to check out all possible exit routes and ask Faulkner to look at any recent tyre tracks on Watershaugh Road. It's been damp the last few days, so we might be lucky. Check for any CCTV cameras, although it seems unlikely there'd be any in a place like this."

Phillips nodded his agreement.

"Easy enough for someone to leave a car parked further up that road," he mused. "All they'd need to do after finishing their business with Charon is row back across the river, dump the boat and walk a hundred yards to find their car. It's almost dark by four-thirty, so there's a good chance nobody would notice."

"Fewer people come out after dark during the winter, especially as the weather's been so cold," she added. "But we'll do a house-to-house and see what that throws up."

"Good thing about small villages is you always get one or two nosy neighbours," Phillips reminded her. "There's a decent chance one of them was twitching the curtains last night and happened to see something."

MacKenzie thought of their unknown perpetrator stealing away into the night under cover of darkness. It was all too easy to imagine.

"Come on," she said. "Let's go and see what Edward Charon can tell us about his killer."

If MacKenzie and Phillips had harboured any notion that Edward Charon might have taken his own life inside the hermitage, it was short-lived. As soon as they ducked inside the billowing forensic tent plastered to the side of the rock-face, they knew immediately that the man had been murdered. The hermitage consisted of an inner chamber and a small chapel comprising three vaulted bays with an altar at the far end. Charon's body rested against the worn step at the foot of the altar, where blood-spatter stained the floor dark red. He was sprawled at an unnatural angle, his legs twisted beneath his torso and his arms outstretched, as if he had been turning to run when he fell.

"D' you see this?"

Tom Faulkner beckoned MacKenzie and Phillips over to where he had crouched down beside the dead man's head. Phillips steadied his nerves and edged a little closer, concentrating on breathing heavily through his mouth. The CSIs had set up freestanding lights to enable them to work but they had the unfortunate side-effect of raising the overall temperature in the small stone cavern and did little to alleviate the ripening scent of death. In all his years of policing, this part of the job had never appealed to Frank. He supposed it was embarrassing for a seasoned murder detective to get the heebie-jeebies at the sight of a cadaver but there was nothing he could do about that. Regardless, he was getting too long in the tooth to worry about whether he could look at the ravages of death without flinching and was more inclined to focus on who was responsible for it.

MacKenzie, on the other hand, seemed to have an iron-clad stomach.

"That's massive blunt head trauma," she said, her suit rustling as she moved beside Faulkner to get a better look at the side of Charon's head. "His skull is completely caved in. Any sign of a weapon?"

Faulkner stood up again, arching his back a bit to ease out the kinks.

"We found a chunk of loose stone lying on the floor over there covered in blood and brain matter," he said, pointing towards a small yellow marker. "I bagged it up for analysis and I'd put money on that being the murder weapon."

Phillips cleared his throat.

"Just goes to show," he remarked.

Two heads swivelled in his direction, each with a blank expression.

"Show what?" Faulkner asked the burning question.

"Goes to show there's nowt new under the sun," Phillips elaborated. "Folk have been doing each other in with bits of rock and chunks of wood since the dawn of time and they're still doing it now."

MacKenzie threw him a pained look.

"All I'm saying is, there's no need for all this fancy novi-whatsit—"

"Novichok," Faulkner put in. "The Russian nerve agent used by spies and KGB moles."

"Aye, that's the one. There's no need for all that, when you can just give somebody a couple of good whacks 'round the back of the head and call it a night."

"I'll remember this, Frank, when we have our first marital disagreement," MacKenzie said, dryly.

Faulkner barked out a laugh.

"Well, fancy methodology or not, our murderer clearly didn't baulk at getting their hands dirty. You can see the blood-spatter stretches halfway across the floor and Charon has almost completely bled out." He paused, running his trained eye over the room. "It's obvious there's been some animal interference during the night, you can see that from the skin on his hands and face. Whatever it was—maybe a fox, or a rat?—has trodden in the blood and spread it all around, contaminating things even more. It'll be a job to sort through it all, once we get the samples back to the lab."

MacKenzie's heart sank, but she appreciated his honesty.

"Just do what you can," she said, looking down at the man's body with sympathetic eyes. "Nobody should die like this."

The two men murmured their agreement.

"Aye, whoever did this didn't mind a bit of blood," Phillips said. "Looks to me like they pummelled the poor feller."

MacKenzie stepped away carefully.

"I've already put the pathologist on standby; he's expecting to take delivery of the body within the next hour or so. After then, we'll see if there's anything else he can tell us."

"Pinter knows his stuff," Phillips agreed, referring to the senior police pathologist. "It's hard to tell if there are any defensive wounds, so maybe he'll be able to help us there. But, judging by the way he fell, it looks as though Charon was surprised from behind."

MacKenzie nodded.

"When I spoke to his manager, Doreen Jepson, she said Eddie Charon was quiet and well-spoken. He kept himself to himself, came into work and did as he was told without any trouble. He always had his lunch at the same time, usually went home at the same time and didn't tend to socialise with any of the other castle staff." She paused and looked up from her inspection of one of the walls. "Do you know what that tells me, Frank?"

"Charon had a routine," Phillips said. "Anybody could have watched him for a few days to see what his habits were."

MacKenzie nodded.

"Exactly. Let's see if we can find a next-of-kin and take it from there," she said. "Nine times out of ten, it's someone the victim already knows."

"And if it isn't?"

"Then we've got one hell of a job on our hands."

As they turned to leave, Phillips paused.

"Is there another way out of here?" he asked.

Faulkner looked up from where he had been taking a series of photographs and shook his head.

"Nope, just the one entrance leading in and out," he replied. "No easy access route from this side of the river, either, although there's a kind of raised stair leading to the top of the cliff. Apparently, it used to be an orchard or a garden of some kind, when the priest lived here. I'll get one of our guys to sweep it, once we're finished in here."

"Thanks, Tom," MacKenzie said. "The rowing boat was on the other side of the river when Matthew found it this morning, which suggests our perp left that way, but it's too early to rule anything out. Let us know if anything crops up."

"Will do," Faulkner said, his voice muffled behind the plastic hood he wore. "Hey, have you heard anything from Ryan?"

Phillips had thought that the sight and smell of human waste were enough to turn his stomach, but the thought of his friend being in danger eclipsed all else.

"Aye," he said gruffly. "He left a message to say they'd landed safely and that some bloke from the Italian CID met them off the plane."

By mutual accord, the three of them stepped outside the stifling interior of the hermitage and breathed deeply of the cool breeze that awaited them on the riverbank. Faulkner slipped off his hood and face mask before speaking again.

"I was the one who swabbed the postcards," he said. "Aside from the saliva on the back of the stamps, we found partial fingerprints. I'd hazard a guess they belong to the handlers in the mail service, because there was no match to Nathan Armstrong."

"You're sure?" MacKenzie asked.

"Positive," Faulkner replied. "We had a set on file after he was arrested and there was no match."

They fell silent and watched a pair of swans gliding over the water, which glistened as the sun reached its pinnacle, sweeping beams of white light across the valley. It might have been an Arcadian scene, timeless and unchanging through the centuries—if they ignored the police personnel roaming the grassy banks.

But it failed to have the same impact, not while they thought of their friend who was far away and without their support.

"If Armstrong sent those postcards, he had to know that Ryan would come after him. He had to know he would never stop searching for the evidence to bring him in," Faulkner said softly. "He couldn't stand knowing he's still out there, living like a king while the families of his victims live with the pain of what he did every day."

"Aye, it's who he is," Phillips agreed. "Armstrong knows that, as well as we do."

Suddenly galvanised, Phillips began making his way down towards the dinghy that would take him back across the river.

"Where are you going?" MacKenzie called after him.

"I'm going to speak to the Chief Constable, that's where I'm going. I want a few days leave."

MacKenzie hurried after him.

"*Frank*! Ryan said he wants to take care of Armstrong quietly. He can't do that if we all turn up with bells and whistles on. Besides, he's over there unofficially, so it won't do any good for us to barge in and start ruffling any Italian feathers."

"I don't need any bells or whistles, I just need an overnight bag and a good chunk of rock—just in case," he replied, darkly.

"I mean it, Frank. You can't go in like a bull in a china shop. If Ryan needs us, he'll let us know."

Phillips slowed down as her words hit home and he came to a standstill on the edge of the wooden jetty. MacKenzie caught up with him a second later and he turned to her in frustration.

"I know you're right, lass. I just can't stand to think of him and Anna over there without a friend in the world."

"They have each other," she said simply.

Then, she overrode their hard-and-fast rule and wrapped her arms around him.

CHAPTER 6

As they were driven through the narrow, cobbled streets of Florence, Anna reflected that it was easy to forget that she and her husband had been born into vastly different echelons of society. Ryan hardly ever discussed his childhood, although it had been a happy one, because to do so reminded him of the sister he had lost, and his grief was still too raw. He seldom discussed money, either, nor the fact he was endowed with quite a bit of it—unless he was planning to give some of it away and felt it prudent to seek her approval first. In the beginning, her mind had boggled at the regular sums he quietly dished out to worthy causes and she'd wondered if he was frivolous or just plain daft. However, she had come to realise that Ryan resented having more than he needed to be happy and would rather share it about with those who had been less fortunate.

Just another reason to love him, she supposed.

In fact, the one and only time they had ever truly argued was to do with her suggesting they draw up a prenuptial agreement before they were married. After all, his family were not merely rich but *wealthy* in an 'old money' sort of way; the kind that was carefully managed, re-invested and handed down through the generations. She, on the other hand, lived simply within her means as a university lecturer and had only modest savings, none of which had been handed down by her family, all of whom were now dead. When she had broached the subject with him, quietly explaining that she felt it was only fair and that she did not want his family to feel she was taking advantage considering the disparity, Ryan had been furious. As far as he was concerned, they were a partnership and whatever possessions he had were hers, too.

"Anna, if anything were ever to happen between us, I'd be happy to share half of whatever I have with you," he'd said. "In fact, if I'm ever stupid enough to throw away the best thing in my life, I'd deserve to lose the lot."

And that had been the end of the conversation.

Ryan was not a man who needed to wear the latest fashions, nor have the biggest, newest car. It was, therefore, all too easy to forget about his privileged childhood before he'd chosen to become a policeman and it was only on rare occasions that Anna was reminded of it.

As it happened, today was one such occasion.

Ryan had been conspicuously vague when she had asked him where they would be staying while they were in Florence and had merely told her everything was 'in hand'. Naturally, she assumed a hotel had been booked in advance and thought no more about it; but, as Ricci's black Mercedes crossed the River Arno and wound its way up the wide, tree-lined avenue known as *Viale Machiavelli*, narrow, shutter-fronted houses gave way to enormous villas set in spacious grounds. Palm trees and other tropical plants crept onto the pavements and formed arches over the road as it curled upward towards *Piazzale Michelangelo,* one of the highest points of the city which held panoramic views of Florence and the hills of Fiesole in the distance.

"Are we nearly there?" she asked him.

Ryan looked across at her, then away again.

"Mm hmm," he said. "Not far now."

Anna's eyes narrowed.

"You never mentioned the name of the hotel," she said, failing to notice that the car had slowed to a crawl and was indicating to turn into one of the gated entranceways set back from the road.

"That's because we're not staying at a hotel," he said cagily. "We're staying in a villa."

"You rented a villa?"

Ryan shifted in his seat.

"Ah, not quite. Here we are."

Anna's head whipped around in time to see a set of giant iron gates give way to immaculately-tended lawns fanning out from what could only be described as a miniature palace.

"Ryan?" she said weakly. "This seems a bit extravagant for what we need."

He said nothing, and the next minute he was out of the car and striding around to hold open the car door for her.

"The villa belongs to my parents," he explained, with a touch of embarrassment. "It belonged to my grandparents before that."

"And your great-grandparents before that?" she teased him, craning her neck to see the edge of a turquoise blue swimming pool just visible around the side of the villa. "Who the heck was your great-grandad, Ryan? Cosimo de Medici?"

"*Ha ha*," he said.

"I wasn't joking," she muttered to herself, as a woman in a smart black dress and heels opened the doors and smiled across at them.

"That's the housekeeper, Magda. Come on," he urged. "Let's go inside."

If Ryan had thought the interior of the villa would settle Anna's jangling nerves, he'd been sadly mistaken. The exterior had been impressive, but the interior was like the palace of Versailles, with acres of marble flooring underfoot, expensive-looking antique furniture and gigantic, Venetian chandeliers hanging from every ceiling. It was a far cry from their home back in Elsdon, with its flagstone floors and homely décor.

Once they had exchanged pleasantries with the housekeeper and installed themselves in one of the many beautiful, airy, drawing rooms, Ryan handed her a strong coffee.

"You look as though you might keel over," he said, then gestured to their surroundings. "Bit gawdy, isn't it?"

She almost choked on her coffee.

"It's luxurious," she said, carefully. "It has your mother's good taste written all over it."

To illustrate the point, she wandered over to a carved sideboard and picked up one of the silver-framed photographs resting on its polished surface. It showed Ryan as a younger man of perhaps nineteen or twenty, during one of his summer breaks from university. In the picture, he was tanned a deep, golden brown and was smiling broadly at the camera as he leaned back against a bright red Vespa scooter, the helmet slung under his arm.

"I'll bet you were a menace," she murmured, running an affectionate fingertip over his face in the picture.

"Why's that?" he asked, walking over to join her. "Because of the scooter?"

Anna set the photograph down and turned to him with laughing eyes.

"No, silly. Because, even at that age, you were a sight for sore eyes. The Italian ladies must have been tripping over themselves to jump on the back of that scooter."

Wisely, Ryan chose neither to confirm nor deny.

"I still have that scooter, you know. It's parked in the garage."

"Is that so?" she said, snaking her hands around his waist. "Well, before this trip is over, I think you'll need to take me for a spin."

"That's a promise," he said.

The villa was not Ryan's choice of accommodation simply because it was the most convenient, nor because it was free. His father was a retired diplomat who had, at the height of his career, held the highest office as the United Kingdom's ambassador to France. Although he had never been based permanently in Italy, David Ryan had fortified each of his homes with the best security that money could buy. Consequently, the villa had been equipped with tall, perimeter fences with CCTV cameras set at intervals, as well as a state-of-the-art internal and external alarm system wired to a dedicated security room which was manned around the clock. He also had access to the best personal security and had made his extensive list of contacts available to his son for the duration of his stay. Safety was of the utmost importance where family was concerned, and Ryan could not have agreed more.

"Armstrong is good with technology," he said, as he talked Anna through the security system inside the villa. "But this place is on another level and it's monitored by security personnel twenty-four hours a day. It helps to know that."

"Does it?" she queried, and thought she understood for the first time why he had not mentioned this aspect of his life before. "You grew up like this?"

Ryan scrubbed a hand through his dark hair.

"That picture you saw—the one with me on the scooter? It makes me look carefree, as if I'd spent that summer riding around picking up girls. The reality was, I had a pair of bodyguards shadowing every move I made. It was the same for my sister," he added, swallowing the sudden pain. "It wasn't my parents' fault, but our childhood was a gilded cage. We wanted for nothing, including love and affection, but we could never stray too far or move out of sight. It was too risky."

"That explains why you've always been such a terrible cynic," she said, matter-of-factly.

Ryan flashed a smile.

"It always pays to expect the unexpected."

They stepped inside the bedroom that would be theirs for the duration of their stay and Anna stopped dead.

"Wow. I'm going to need a minute, here."

Hazy afternoon light beamed through floor-to-ceiling sash windows. Floaty curtains swayed on the breeze and gave the impression of calm. Parquet flooring softened the large space and a giant super-king-size bed stood in the middle of it all, dressed in plain white linens.

"I don't know whether to call your mother and tell her I love her, or shout at you for keeping this place a secret for so long," she confessed.

Ryan huffed out a laugh.

"I don't know what Phillips is going to make of all this," he said. "I mentioned a trip to the Lake District last month and he almost bit my head off, so I dread to think what he'll have to say when he finds out there's a villa in Tuscany at his disposal."

"Perish the thought," Anna said, gravely.

CHAPTER 7

While Ryan and Anna settled into their home for the next few days, another man touched down in Florence. He paused to sniff the air, smiling at the unmistakeably rich scent of Tuscany with its olive groves and warm winds circling the valley. It had been too long since his last visit, but he intended to make up for lost time and enjoy everything the city had to offer.

Nathan Armstrong cut a dapper figure as he crossed the tarmac towards the terminal building, dressed in a sharp suit complete with silk pocket square and matching cravat he'd tucked casually around his neck. Of course, he'd changed into a fresh shirt before exiting the plane and had taken the time to replenish his aftershave; a man in his position must always be ready for the flash of a camera or the unexpected attention of one of his fans.

A liveried chauffeur hurried across to take his bags and lead him through fast-track customs—the province of VIPs like himself—and into the limousine his Italian publisher had arranged to collect him from the airport. Appearances were important, and a man of his stature needed to look the part. It would hardly do for him to be seen arriving into Florence in the back of a poky little Fiat; people might think his popularity was starting to wane.

Armstrong was distressed to find that he had almost passed through the terminal building without having been noticed, when a woman standing beside a carousel of his books looked up and spotted him.

"Nathan Armstrong!" she squealed as she hurried across, and he only just held back a grimace when he noticed her wide feet with unpainted toenails flapping about in the dusty old flip-flops she wore. If this was his reader demographic, perhaps it was time he sought a new profession.

"Yes?" he affected an air of surprise at having been recognised.

"I thought it was you!" she gushed. "I've read all of your books and loved every single one! I cannot believe it has been twenty years since I first read *Il Mostro*."

He schooled his features into a modest expression and inclined his head.

"It's very kind of you to say so, *signorina*," he replied. "*Il Mostro* will always be very special to me. Indeed, that's why I'm here in Florence, to celebrate its anniversary."

"And the movie," she went on, gazing up at him. "I must watch it again, soon. I remember the first time I saw it at the cinema. I was terrified for weeks."

Armstrong managed to hold back a laugh. He'd found the film rather tame, when compared with reality.

"Well, I'm so pleased to have met you," he said, with every appearance of sincerity. "But I'm afraid I'm in rather a hurry."

He half-turned, but paused just long enough for her to thrust a copy of the 20th Anniversary Edition of *Il Mostro* in his face, begging him to autograph it.

He sighed, checking his slim gold watch as a matter of form.

"I suppose…just for you, *bella*. What's your name?"

She giggled, and he made a show of signing the book, which inevitably drew attention from passing travellers who slowed down to see who he was. While Armstrong enjoyed the attention, his chauffeur stood a respectful distance away and decided to light a cigarette, rightly assuming he could be there for a while.

Fifteen minutes later, Armstrong managed to tear himself away from a gaggle of fans and was bidding them a modest farewell when he saw the policeman standing patiently beside the exit doors. He made him straight away—after all these years, he could spot them a mile off—and told himself not to react. Instead, he strolled across to his chauffeur and together they headed towards the car park, beyond the automatic exit doors leading out of the terminal building.

"Signor Armstrong?"

He wheeled around with a pleasant smile already painted on his face.

"Yes?"

"I am Inspector Alessandro Ricci," the policeman said, showing Armstrong his identification card. "Might I have a word?"

Armstrong looked confused.

"What about, Inspector?"

"*Signore*, I would rather not discuss these matters on the street," he replied, casting his eyes around the busy 'Arrivals' area. "But, if I may ask you to call into the station tomorrow morning at, say, ten o'clock?" Ricci handed him a card with the address.

Armstrong told himself to stay calm.

"I have a rather busy schedule, Inspector—"

"It will not take long, *signore*. An hour, at most."

"What does it concern?"

He scanned Ricci's face but could read nothing there.

"It concerns two missing persons," Ricci said, without expression.

Armstrong shook his head, affecting an air of confusion.

"None of my acquaintances have been reported missing," he said. "If it concerns strangers, I must say that I meet so many people, I can hardly see how I can help you."

Ricci merely smiled.

"Until ten o'clock," he said, and was about to turn away when Armstrong's voice stopped him. This time, there was no cajolery or affected confusion, but a thread of steel.

"Do I need to call my lawyer, Inspector?"

Ricci gave one of his shrugs in response.

"I cannot say, *signore*. That will be up to you, if you feel it necessary."

"For a man in my position? Yes, I think it's necessary." He paused, lowering his voice so that only Ricci could hear. "I take it you're not suggesting that *I* have anything to do with these unfortunate souls having gone missing?"

Ricci's tone remained friendly.

"I am not suggesting anything, *signore*. I merely seek your cooperation with our investigation in answering some questions."

"And if I refuse?"

Ricci spread his hands in an apologetic gesture.

"It would be unfortunate," he said. "We may then need to compel your attendance at an interview. It would be preferable, for both of us, to keep things as quiet as possible. Do you not agree?"

Armstrong's lips twisted.

"I'll be at the station for ten o'clock," he snarled.

As Ricci strolled off, Armstrong's eyes followed him until he had disappeared out of sight. Only then did he turn to the chauffeur standing a discreet distance away.

"Speak a word of this to anyone and I'll have you sacked."

Much later, when he was ensconced in the privacy of his apartment, Armstrong locked the door and sank into one of the comfortable leather armchairs arranged in the seating area. He sat there for long minutes in the surrounding silence and thought of one thing.

Ryan.

He was behind it, of that he was certain.

Ryan stood on the terrace of the Villa Lucia, his forearms resting against the thick stone balustrade as he looked out across the city, spread out before him in a tapestry of terracotta and peach, with cypress trees dotted here and there. The sun dipped low against the horizon, washing the landscape in misty rays of rich ochre as it made its final descent over the edge of the world.

But he hardly noticed. His thoughts were far away as he watched the distant lights of a plane coming in to land, blazing a trail through the cloudless sky as it made its gradual descent into Florence.

"It looks like an oil painting," Anna said, from the doorway behind him.

Ryan straightened up and turned to face her, hitching his hip onto the edge of the wall. He'd changed into casual chinos and a plain white cotton shirt rolled up at the sleeves, since it was a warm evening. Anna felt suddenly awkward. He was her husband, the man she shared a bed with each night, but Ryan seemed different here. He looked very much at home in his surroundings and it was a sharp reminder that he had lived for more than thirty years before she'd met him; a life filled with grand villas and God only knew what else. It was disconcerting to find that there was still so much of him to discover, especially as her own history seemed to have been laid bare in comparison.

Sensing her turmoil, Ryan reached out to take her hand and tugged her towards him.

"How are you doing?" he murmured, touching his lips to hers.

"Better now," she admitted. "I was feeling a bit like a duck out of water."

"You're never out of place when you're beside me," he replied, with irrefutable logic.

"You know what I mean," she muttered. "All this…it's a bit above my pay bracket."

Ryan surprised her by laughing.

"It's a bit above mine, too," he assured her. "I'm a lowly murder detective, remember? Don't start thinking we can afford crystal chandeliers in the hallway back home, especially with the next round of funding cuts coming from the Home Office."

She gave him a none-too-gentle nudge in the ribs, and he became serious once more.

"Anna, it's just *stuff*. None of it matters," he said, gently.

"Easy for you to say, since you grew up with it," she pointed out. "All this will be yours one day, won't it?"

The corners of his lips twitched, and he considered cracking a joke about him taking out more stringent life insurance, but he guessed—correctly—that it would not be well-received in her present mood.

"I suppose you're right, but it just goes to prove we can't take anything with us when we die. I don't need bricks and mortar to be happy, Anna. I need you, especially now."

She searched his face, noting the lines of worry etched into his skin.

"Armstrong's here in Florence, isn't he?"

Ryan scrubbed a hand over his face and then nodded.

"Yes, he's here. Even if I hadn't just heard it from Ricci, I would have known," he muttered. "There's a tension in the air...It sounds ridiculous. I can't explain it."

"I understand," she said. Ryan was a man who relied upon evidence and fact, but he never overlooked his instinct, either.

"Ricci caught him at the airport," he continued. "He's set up a meeting tomorrow morning at the police station."

"So soon?"

Ryan shrugged.

"The sooner the better," he said. "Ricci also told me that Armstrong's staying at one of the old palazzos in the centre of town, it's recently been converted into apartments."

"Now you know where he'll be."

"Yes. I want to be there in the room when they question him, but I can't." It hadn't stopped him from trying to persuade his new colleague in *GIDES* to let him observe, at least. He'd have to be content with that.

"It wouldn't help if you were in the room with him," Anna was bound to say. "Armstrong would be more inclined to be antagonistic. Besides, Ricci seems like a capable man."

Ryan made a non-committal sound in his throat.

"I don't know him, so I don't know if he's capable or not," he said. "Plus, Ricci's not invested, yet. He still believes

Armstrong's a celebrity and that it makes him above the law. He can't see it, yet."

"It?" she queried.

The last rays of sunlight were reflected in Ryan's blue-grey eyes as he looked across at her.

"The man behind the mask," he explained. "I saw flashes of the real 'Nathan Armstrong' during the investigation in Kielder, but then the mask slipped back into place and he was the arrogant author again, just another quasi-celebrity. I want to peel back the mask to see what's festering beneath."

There was a short pause while they watched the sun disappear behind the distant silhouette of the Duomo, the cathedral whose famous curved outline dominated the skyline. Lights flickered as the night came alive and, Ryan knew, there would be thousands of people roaming the city's quaint streets without a care in the world. Lovers would be walking hand in hand over the Ponte Vecchio while students and tourists strolled through the grand piazzas, never thinking of the danger lurking in their midst.

Darkness masked all kinds of misdeeds.

"Tomorrow can't come soon enough," he muttered.

CHAPTER 8

In the village of Warkworth, Phillips accepted a second custard cream biscuit from the last calling point on their house-to-house interviews. From her position on the sofa beside him, MacKenzie rolled her eyes and thought that, at the rate he was going, they'd be lucky to finish before midnight.

"Thank you again for the tea, Mrs Mackie," she said, setting her mug on a nearby coaster.

As a rule, she seldom drank the teas and coffees she was offered during an investigation, but she found they worked as a good ice-breaker, giving a nervous or elderly witness the chance to settle themselves by performing a humdrum task like boiling the kettle.

Alice Mackie sank down onto one of the over-stuffed chairs in her sitting room and smiled at them both. As a widow of over fifteen years, she kept herself as busy as she could with her friends and did all she could for those less able in the little coastal village. But once the front door to her cottage shut behind her, the walls seemed to close in. Consequently, she'd been glad to find two friendly faces on her doorstep, even if they *were* investigating a murder.

"No trouble at all, pet," she replied. "Can I get you anything else? What about a nice cheese scone?"

Phillips' head popped up like a meerkat, but one stern look from Denise silenced him.

"You've been more than kind, Mrs Mackie," she said, pointedly. "If it's alright with you, we'd be grateful if you could answer one or two questions for us?"

Alice folded her hands and leaned back.

"O' course," she said. "What would you like to know?"

"Can you tell me how long you've lived here, Mrs Mackie?"

"Oh, well, now. When we first got married, Dougie and I—that's my late husband—we lived in Berwick for a while, because he had a job up there. He was a dentist, you know. Anyhow, a partnership came up at the surgery here in Warkworth…gosh, it must have been back in 1982. No!" she corrected herself. "It must have been '83, because that was the year before our Paul was born."

MacKenzie nodded politely.

"Have you lived in this house since 1983, then?"

"No, love," the other woman chuckled, as if it were obvious. "We lived in a *much* bigger house attached to the surgery but, after Dougie died and the kids moved on, it was too large for me. I moved into this little place about ten years ago."

"Right," MacKenzie murmured, wondering how the answer to a simple warm-up question could have become so convoluted. "And how long had Edward Charon been your neighbour?"

"Eeh, I still can't believe he's dead," Alice said, in a dramatic whisper. "He seemed so full of life. He must have been fit as a fiddle, doing all that rowing, as well."

Phillips caught MacKenzie's eye and picked up the thread of conversation without a hitch.

"Had he lived in the area long?"

"No, not long at all," she replied. "Must've been last March when he moved in, so that's nearly a year ago now. As far as I know, he was new to the area."

"Friendly, was he?"

She pursed her lips, considering how much she should say.

"Well, he wasn't *un*friendly," she said. "But he kept to himself, mostly, and didn't have many visitors, either."

"No?"

She shook her head and took a sip of tea, cradling the mug in her hands to warm them.

"No. In fact, I never saw anybody visiting him, unless you count Jehovah's Witnesses and the young man who helped him home a couple of weeks ago."

MacKenzie looked up from her notepad with interest.

"When was this?"

"Must have been a week last Friday," Alice replied. "I remember, because I had my ladies around for some dinner and a natter. Moira was leaving for home at around half past ten or quarter-to-eleven and saw them both trying to get the front door open."

"Was Eddie a bit worse for wear?" Phillips asked.

"Aye, he was," she said, not wishing to speak ill of the dead. "The lad was helping him indoors."

"Did you recognise him? The lad, I mean."

Alice nodded.

"It was Matthew Finch. He's Barbara's grandson," she told them, although they had no idea who Barbara might be. "Always was such a helpful boy. He works up at the castle, too, you know."

They nodded politely, choosing not to disclose the fact it had been Matthew who found Edward's body.

"Do you remember the last time you saw Eddie?"

Alice leaned down to rub her ankle while she thought back.

"Must have been a couple of days ago, on Tuesday," she decided. "I heard him come in from work at around twenty-past-five and I went around to knock on his door. I needed to ask him a favour," she said, and flushed a bit at the lie she'd told.

Reading the situation correctly, Phillips cleared his throat.

"And, did he come over for dinner, then?"

She smoothed a hand over the material of her skirt and lifted her chin a bit.

"He didn't," she said, in dignified tones. "I only asked him to be *neighbourly*. The poor man seemed so lonely;

never having anybody over, hardly speaking to a soul. I thought it might do him good to have some company."

It might have done them *both* good, she added silently, then pushed the thought away. There was another soul lost to the world.

"Does he have any family?" she asked softly. "I'd like to send them a card."

MacKenzie didn't answer directly.

"We haven't found Edward's next-of-kin, yet, Mrs Mackie. He didn't happen to mention anybody, did he?"

Her brow furrowed.

"No, he didn't mention a soul," she replied. "And I don't just mean family. He never mentioned friends or even talked about anybody from work. Come to think of it, that's a bit odd, isn't it?"

MacKenzie smiled slightly.

"Yes, Mrs Mackie, you could say that."

When Phillips and MacKenzie stepped outside thirty minutes later, night had fallen. The air temperature was well below zero and seeped through the layers of their clothing to penetrate the bones beneath. But the sky above was peppered with stars, so many they lit up the heavens like fairy lights on a Christmas tree.

They took a moment to appreciate the view and then headed off towards their car, which was still parked at the castle.

"Can't make out the bloke's character, can you?" Phillips thought aloud.

"Mm? No, no. Not much."

"All people seem to agree on is that Charon liked his own company, but he liked a drink even more."

"Mm hmm."

MacKenzie could hardly muster the strength to give him more than single-syllable answers. It had been a long day, filled with procedure and red tape, and her leg was so painful she was almost hobbling.

"Hey," Phillips murmured, taking her arm in a gentle grip. "Is your leg hurting you, love?"

She bit off the angry, defensive response that sprang to her lips and drew in a shaking breath instead.

"It's a bit sore," she admitted. "It must be all the cold weather."

Phillips battled against the powerful wave of anger which coursed through his body as he thought of how she'd come by her injuries. Most days, he tried to forget the anguish and focus on the here and now, reminding himself to be grateful that she'd been returned to him alive and not hacked to pieces, as had been the case with some of the Hacker's less fortunate victims. Still, he'd rather she had never been hurt at all.

"Here," he said gruffly. "Let me give you a carry."

"*Frank*," she tried to slap his hands away, fearful of who might see, but could only be grateful when he scooped her up into his burly arms and allowed her to lean on him.

Phillips had been a keen amateur boxer for years, but it was easy to forget the layer of muscle that lay hidden beneath what she affectionately called his 'custard cream layer'.

"Just this once, mind," she mumbled. "I don't know what people would think, if they saw—"

He looked across at her pale face and gave a roguish smile.

"They'd think I was a better-lookin' version of Prince Charming, carrying you off to the castle," he said, and then pretended to drop her, which elicited a squeal of panic.

"*Frank*! Put me down, y' old fool!"

"Not a chance," he said, hitching her a bit higher against his chest. "If I have a heart attack, I'll die happy."

But when he spied the car, he sent up a silent prayer of thanks. A minute later, he deposited her on the passenger side and insisted on driving home.

"You're not insured on this car," she said, worriedly. "What if anything were to happen?"

"I'll take my chances," he said, snatching up the keys. "I know a few officers in the traffic team who'll put in a good word for me."

MacKenzie was about to argue further, when another spasm of pain shot up her leg, causing her to buckle.

"Alright," she capitulated, gritting her teeth. "I suppose the chances of you getting caught speeding are pretty low, anyway."

He shot her an affronted look.

"What's that supposed to mean?"

She strapped on her seat-belt and leaned back with a grateful sigh.

"Frank, being in the car with you is less like *The Fast and the Furious* and more like *Driving Miss Daisy*."

"Slow and steady wins the race," he said.

After what seemed like an endless journey to re-join the dual carriageway, Phillips picked up their conversation once they were heading back towards the city of Newcastle upon Tyne, thirty miles further south.

"What do you make of what Alice Mackie had to say? Seemed like the old boy was a bit of a loner."

MacKenzie agreed.

"I've asked Yates to pull together a file on Charon," she said, referring to the trainee detective constable in their team. "So far, she's having trouble finding any next-of-kin, or anything dating back to more than a year ago."

"Changed his name?" Phillips queried. "Or could be witness protection."

"That's what I wondered, so I've asked her to look into both. Might take a while yet."

Phillips reduced his speed, careful not to go above sixty.

"What about the castle? Didn't they check his references?"

"We can speak to them about that," she said. "I'd be surprised if they didn't, which means it's possible he may have provided false ones if he went by a previous name."

She paused, trying not to notice that they'd been stuck behind the same slow-moving lorry for the past three miles.

"Alice Mackie says he only moved into the house next door last March," Phillips said, blissfully unaware that anything was amiss, despite seven or eight cars in a row having overtaken them. "We couldn't see anything much when we had a nosy around his house earlier, but we could have a proper check tomorrow when the CSIs go in. Maybe we'll find some documents, or the house deeds. That should tell us how he paid for it."

"If not, we'll request it from the Land Registry," MacKenzie said. "The man we know as 'Edward Charon' has a clean sheet as far as previous convictions go, but doesn't even own a car. He couldn't have been more than sixty-five."

"Maybe he couldn't drive," Phillips suggested.

"It's possible, I suppose."

They fell into a comfortable silence while MacKenzie found herself reading a variety of lewd stickers that had been fixed to the back of the lorry in front of them.

"Why would a man in his sixties move to a remote coastal town and take up a job as a ferryman, Frank?"

"Maybe he liked the quiet life."

"Aye, or maybe he was running from something."

Phillips made a low sound in his throat.

"You're thinking he's linked to one of the firms?" he asked, and thought of the various organised crime syndicates operating in the North East. "Could have got himself in a bit of hot water and tried to start again. It was brutal, the way he died, so it wouldn't be outside the realms of possibility."

"True, but we usually see punishment killings with knives or guns, not with bits of rock, and some mafia stooge wouldn't bother to wait for him in the hermitage; they'd go 'round to his house or take him down some back alley."

"Aye, there weren't any markers on him that I could see."

Sometimes, they found a victim's tongue had been cut out, if one of the families thought the unfortunate soul had spoken to the police. However, Edward Charon's tongue and extremities had all been intact.

Phillips drummed his fingertips on the steering wheel in a cheerful rhythm.

"Nothing I like more than a challenge," he declared.

"D' you know what I like, Frank?" MacKenzie said, sweetly. "I like to get home before the early hours of the morning. For pity's sake, overtake this lorry before you drive me demented."

"Now, now," he teased. "Nobody likes a backseat driver."

He laughed when the air turned blue inside the little black Honda.

CHAPTER 9

Friday, 23rd February

The new day brought with it a layer of mist which curled over the rooftops and spires of Florence, weaving through the streets like long fingers as it spread through the city. Ryan leaned against one of the terrace doors to watch it, lifting an espresso to his lips. Having been unable to sleep, he'd wiled away the long hours of the night researching his quarry. It hadn't taken more than a few Google searches to find out that Florence was the last stop on Nathan Armstrong's world tour and that it had been chosen to celebrate the twentieth anniversary of the publication of his worldwide bestseller, *Il Mostro*.

Like many people, Ryan had seen the film that had been made a few years after the book was released, back in the early noughties. He remembered thinking it was overly gory, which was not to his taste. In his business, he hardly needed to seek out further evidence of the damage that one human being could do to another, let alone pay for the privilege. Further internet searches had supplemented his basic knowledge of the book's storyline, which relied heavily on the real-life events surrounding the infamous serial murders attributed to *Il Mostro di Firenze*, the 'Monster of Florence', which remained unsolved. Several books had been written on the subject, but Armstrong's thriller had surpassed them all, selling millions of copies around the world and setting him up for life.

It made for difficult reading when Ryan discovered that the book had not only been a commercial hit, but had been critically acclaimed by industry pundits and reviewers alike. Given Armstrong's character, it would have been preferable to find that his literary efforts had been met with a lukewarm reception, but the opposite had been true. Accolades and awards had been rained upon the author by a variety of dubious publishing entities, which was enough to turn Ryan's stomach.

"Sycophants," he muttered, scrolling past another nauseating write-up from somebody with a triple-barrelled name.

By the time Anna awakened, Ryan had read two-thirds of *Il Mostro*, which he'd downloaded onto an e-reader, to find out for himself what all the fuss was about. Having already subjected himself to one of Armstrong's later works of fiction, Ryan hadn't held out much hope, but found himself pleasantly surprised by the higher standard of the man's earlier effort.

Apparently, Nathan Armstrong had grown lazy sometime during the intervening years.

"What time is it?" she yawned, searching for her smartphone to check the time.

"Just after eight," Ryan replied, stepping away from the open doorway. "Go back to sleep, if you like."

Anna stretched and shook her head, focusing on him properly.

"You're showered and dressed already—"

"I couldn't sleep," he said. "I've been catching up on some reading."

She raised an eyebrow.

"I thought you said this wasn't a holiday?"

He laughed shortly.

"Trust me, it isn't. I've been reading *Il Mostro*, by our illustrious friend."

Anna wrapped her arms around her knees, eyeing the shadows beneath his eyes with concern.

"Any good?"

He opened his mouth to say something scathing but, since he prided himself on being an honest man, thought better of it.

"It's not bad," he admitted. "Well researched, for one thing. Though it pains me to say it, I can understand why it did so well. Small wonder Armstrong has an ego the size of a small planet."

Anna laughed at the look of derision marring his handsome face.

"He's still a killer," she reminded him.

Ryan polished off the last of his coffee, then moved across to the machine in the corner of the bedroom to pour a cup for his wife.

"They do say you should write about what you know, in which case Armstrong ought to be well placed to write a serial killer thriller."

"He'd be no good at writing a self-help book," she quipped.

Ryan handed her a steaming cup and sat on the edge of the bed.

"Thank you," she murmured, and thought privately that it was small, seemingly insignificant gestures such as a cup of coffee in the morning that made up the fabric of her love for him. It cost him very little, but meant so much.

"What else did you find out?" she asked.

"We already know Armstrong's in Florence for a special event," he replied. "His Italian publisher is throwing him a big, swanky party at the Uffizi Gallery on Saturday to celebrate twenty years of him being a demi-God. That means he has today and most of tomorrow to maraud around the city, enjoying himself."

"You think he'll hurt someone?"

Ryan's eyes turned flat.

"People have gone missing from the major cities he visited on his tour," he said quietly. "People who had come into contact with him, at one stage or another. There may even be more that we haven't found yet. That tells me he's good at planning and execution—so good that he leaves no evidence trail—but he isn't so good at delaying his own gratification."

Ryan stood up to pace around a bit, working off some of his frustration.

"You asked me whether I think he'll hurt someone in Florence? The answer is 'yes', because I don't think he can deny himself the pleasure."

"Even when he knows you're tracking him?" Anna put in. "Because he must know you'd follow him here. He sent you those postcards, after all. What else were they, if not an invitation?"

"Yes, he knows," Ryan said. "And no, it isn't enough to stop him. In fact, I think my being here heightens the challenge for him not to get caught. I don't know what else motivates him yet, not deep down, but I need to find out. When we know *why*, it'll be easier to work out *who* he'll target next, and *when*."

Anna listened with a growing sense of unease. She'd known the type of man her husband had come to find, of course she had, but hearing Armstrong's character and exploits spoken of so plainly made her blood run cold.

"What will you do? What can *we* do?" she corrected.

Ryan stuck his hands in his pockets.

"We do things by the book, as far as we can. Ricci's due to speak to Armstrong in a couple of hours and we'll find out where he says he was when Bernard and Spatuzzi went missing."

"Both male," Anna thought aloud. "Like Duncan Gray, all those years ago."

Ryan thought of the young teenage boy whose mummified body had been discovered four months ago, and of his mother's grief. Angela Grey had lived for thirty years thinking her son had run away from her, knowing in her heart that he was gone for good. She'd never suspected that he'd lain less than half a mile away from where she lived and worked, buried in a clay tomb by a man who believed his past deeds would never rise up to haunt him.

But he'd been wrong.

Ryan had done all he could to prove Armstrong had been the one to kill Duncan Gray, but on the cusp of charging the man with murder, he'd been overruled from above. He'd never forget the anger he'd felt as he watched the man walk out of Northumbria Police Headquarters, free to do as he pleased.

"Yes, the missing persons are all men, as far as we know."

"Can we draw any conclusions from that?" Anna wondered.

Ryan considered the question.

"It was impossible to say conclusively whether Duncan Gray had suffered any sexual assault before he died but, if the police are able to find the bodies of Riccardo Spatuzzi or Luc Bernard before too long, we'll be able to check for any obvious motives."

"You think they're definitely—"

"Dead? Yes."

Anna swallowed.

"How do you know?"

"Put it down to instinct, again," Ryan said. "But I've also read the police reports from Paris and Vienna. Both men were, by all accounts, content and happy in their lives, give or take the usual gripes about money or job satisfaction. There was nothing to suggest suicide as a possibility, or that either man was likely to pack up and leave one day without a word to anyone. The only logical reason why Bernard or Spatuzzi would go missing is that they were taken against their will..."

He trailed off, thinking of Armstrong's general character, then gave a small shake of his head.

"I can't say whether the gender makes any difference because I don't have enough information. But I can tell you one thing: if either of those men had injured him, humiliated him or otherwise bested him, I think it would be enough to send Armstrong over the edge."

Anna was silent for long seconds as she thought of another man, at another time, who had harboured similar delusions of grandeur. It would be all too easy to dismiss the thought as fanciful, to laugh off the idea that a person could be so megalomaniacal as to commit murder. But she had seen that type before and could even remember the warmth of his breath as Steve Walker had loomed over her with a knife in his hand, ready to kill or be killed.

"He needs to be stopped," she said, flatly, and rolled out of bed in one fluid movement to reach for the dressing gown draped over a nearby chair. "Tell me what I can do to help."

Ryan opened his mouth to tell her there was nothing, but stopped himself just in time. His wife was no trophy to be cosseted or protected; she needed neither. Anna Taylor-Ryan was a survivor who had lost every member of her family and had nearly been lost herself. There was nothing new he could tell her about the kind of dark, nefarious men and women he hunted each day, nor about the kind of destruction they left in their wake. She had been witness to both and would carry the memories with her, probably for the rest of her life.

This was not a woman who would be satisfied with some menial task, paying lip service to her considerable talents rather than using them as a force for good. He could not have loved her, otherwise, nor would he wish her to be anything less than who she was.

"I need to know who Riccardo Spatuzzi really is," he said firmly. "Inspector Ricci knows the name but either can't, or won't, tell me the connection. I suspect it has to do with the mafia, but I have no idea to what extent. Without the full picture, we can't eliminate the mafia as having a possible connection to his disappearance."

Anna thought for a moment.

"The best person to speak to would be a journalist," she decided. "Somebody in the local press, who knows the city inside out. I can try to find one."

Ryan nodded his thanks.

"Make a few calls, speak to some people, but wait until I come back before heading into the city."

"He won't come after me," she said, but Ryan shook his head.

"We don't know that. Please, Anna."

Before she had an opportunity to answer, they were interrupted by the familiar, tinny rendition of the *Indiana Jones* theme tune ringing out from Ryan's smartphone.

CHAPTER 10

The Criminal Investigation Department was based out of Northumbria Police Headquarters, east of Newcastle upon Tyne in an area known as Wallsend. It was the old heartland of the city, a cemetery of shipyards and Roman forts, as well as being the hub of a proud community that weathered whichever storm rolled in and battered them from the sea. There was *spirit* here, MacKenzie thought, as she and Phillips turned into the staff car park. There was still plenty of industry, too, if the queue for their local Pie Van was anything to go by. What had started out as a humble operation outside the gates of the constabulary's former office building had, by now, grown into several high-end kitchens-on-wheels serving everything from ham-and-pease-pudding stotties to vegan-friendly falafel.

When she mentioned as much to Phillips, he pulled an expressive face.

"Aye, that's the price of capitalism," he said. "I remember the days when I could pop down for a corned beef pasty and an Irn Bru and it'd take two minutes. Now, it's all, *diet* this and *organic* that, and the pasties are the size of postage stamps."

He patted his stomach.

"I s'pose it's for the best," he said, sounding unconvinced.

MacKenzie turned to face him.

"I think you're looking just fine, Frank."

It didn't matter that Phillips considered himself an experienced Man of the World. One look from Denise MacKenzie was enough to turn him weak at the knees and, paired with the kind of suggestive smile she was deploying right now, he might as well wave a white flag and surrender.

"Aye. Well," he said, eloquently. "I've, ah, well…I wanted to look smart for the wedding."

"You'd always look smart, to me," she said.

He made a valiant effort to pull himself together.

"I don't know if this counts as workplace harassment but, if it does, I want you to know that I'm consenting."

MacKenzie burst out laughing and planted a quick, smacking kiss on his upturned face.

"Take it easy, sergeant. We've got a full day's work ahead of us before anybody's getting harassed."

With that, she gave him a wink and stepped out of the car while he sat there for a couple of seconds grinning like a fool.

"What a woman," he sighed.

If the exterior of Police Headquarters was a triumph of boxy, uninspiring architecture, then its interior was a triumph of cheap, clinical décor. There was a sweepstake running on how long it would take for the first leak to start in the ceiling above the reception foyer and Phillips' bet was that a damp spot would appear by the end of the week. He peered closely at the foamy ceiling tiles as they passed underneath, tutting when he found them all intact.

"Told you it would take longer," MacKenzie said. "My bet was for six months, on the nose."

Phillips waved that away, good-naturedly.

"I'm sticking to my guns," he said. "I've spent nearly thirty years working in and out of government buildings and, I'm telling you, that ceiling will spring a leak by the end of the week."

She stopped dead in the foyer and turned on him with narrowed eyes.

"Now, Frank. Don't think you can go and hurry things along by leaving a tap running on the floor above," she warned him, pointing a red-tipped fingernail above her head.

He had the grace to look abashed.

"As if the thought had ever crossed my mind," he said, gravely.

"Mmm."

They buzzed through a set of security doors leading to the office suite that housed CID and made their way up to the first floor, passing along what seemed like miles of carpet-tiled corridor until they reached the open-plan space where they spent at least half their lives. MacKenzie slung her shoulder bag onto the back of her chair and her eyes strayed to the empty space further along the row of desks, where they would usually find Ryan seated with his head bent industriously over a stack of files or his flinty blue gaze trained on the computer screen.

She glanced around the room at the motley crew of men and women belonging to Ryan's stable of detectives. Despite the recent shift change, they looked tired. Outside, rain had started to fall, pattering against the window panes lining one wall of the room and it was having a soporific effect on them all. At moments like these, it was hard not to miss Ryan's natural leadership; the energy he carried with him when he entered the room and the passion for his work that couldn't help but inspire others to feel the same.

But there was no time to miss him while there was work to be done and, sensing that the energy in her workforce was low, MacKenzie called an impromptu meeting.

"Alright, listen up!" she called out. "Can everybody gather around, please?"

Chairs were scraped back, and the muted rumble of conversation died down as the men and women of Ryan's division formed a semi-circle around her desk.

"Morning, everyone," she said, injecting a bit of cheer into her voice. "As you know, the Chief has asked me to keep an eye on things while DCI Ryan is away for the next few days. We all know one another," she added, with what she hoped was a friendly smile. "We've all worked together on countless cases over the past few years, so I hope you feel you can come to me if there's a problem."

She saw nods around the room, which was encouraging.

"Look, I want to make one thing clear," she continued. "I'm just keeping his seat warm, I'm not looking to take it."

She paused to let that sink in.

"With that in mind, I want us to focus on keeping things on an even keel over the next few days. I'd like each of you to let me have a summary of your caseload and how it's progressing, so that we can divvy up the resources as efficiently as possible. I'll start by saying that Phillips and I caught a new case yesterday morning, one we're treating as a murder enquiry, so we may need to reassign resources depending on how things pan out."

Although serious crime was their bread and butter, the truth was that murder remained a rare occurrence, for which they could all be grateful. Rarer still did they find a murder that did not conform to the usual tropes of gang or inter-family crime but appeared to be entirely without motive. As she looked around the faces of her colleagues, she saw their eyes sharpen.

"The victim is Edward Charon, a sixty-five-year-old resident of Warkworth and former ferryman to the castle hermitage. He was found bludgeoned to death inside the hermitage around ten-fifteen, yesterday morning."

"How long had he been lying there?" somebody asked.

"We're waiting to hear from the pathologist about post mortem interval," MacKenzie replied. "The temperatures fell to well below zero last night, so it's hard to estimate, but judging from experience I'd say he'd been dead at least twelve hours."

"Why would anybody bump him off?" one of the DCs asked. "Was he dealing on the side?"

Nine times out of ten, drugs or some other illegal commodity lay behind an otherwise motiveless crime, so it wasn't a foolish question.

"We haven't ruled anything out," MacKenzie said. "We're having trouble finding a next-of-kin for the victim and the process has thrown up some questions surrounding Charon's identity, which Mel has been looking into."

She sought out trainee DC Melanie Yates, who poked her head around the side of one of her taller colleagues.

"Maybe you could give us a quick run-down of where you are with Charon's background check?"

Yates was a quiet, no-nonsense woman in her twenties. Her work on the fringes of several investigations had been sufficiently impressive for Ryan to pluck her from the realms of obscurity and offer the opportunity to train on the detective's pathway, as he had done with others before. Melanie was honest enough to admit that, having idolised Ryan from the very first time she'd seen him in the corridors of CID, it was a dream come true to find herself working within his team. She learned something new almost every day from her more experienced colleagues and she had almost overcome the foolish, schoolgirl crush she harboured for her very-married boss.

Almost.

As it was, she was worrying about his welfare in Italy and had limited herself to a maximum of three enquiries as to his wellbeing per day. Anything more would look far too familiar.

"Mel?"

"Right, yes. Umm," she scrambled her thoughts together, never more aware of several sets of eyes having swivelled in her direction.

"A simple search of the victim's home and local enquiries elicited no information on Edward Charon's next-of-kin, so I ran a standard check on his background. He had no criminal record or cautions to his name, but it appears that Charon changed his name by deed poll in February of last year."

"What was his name before?"

"Edward Clarkson," Yates replied. "Aged sixty-five and a former resident of Gosforth."

"What did he do for a living?" Phillips asked.

"He was a barrister," she replied.

There were murmurs of surprise around the room.

"Eh?" Phillips said, capturing what they were all thinking. "Why the heck would a barrister change his name and move out of the city? Unless he fell in with the wrong element," he added, answering his own question.

"I don't know yet," Yates replied. "We need to speak to his former colleagues in the chambers where he worked— ah, *Riverside Chambers*—down by the Crown Court on the Quayside."

"What about family?" MacKenzie asked.

"Edward Clarkson was unmarried, although he cohabited with a woman by the name of Jill Grant from 1991 to 2004 at his home in Gosforth."

Yates reeled off an address on one of the most expensive streets in the city.

"See if you can contact her," MacKenzie said. "She's the closest thing to family we've found, so let's see what she can tell us."

"Will do," Yates murmured.

"Something's off here," Phillips burst out. "A man of his age and means doesn't leave it all behind and bugger off to Warkworth for no reason, unless he's had some sort of mid-life crisis."

"Some people crave the quiet life," MacKenzie said.

"That's all well and good, but he didn't need to change his name for that, did he?" Phillips folded his arms and shook his head. "Naht. The bloke was running from something, that has to be it."

MacKenzie was minded to agree.

"Frank, you look into that connection with Yates, while I'm paying a visit to the pathologist."

She turned back to the rest of the team and proceeded to divvy up the remaining tasks, appointing a reader-receiver and several analysts to manage the influx of data that was already starting to come in.

"Boss?"

MacKenzie paused in the act of retrieving her coat.

"Ah, yeah?"

"What's the name of the operation? For the board, I mean?"

Her mind was blank for a moment, then it cleared.

"Let's call it 'Operation Hotspur,'" she said, as a nod to the young Percy Earl of Northumberland whose exploits had even inspired Shakespeare, in his day. "Maybe it'll bring us luck."

CHAPTER 11

The streets of Florence sang with the chatter of Italian voices raised in the kind of friendly to-and-fro that Ryan remembered so well from his youth. Friends waved at each other across the street or stopped traffic just to say 'hello' and nobody seemed to mind. Having left Anna in the safe hands of his housekeeper, Magda, Ryan had uncovered his old scooter from the dusty confines of the garage. He'd been delighted to find that its engine revved into life with a smooth, purring roar and, moments later, he'd exited the high-security perimeter of the Villa Lucia to rattle through the streets, blending in with a stream of dark-haired men and women making their way into the city centre. As the wind rushed against his face, it was a journey of rediscovery, like a sepia-hued snapshot of an old memory he'd cherished from boyhood and had been afraid to uncover in case it would be spoiled. It struck him how difficult it was to come back to investigate the possibility of murder, especially when his heart urged him to forget about

Nathan Armstrong and lose himself in the cultured scents and tastes of Tuscany instead.

He slowed down as morning traffic grew heavier towards the centre and didn't stop to admire the River Arno as he crossed it, focusing instead on reaching his destination in one piece as he wove between the line of stationary cars, their horns blaring as a delivery van pulled to a stop in the middle of the road and began to unload its goods. Eventually, Ryan navigated his way through the side streets, circumventing the Duomo and working mostly from memory until he found himself outside *GIDES* headquarters at the *Commissariato San Giovanni* once more.

After slotting his scooter into one of the bays on the road outside, he entered the building ahead of Armstrong's allotted time and according to Ricci's express instructions, exactly at nine-fifteen. He was a man of his word and Ryan agreed it would serve no purpose to antagonise Armstrong any more than was necessary, so it was best he avoided any uncomfortable run-ins.

Inspector Ricci was waiting for him inside the cool foyer and, this time, was joined by one of his colleagues at the *Gruppo*, a female detective by the name of Chiara Banotti.

"Good morning, Chief Inspector," Ricci welcomed him. "Allow me to introduce Sergeant Banotti to you. She will be accompanying me during the interview with Armstrong."

Ryan shook the woman's hand and found it firm. Her dark hair was held back in a professional chignon and her face was sober, signalling to him that she, like Ricci, would be taking their duties seriously.

"Sergeant," he said, politely. "Thank you for taking the time to pursue things with Armstrong. I appreciate how busy you must be."

She gave a slight shrug.

"It is my city," she told him, and he understood what she meant without seeking further explanation. She had pride in her birthplace and would not tolerate anything that threatened to sully its beauty.

"This way, please," Ricci murmured.

Ryan was shown into an observation room not dissimilar to those back at CID Headquarters. One long wall had been built from reinforced glass, allowing him to view the neighbouring interview room whilst remaining unseen from the other side. It was slightly old-fashioned, he supposed, now that television links were more widely used to replay recorded interviews. However, he was of the old-school approach that nothing quite matched the immediate impact of watching an interview in real-time. It afforded him the ability to assess body language and pick up on the kind of tiny facial tics which so often told him more than words might say.

Not that it carried much weight in court, he had to admit.

"Coffee," Ricci said simply, nodding towards a tray holding a cafetière and a small jug of milk. "Some things are universal."

Ryan flashed him a smile of thanks.

"I don't need to remind you that you should, on no account, enter the interview room without my express permission," Ricci said.

Ryan bobbed his head.

"I already told you, this is your baby. I won't interfere."

But, as Ricci and his sergeant turned to leave the room, Ryan offered one small piece of advice.

"One thing," he said, choosing his words with care. "Armstrong responds to flattery. If he feels threatened, intellectually or otherwise, he'll clam up and give you nothing. Your best bet would be to appeal to his ego."

Ricci nodded.

"Thank you."

Ryan watched the door click shut and then settled down to wait.

While Ryan sipped a cup of coffee and awaited the arrival of Nathan Armstrong, Anna found herself engaged in a Mexican standoff. She stood in the shiny marble hallway of the Villa Lucia, her straw bag in one hand and sunglasses in the other, fully intending to head out into the city.

But Magda had other ideas.

The older woman stood guarding the doorway in her smart uniform of black trousers and plain white shirt, her short hair cut into a stylish yet practical bob around a beautiful face. At first, Anna had been fooled into thinking the woman was a mere housekeeper but everything about her eyes and general stance now told her otherwise.

"This is ridiculous," she said, for the third time. "I'm not under house arrest!"

"Mr Ryan asked me to watch over you," Magda said, in the same maddeningly calm tone she'd used for the past ten minutes.

"And that's very nice of him—and you," Anna replied, sweetly. "But I don't need a bodyguard, thanks. I'm perfectly capable of getting around the city without a chaperone."

Even saying words like *bodyguard* and *chaperone* was enough to make Anna grimace. She was hardly the Prime Minister, for goodness' sake.

"I have no doubt that the *signora* is very able," the other woman said. "But my instructions are to protect you and stay with you at all costs. I cannot do that if you are not with me, can I? Would you wish for me to lose my job?"

Anna gave a hefty sigh, acknowledging that the other woman had scored a direct hit with that last below-the-belt remark. Magda knew fine well that Anna would never want to be responsible for depriving the woman of her livelihood and had used her own good nature against her, mercilessly.

She may have won the battle, so the saying went, but she had not won the war.

"Fair enough," Anna said, taking the wind out of her sails. "You can come with me."

Magda looked uncertain.

"It would be easier if we stayed at the villa," she said.

"I'm sure it would, but that's the coward's way," Anna snapped. "A woman like you must agree that we're just as capable of defending ourselves on the street."

Magda nodded slowly. As a woman with twenty years' experience defending important but vulnerable men, she could hardly disagree.

"Besides," Anna said, playing her trump card. "Top spec security is one thing but, if a madman was intent on getting behind it, he'd find a way. They always do."

Magda wavered, once again unable to argue with the logic.

"Where is it you wish to go?" she asked, cautiously.

"Only to the Piazza di Santa Trinita," Anna replied quickly. "I'm meeting a journalist from the *Florence Daily News* at one of the cafes there. I'm already running late," she added, to hurry things along.

Magda shuffled her feet, clearly unsure what to do for the best.

"Armstrong will be in an interview at the police station for the next hour, probably," Anna said, dealing a final blow. "He won't be out on the streets looking for me, so it's the ideal time to go."

Magda's face cleared.

"That's true," she admitted, and then smiled grudgingly. "You are well matched."

"I don't—?"

"You and Max are both as stubborn as mules."

"Thank you," Anna said, meekly.

While Magda muttered something unintelligible about bringing around the car, Anna smiled to herself at the woman's reference to 'Max'. It was true that Ryan was possessed of a series of names, none of which he responded to on any regular basis other than simply, 'Ryan'. But here, she could imagine a young Maxwell Charles Finley-Ryan scampering around the Tuscan hills or splashing around with his sister in the pool outside.

As she thought of the late Natalie Ryan, her eye fell on another set of family portraits, this time professional black and white shots taken at least fifteen years ago. There, hung proudly in the centre, was one of Ryan's sister. Natalie had been a beautiful young woman, one who had barely lived enough of life to know what womanhood meant. Seeing their photographs side-by-side, it was impossible not to notice the strong family resemblance between the siblings, each with striking eyes and coal black hair they'd inherited from their father. Anna closed her eyes for a moment and remembered her own sister, Megan. They hadn't shared much in common, either in looks or in temperament, but she mourned her loss all the same.

Her eyes flickered open again and she found herself looking at the face of her husband, captured as a much younger man. There were fewer laughter lines around his eyes, but they were open and carefree; not so guarded as they were now.

Life had taught him that.

Anna never needed to ask why he pursued a constant quest to avenge the dead, nor why it mattered so much to him. The reason was there, hanging on the wall right in front of her. He still felt responsible for what had happened to Natalie three years earlier and, until he could forgive himself, he would never stop trying to atone. It made no difference how many people had told him that he was not to blame for her death; he carried the guilty weight of it on his shoulders every day. He would never be one to stand by and risk more families being devastated, as his own had been, not if there was anything he could do to prevent it.

She heard the hum of a car engine on the driveway outside and broke out of her reverie, slipping on her sunglasses and stepping outside into the morning sunshine to join Magda.

Ryan might be on a quest, she thought, but he didn't have to do it alone.

CHAPTER 12

"My client wishes it to be on record that he has agreed to cooperate with your enquiries entirely as a gesture of his own goodwill and not because he has been compelled to do so."

The words were spoken by Nathan Armstrong's high-ticket Italian lawyer, who was seated to the right of the man himself as they gathered around a small table in one of the more attractive interview rooms at the *Commissariato*. Every inch of him looked expensive, from the cut of his suit to the hideously pricey watch weighing down his wrist. Even his hair looked expensive, Ryan thought, as he watched from his position in the observation room. It remained to be seen whether he was worth the top dollar Armstrong would be paying for the privilege of such a well-dressed legal representative.

"It's noted," Ricci was saying. "And we would like to thank Signor Armstrong for being so cooperative."

Ryan smiled as he noted the deferential doffing of the cap.

"Let's get on with it," Armstrong said. "I don't have all day."

"Surely," Ricci replied. He recited a standard caution and then made a show of fiddling with his paperwork. Ryan raised an eyebrow at the small display of theatrics but couldn't fault the objective which was, of course, to appear unthreatening.

It seemed his Italian counterpart had decided to take his advice.

"We are investigating the disappearance of Riccardo Spatuzzi, an Italian national. Do you recognise the name?"

Armstrong didn't so much as blink.

"Of course," he said. "His disappearance was reported in the Viennese press just before I left for Barcelona."

Ricci linked his fingers on the table top.

"I understand from the schedule published on your website that you were due to appear at a signing event in Vienna on Thursday 1st February, is that correct?"

Armstrong nodded.

"If you could speak up, for the microphone?"

"Yes," he snapped.

"Thank you," Ricci murmured. "Did you attend a gala dinner at the British Consulate in Vienna on Friday 2nd February?"

"You are well aware that my client was on the guest list to attend," Armstrong's lawyer chimed in.

"Being on the guest list and being in attendance are two different things," Chiara Banotti said quietly.

"I *did* attend," Armstrong said. "Hundreds of people could tell you I was there, so I'm hardly likely to say otherwise."

In the observation room, Ryan barely held back a snort. Once again, the man's arrogance revealed itself in the notion that, amongst a gathering of nearly three hundred, he would be so distinguished as to be remembered by the majority.

"Our Austrian counterparts are in the process of re-interviewing everyone who attended the gala dinner," Ricci said quietly, to give them all something to think about, then came straight to the point. "Do you remember seeing this man at the gala?"

He retrieved an A4-sized picture of Riccardo Spatuzzi from his folder and placed it on the table. Ryan leaned forward, almost pressing his face to the glass, to watch Armstrong's response closely. His eyes flicked down once to look at the photograph, then away again.

"Perhaps," Armstrong said. "I can't remember. I met any number of UN officials, but he certainly wasn't seated on my table at dinner. That's Riccardo, I take it? Who was he?"

Ricci said nothing, being of the same opinion as Ryan that silence could be a powerful tool.

"Look, Inspector, I'm sorry to hear the man's gone missing but I didn't know him and never met him before in my life. I think I've made myself very clear."

"And any further badgering could be construed as harassment of a witness," his lawyer put in, ladling it on thick for the benefit of the recording. "So far, you've provided no reasonable grounds for my client to be here."

"I'm coming to that," Ricci told him. "As a final point, then, our records show your outbound flight from Vienna to Barcelona was at midday on Saturday 3rd February, the day after the gala. Is that correct?"

"I believe so," Armstrong said. "Again, that's a matter of record."

Ricci nodded, fiddling with his paperwork again.

"Except…the flight records show that you did not turn up for that flight and instead purchased a ticket for a later flight, at 13:50. Is that correct?"

A muscle in Armstrong's jaw ticked.

"Yes, come to think of it, you're right. I was running late that day."

"May I ask why?"

"I spent a late evening at the gala and slept in," he said, injecting a layer of charm into his voice and shifting his body ever so slightly towards Chiara Banotti.

Hell, it had worked in the past.

"And, I suppose, if we were to contact your hotel they would confirm you were late to check out?"

"I doubt it," Armstrong drawled. "Since I stayed in a serviced apartment, which I was free to use all day, if I wished."

Ricci nodded. He was already aware of the address of the luxury apartment where Armstrong had stayed. It was very similar to the apartment owned by Armstrong in Florence, so it seemed the man was not a fan of hotels, in general.

"You prefer your privacy, *signore*?"

"That question bears no relation to your enquiry," the lawyer said. "Move on to your next point, Inspector."

Ricci gave one of his shrugs.

"The week before your stay in Vienna, I understand you were in Paris for a signing event on Friday 26th January. Is that correct?"

"Yes," Armstrong replied.

From the observation room, Ryan saw that, beneath the table, Armstrong's index finger had begun to tap irritably against his knee.

Ricci reached for a second folder and took his time searching for a photograph of Luc Bernard, which he placed beside the picture of Riccardo Spatuzzi. Ryan didn't need to see either photograph, since their faces were already imprinted on his mind from the copies he held at home.

"Do you recognise this man?"

This time, Armstrong didn't so much as look.

"No, I don't."

Ricci was not deterred.

"Would you look again, please?"

Armstrong looked for several seconds, to make a point, and then away again.

"I still don't recognise him."

"This is Luc Bernard, a waiter from Paris. He attended your book signing at *Shakespeare's* bookshop on 26th January."

"How can you be so sure?" his lawyer asked. "People often register their name ahead of time but don't turn up on the day."

"The bookshop have provided CCTV footage which confirms it, as does his social media accounts. He uploaded an image of himself standing next to your client, who was seated at his signing table in the image."

Ricci slid his hand inside the folder again and produced the requisite images taken from the Facebook and Instagram sites.

"So I signed his book? So he took a photo beside me?" Armstrong scoffed. "I still don't remember him. If you think I would, you clearly have no idea how many people I meet on a weekly basis, Inspector."

"I'm sure I don't," Ricci said. "I've never been a celebrity like you, *signore*."

Behind the safety glass, Ryan grinned. He had a feeling he was going to like Alessandro Ricci, once this was all behind them.

"So, to confirm, you have no recollection of having met this man, although you acknowledge that you *did*, in fact, meet him during the course of your signing event?"

"My client has made himself perfectly clear."

Ricci and Banotti exchanged a look. Without further evidence, there was not much else they could use to try to draw Armstrong out.

"Is it true that you left Paris for Vienna on Sunday 28th January?"

"I presume you've already checked my flight details, Inspector. Yes, it's true."

Ricci ran a hand over his jaw, considering how far he could go.

"Would you be willing to provide us with a list of your movements during your stay in Paris and Vienna?"

"Absolutely not," his lawyer broke in. "My client has a right to his own private life, the details of which he is not compelled to discuss without the proper order. If you wish to charge him with an offence, then do so. Without it, he won't be telling you anything more."

"I couldn't have put it better, myself," Armstrong smiled, once more the charming raconteur. "Incidentally, Inspector, why is it that I'm singled out as a suspect—"

"We did not say you were a suspect, *signore*," Ricci put in.

"—as a *suspect*," Armstrong repeated. "When these two missing persons may be wholly unconnected. Why are the police so sure there is a connection and, moreover, that I am connected? There must be thousands of people who can claim to have been in Paris and Vienna around the same time as these two unfortunate souls went missing."

When neither detective answered him, Armstrong laughed shortly.

"Something to think about," he said to himself.

Throughout the interview, Armstrong had given no hint at all that he was aware of anyone observing him through the mirrored-glass wall but as he was leaving the room, he stopped dead in front of it. On the other side, Ryan took an automatic step backwards, although he knew that the man could neither see nor hear him.

On the other side, Armstrong smiled slowly.

"Well, well," he purred.

CHAPTER 13

By the time they reached the Piazza di Santa Trinita, Anna had a newfound respect for life and limb. Although it was only a mile from the Villa Lucia, traffic conditions and speed restrictions meant that the journey should have taken up to fifteen minutes.

It had taken five.

Magda, it seemed, was a woman of many talents.

"*Eccoci qui.* Here we are," she said, after zooming along the *Via de' Tornabuoni* and executing a perfect parallel parking manoeuvre into a space Anna would have sworn was too small.

Anna stepped out of the car onto terra firma and looked around the square which was, somewhat ironically, triangular. In its centre was an ancient Roman column inscribed with the word 'JUSTICE' at the top and it was surrounded by several palaces and the church from which the square took its name. It was an upmarket part of the city, if the high-end designer fashion outlets and clientele were anything to go by. On the corner, an old fourteenth-century palazzo was now the global headquarters of one such brand and she watched a woman with an improbably small dog step out of its glass doors to teeter along to the next shop further down the street.

"The café is this way," Magda said, walking around to stand close to Anna.

"You don't have to—"

Magda's expression was unwavering.

"I go where you go," she said, simply. "Get used to it."

Anna's eyebrows flew into her hairline at the woman's tone, but she had to admit she respected her for it. Not many would have stood their ground against their employer's wife, after all.

They walked a hundred metres down a side street until they came to a pretty café with wrought-iron bistro-style tables set out on the pavement and creeping wisteria crawling up its ancient walls. It was set inside the ground floor of one of the many narrow old buildings that made up the city of Florence, with narrow, shuttered windows to the front. Ryan had told her that the buildings had been fortified in such a way as to protect its inhabitants from intruders, but they were often large and impressive inside, with blooming gardens hidden behind the austere frontage.

"This is it," Magda said, casting her eyes up and down the street. "Who are you meeting?"

"Ah, his name is Andrea Conti," she replied. "He's a journalist with the *Florence Daily News*."

Magda nodded.

"I recognise the name," she said, clearly relieved.

"Let's go and sit down," Anna suggested, moving towards a pretty table beneath a twine of wisteria. "We still have a while before he's due to arrive."

Magda shot her a look.

"We're early? I thought you told me we were running late?"

Anna gave her a breezy smile.

"Did I? Silly me."

Andrea Conti was widely regarded as being the most knowledgeable newspaper hack in the city of Florence. He'd worked on most of the beats over the course of his thirty-year career but had settled on reporting crime which, for the main part, centred around petty misdemeanours. Mafia-related crime had reduced in recent years thanks to a national crack-down, although whether it had succeeded in higher regulation and reduced corruption or the other way around, he couldn't say with any degree of certainty. Conti's world was filled with spider diagrams and torn bits of paper tacked to the cork board which covered an entire wall in his respectable one-bedroomed apartment. Information flowed towards him like irrigation channels from numerous sources dotted around the city and far beyond, informing his hard-hitting articles and weekly round-ups. He had a reputation for being immune to bribery, which had been the deciding factor when Anna had made her calls earlier that morning. She wanted someone whose information she—and Ryan— could trust, and who better than a man who would, by all accounts, have made a good policeman himself?

"Signora Ryan?"

Conti did not conform to the stereotype of a world-weary newspaperman. For one thing, he wore his fifty-one years with a certain irreverent flair and might have passed for any one of the affluent tourists who wandered past him.

"Signor Conti?" she replied. "Come and join us."

He looked across at Magda with a question in his eyes and Anna cursed herself for not coming up with some plausible excuse.

"Ah, let me introduce Magda," she began. "My—"

"I am her aunt," Magda lied seamlessly in her native tongue. "Anna is visiting with me. I hope you don't mind me tagging along."

He looked between them and thought that, had he not been adept at reading human behaviour, he might have swallowed it. The age gap was about right and, although the younger woman's skin was a shade or so lighter, they both had dark hair and eyes, and the kind of symmetrical features that *might* have belonged to the same gene pool. As it was, the young Mrs Ryan had need of company to look out for her wellbeing, which was interesting in itself. The only Ryans he knew of that might be of sufficient importance as to warrant personal security were the English family who owned the Villa Lucia, up on Viale Machiavelli.

They'd visited the villa over the summer, he happened to know, but he hadn't seen this woman before.

He'd look into it, he decided.

"Of course not," he said aloud, settling himself at the table beside them. "How may I help you? I understood from your telephone call this morning that you have some information for me?"

Anna cleared her throat nervously. She'd only been able to secure a meeting at short notice on the promise of a juicy new lead but, now it came to it, she realised there was nothing she could tell him.

At least, nothing on the record.

"Before I come to that, I'd like you to tell me everything you know about Riccardo Spatuzzi," she said, signalling a waiter for some drinks.

Conti placed an order for a beer and smiled again.

"Mrs Ryan, why should I tell you my secrets, if you will not tell me yours?"

"You shouldn't but, if you don't, we're at a stalemate," she said, taking a delicate sip of her water. "I'm sorry you've had a wasted journey."

He let out a booming laugh which caught the attention of the neighbouring table.

"You're a tough cookie," he said, appreciatively. From the look of her, a strong gust of wind could take her away, but he was delighted to find there was backbone beneath.

"Alright, I'll tell you this much," he said, leaning forward so that only they could hear him. "Be careful who you speak to about Riccardo Spatuzzi. There are people who would pay a lot of money for information on his whereabouts and others who would kill for it. Ask too many questions and they may start to believe you know something about it."

He paused, clearly wondering the same thing himself.

"Perhaps that's the lead you spoke of, *signora*? You know what happened to Riccardo Spatuzzi?"

His face became animated and he began to reach for his phone so that he could record the conversation.

"No! No, I don't. I—look, all I want to know is whether he was embroiled in something…something bad. Were you investigating him at all before he died?"

Conti looked between them, weighing up his options, then blew out a long breath and leaned forward again.

"You must know that Riccardo is the son of Monica Spatuzzi?"

Anna stole a glance at Magda, who gave a small shake of her head to signal that she had no idea who he was talking about.

"Who is Monica Spatuzzi? Someone famous?"

Conti laughed again and ran a hand over the back of his neck.

"You could say that," he replied. "Spatuzzi is *mafiosa*. The head of the family. Riccardo is her eldest son."

Anna gulped down another mouthful of water.

"They have a villa in the hills in Fiesole. They say it used to belong to Michelangelo," Conti continued. "My sources tell me Spatuzzi was beside herself when she heard Riccardo was missing. There's been a rise in local crime since it happened."

"So you're telling me Spatuzzi believes another one of the families has taken her son and she's given the order for punishment?"

"You're catching on," he said, downing the last of his beer before signalling for another. "They're trying to find out who is responsible, and she's promised a fortune to whoever can bring her information. Be careful, *signora*, people would do a lot for money like that."

Anna nodded.

"I understand—and thank you—but I don't really know anything."

"You know more than you think and, as for the rest, people can guess. For example, I know that you must be the wife of Max Ryan, the son of David Ryan, the former diplomat who has the Villa Lucia. I heard that Ryan became a detective in London, years ago, and the papers reported the death of his sister around the world. I wrote a piece about it, myself," he added, with a timely pause as a mark of respect. "It would not be unusual for Ryan to have brought his wife to visit his family's villa, but he is not here with you, he is at the *Commissariato San Giovanni* this morning."

Anna was shocked.

"You are surprised, *signora*, but it is my business to know these things. When a little bird tells me a senior inspector goes to the airport twice in the same day and brings back an English detective with his beautiful wife," he raised his glass of beer towards her. "My interest is piqued. So, I asked another little bird, who told me the English detective is visiting to assist an enquiry into a missing person."

He wiped the edge of his mouth with a napkin.

"And, here you are, asking me about Riccardo Spatuzzi," he finished. "It would seem, *signora*, that you know who has taken him and, moreover, that your husband is working with the police to charge that person."

Magda shot Anna a look of sheer panic, but Anna put a hand on her arm to reassure her and then looked Conti straight in the eye.

"What do you want, *signore*?"

He polished off the last of his beer and set the glass down on the table before answering.

"I want full exclusivity," he said. "Everyone is going to want a piece of this story when it breaks but I want to be the first. If your husband speaks to anyone, he speaks to me. In exchange, I'll keep this to myself. For now," he tagged on.

Anna thought of all the unknown faces passing them in the street and wondered how many might work for the Spatuzzi family. How many might, even now, be reporting back to her. If Conti knew of their arrival and of the reason for it, there was no telling how many others.

"Deal," she said simply.

CHAPTER 14

By the time MacKenzie reached the Royal Victoria Infirmary, she was deeply regretting her decision to stop off at the Pie Van for a bite to eat on the way. The organic couscous salad was sitting heavily in her stomach and she knew that it would take a monumental effort to keep it all down once she had completed the next unenviable task on her 'to do' list.

The mortuary at the RVI was home to the senior police pathologist attached to the Criminal Investigation Department, Doctor Jeffrey Pinter. He was a lanky man in his mid-fifties who had the misfortune of reflecting some of the physical characteristics of the dead he cared for, owing to a long-term deficit of Vitamin D. However, he was a cheerful man whose idiosyncrasies she was prepared to overlook because he was the best pathologist across several command divisions by a country mile.

"Morning, Jeff!" she called out to him as she keyed in the security access code and stepped inside the chilly interior of the mortuary.

"Morning!" he called back.

She looked around the room, seeking out the direction of his voice, then a balding head popped around the side of one of the large immersion tanks.

"Lovely to see you, Denise," he gushed, in the manner of a man who had never quite lost hope of a last-minute change of heart before her forthcoming wedding. "Ah, no Frank today? How's he faring?"

"He's well, thanks Jeff. Can't say the same for poor Edward Charon."

Taking his cue, Pinter turned to the business at hand.

"Yes, indeed. Well, I've finished my preliminary report. I've got a couple of the technicians working on the last few details before I submit my final report, but the overall opinion is unlikely to change."

"I appreciate you turning this around so quickly," she said.

"It's been a slow week, as it happens," he remarked, scratching a bony finger against his earlobe in a manner she found vaguely nauseating. "Come on through and I'll give you the lowdown."

She followed the billowing tails of his lab coat through the main, open-plan mortuary room with its bank of metal drawers and overpowering lemony stench mingling with something undoubtedly rotten. It was a unique scent, one she would recognise anywhere but could never quite find the words to describe. It was unlike anything else, being both chemical and organic fused into one noxious-smelling gas.

"Bit heavy today, isn't it?" Pinter threw over his shoulder, as if he had known what she had been thinking. "We had a lady in here earlier who hadn't been found for rather a long time, I'm afraid."

"How sad," MacKenzie murmured, and wondered what kind of woman she had been; the lonely *Eleanor Rigby* character the Beatles had so deftly written into song or something else entirely? She supposed there was no sense in worrying about things she could not change.

"I've put our Mr Charon in here," Pinter said, opening a side door marked 'EXAMINATION ROOM A'.

As she stepped inside, MacKenzie thought briefly of all the other victims of crime she'd visited in the same room, with its clinical white-washed walls and impersonal metal trolley, and of how many more to come. The strip-light buzzing overhead shone a stark, grey-white light, serving to enhance the overall sense of gloom, and there was no time to prepare herself before Pinter whisked away the paper shroud covering what remained of Edward Charon.

"What can you tell me?" she asked, after a few seconds' adjustment.

"Well, for starters, it was tricky to estimate the precise time of death," Pinter said. "Charon's core temperature had regulated itself to the ambient temperature of his surroundings, which were below zero for most of the night he was lying in the hermitage. Set against that, the low temperatures effectively delayed the process of putrefaction we would ordinarily expect to see in predictable stages, which made life harder."

"I understand," she assured him. "I just want your best guess."

"In that case, I'd put the time of death at anywhere between fourteen to twenty hours before he was found."

MacKenzie winced.

"That's quite a gap," she said. "On the other hand, we may be able to narrow it down looking at the other facts. If we put his death at somewhere between two o'clock and eight o'clock on Wednesday, give or take, I can tell you straight away that he was still alive and rowing visitors across to the hermitage until four o'clock on Wednesday afternoon, when the castle closed. Apparently, he liked to have a final row up and down the river until around four-thirty, when he would stow the boat and the oars and head home. He spoke to his colleagues at around ten past four on Wednesday as a couple of them walked home via the riverbank. They seem to have been the last to see him alive."

"So, the post mortem interval reduces to somewhere between, let's say, four and eight o'clock on Wednesday evening."

"Much better," she said, with the hint of a smile. "I can work with a four-hour window. What about cause of death?"

Pinter pulled out a retractable pointer from some unseen orifice and unfolded it with a loud *click*.

"Massive cardiac arrest following organ failure. I've cleaned him up as much as possible, so you can see pretty clearly that he was dealt a fatal blow which was then followed by a series of lesser blows. They all seem to be centred on the same area of his head, which is unusual."

MacKenzie made a small sound of agreement.

"If Charon had turned to run or otherwise tried to defend himself, it would be harder to aim for the same spot again, wouldn't it?"

"Exactly," he said, in the sort of tone one might use to praise a good pupil. "Taking into account the direction of the blow, which is from behind, it seems safe to assume Charon was taken by surprise."

"That's what we thought at the scene," MacKenzie told him, but asked the next question as a matter of good procedure. "Any defensive wounds, or signs of tampering?"

Pinter shook his head.

"Nothing obvious," he said. "We've swabbed beneath the nails and I'll let you know when those results come through, or Faulkner will be in touch directly. That'll be a hard job, too, given the number of animal DNA profiles contaminating the scene."

MacKenzie looked down at Charon's hands which were encased in small plastic bags that were slowly ballooning as natural gas emissions left his body.

"We thought that, too," she said, and signalled that he could cover the man's body. "Thanks, Jeff."

"If I come across anything important, I'll be in touch."

She nodded, casting one last thoughtful look at the shrunken figure on the trolley.

"I don't mind telling you, Jeff, this one may turn out to be a tough nut to crack. It seemed obvious how Charon died, even when we saw him *in situ*, and everything you've told me today confirms it."

She half-turned to leave.

"It isn't so much the *how* that I'm worrying about, it's the *why*. I've got a terrible feeling that question won't be easy to answer, not this time."

Pinter gave her a lopsided smile that transformed his narrow face into something approaching human.

"If anyone can do it, you can."

She smiled in return, then a moment later she was gone.

Across town, Phillips and Yates crossed the River Tyne and made their way south towards the village of Cleadon, which straddled the county lines of South Tyneside and County Durham. It was one of the oldest villages in the region, with a history spanning over a thousand years, and was a well-to-do suburban area with the kind of amenities that made it popular to professional couples and families alike.

"Nice 'round here," Phillips remarked.

Just recently, he'd been wondering whether it was time for a change of scene. MacKenzie had sold her house after... well, after what happened, and had been living with him ever since. But the house he owned had been his late wife's too, and her taste was painted on every wall. He'd done his best to spruce the place up and had told MacKenzie time and again that she should change whatever she liked to make the place her own. All the same, he suspected she had too much respect to want to change much, even after all these years.

So perhaps it was time for a fresh start.

"My cousin lives near here, in Boldon," Yates said. "There's a nice charcuterie where you can get an eggs benedict that's to die for."

Phillips almost performed an emergency stop, but managed to hold off.

Twelve-thirty, the clock on the dashboard read. Maybe after they'd paid their house call, there'd be time for a quick nibble.

"It's just along here, to the left," Yates said, pointing towards a smart street of houses not far from the village green.

They pulled up in front of a red-brick detached property bearing a slate name plaque which read, 'LITTLE GABLES.'

"Sounds about right," Phillips muttered. "Howay, let's see what Eddie's former girlfriend has to say about him."

CHAPTER 15

Their enquiries had already confirmed Jill Grant was a self-employed graphic artist, with a studio at home which meant there was a good chance she would be in residence. Sure enough, it only took a couple of rings of the bell before the door swung open to reveal an irritated-looking woman in her late fifties.

"Yes?" she demanded.

"Jillian Grant? My name is Detective Sergeant Phillips, and this is trainee Detective Constable Yates. We were wondering if you could spare us a few moments of your time?"

They held out their warrant cards for her to inspect and watched her demeanour change rapidly.

"CID? That's serious crimes," she said, in a detached, faraway sort of voice. "Has something happened to Mark or Hannah?"

Her hand crept upward to clutch her neck.

"No, no. It's nothing to do with your family, love," Phillips said quickly, defusing the situation with the ease of long experience. "Actually, it's concerning someone you lived with a few years ago—Edward Clarkson?"

"Eddie?" she swallowed, clearly confused. "Yes. Yes, come in."

They followed her through an impressive hallway filled with modern pop art they presumed she had created herself and into a large kitchen-diner, where she invited them to sit at the dining table.

"Would you like some tea, or something?"

"That's kind, but we're fine," Phillips replied, deciding to hold out for the charcuterie down the road.

Jill sat down at the table beside them and linked her hands, which were covered in silver rings of varying designs.

"What's happened to Eddie?"

For once, Phillips remained silent and Yates looked across at him in surprise. He raised a single bushy eyebrow and she realised with dawning panic that he expected her to deliver the news, which was something she usually managed to dodge. Delivering bad news was one of the worst parts of the job but she knew it was something she needed to practice, which was precisely what Phillips intended.

She shuffled a bit in her chair.

"Ah, I'm sorry to tell you that Mr Ch—Mr Clarkson was murdered on Wednesday evening. I'm sure this must come as a shock, so please take all the time you need."

Not bad, Phillips approved silently.

"We're also hoping you might be able to fill us in on a few details about Eddie," he added, to give the woman something to focus on.

"I—I hadn't seen Eddie in quite a few years," Jill mumbled, kneading a sudden tension headache at the base of her neck.

"That's alright," he said reassuringly. "We just want to talk through whatever you can remember of him."

She laughed suddenly, but it was far from being a happy sound.

"What I remember?" She touched her fingers to her lips as she fought for composure and when she spoke, she sounded ten years older than she had moments before. "I remember the last time I saw Eddie, he was threatening to kill me. He was looming over me in the bedroom, naked after a shower, demanding to know who I'd seen that day. He was almost psychotic."

Phillips and Yates exchanged an eloquent look. This was not what they had been expecting to hear, although they couldn't say what they had expected, really.

"Was Mr Clarkson violent towards you?" Yates asked, gently.

The woman's eyes spoke of many things, but her lips pressed tightly shut.

"I'd rather not discuss that," she said.

"Of course," Yates replied. "Would it be better if we came back another time, perhaps when you have someone with you?"

Jill rubbed the back of her hand against her forehead and then let it fall away, staring off into the distance as memories swirled.

"No," she said eventually. "No, I'd rather get this out while Mark's at work. He knows...I told him all about Eddie, but I'd rather not go over it all again in front of him. He gets angry on my behalf."

They both nodded.

"Take your time," Phillips said.

"I met Eddie at a friend's party in 1990 or maybe 1991," she began. "Must've been 1991 because I had just turned thirty."

She sucked in a quivering breath.

"Eddie wasn't the most handsome man in the room, but he had charisma," she recalled. "He was very charming and, of course, he was a barrister working for the Crown Prosecution Service, which I thought was very important and glamorous."

Her lip curled, presumably at her former self.

"Eddie was a selfish man," she said. "I'm sorry to say it, now that he's dead, but it doesn't change the truth."

"It's okay," Yates murmured. "We're not here to judge anyone, we just want to know anything you might be able to tell us, so that we can try to find who killed him."

Jill nodded again and then drew in a shaky breath before rising to her feet.

"If it's alright with you, I think I'll make a pot of tea, after all. It'll give me something to do with my hands."

They waited while she found some cups and saucers, which rattled against the granite worktops as she lost her grip.

"Sorry," she muttered.

They said nothing and then, after a moment, she started talking again.

"As I said, I met Eddie in 1991 and fell head over heels in love with him. He was...*dashing*, I suppose."

Phillips thought of the man he'd seen lying dead on the hermitage floor and tried to imagine what he might have been like, years before.

He couldn't even begin.

"Eddie had just bought an enormous house in Gosforth and, within a couple of months, I agreed to move in with him."

Jill paused in the act of finding a tin of biscuits to look over her shoulder.

"I realise now how foolish that was," she said. "With Hannah—my daughter—I'd be up in arms if she agreed to live with a virtual stranger after only eight weeks. And she probably wouldn't listen to me," she added, with an air of acceptance. "Just as I didn't listen to anyone back then. As far as I was concerned, Eddie and I were going to get married one day and I'd be Mrs Edward Clarkson who lived in the fabulous house, wore fabulous clothes and whose husband was the toast of the town."

"But?" Yates prompted, gently.

"Exactly. *But*. It didn't take long for the cracks to show," she said bitterly. "Soon enough, he was criticising what I wore, how I behaved, even my accent. Apparently, the wife of a barrister isn't entitled to a regional accent. It was the height of hypocrisy, looking back, considering Eddie was born in Walkergate, himself."

Phillips knew the area well and its people were the salt of the Earth.

"So he was a bit of a snob, our Eddie?"

"That's putting it mildly," she replied, setting a polka-dot teapot on the table. "It started out with a couple of slaps here and there, if he thought I'd embarrassed him at a party, or said the wrong thing. He was such an insecure man, always wanting to be fashionable, never wanting people to think he wasn't anything other than perfect and successful. It was an impossible standard."

She sank down into a chair, weary with the effort of remembering.

"You said Eddie was born in Walkergate," Phillips prompted. "Do you happen to know the name of his parents, or whether he kept in touch with any family? Brothers, sisters?"

"He told me once that his parents ran an Italian restaurant, but that could have been a load of old hogwash. He lied frequently," she explained. "But he never told me their names or whether they were still alive and, frankly, I learned not to ask."

Phillips was undeterred.

"How about close friendships, or his work colleagues?"

"Ah, well, when I knew him, he worked at Riverside Chambers, down on the Quayside," she said. "I think he knocked about with some of the other blokes there, and their wives, but it was all superficial friendships and golfing on Sundays. They loved fine dining, seeing whether they could out-do each other on a Saturday night, you know? But there was nobody he could have called in a crisis."

Yates opened her mouth, but then Jill added, "I suppose you could speak to his clerks. They knew everyone in chambers and all the gossip. They'd probably know more about Eddie than he knew about himself."

"Okay, thanks for the tip," Phillips said. "Let me ask you this: do you remember Eddie ever being frightened of anyone? Did he mention getting himself into any trouble, or getting in with the wrong people?"

Jill looked up with tired eyes.

"Eddie was a shark," she told him. "He didn't care who he upset, so long as he stayed at the top, ahead of everyone else. He could have offended half of the city and it wouldn't surprise me but, as for him ever telling me about being worried, he just wasn't that sort of person. He probably would have considered it a weakness to confide in me that way."

Phillips caught Yates' eye and she nodded, reaching for a card with her contact details printed on the front.

"Thanks so much for your help, Jill. If you think of anything else, please contact us right away. My number is on the card, or you can call the incident line."

Jill nodded, turning the little piece of rectangular card around in her fingers.

"Is it wrong to feel nothing?" she asked them, softly. "Shouldn't I feel sad that he ended up the way he did?"

Phillips laid a hand on her shoulder in a gesture of silent support.

"None of us are saints," he said. "We can't perform miracles."

She nodded and only after they left her alone in the silence of her own home did she allow the tears to fall.

CHAPTER 16

"There's nothing more I can do."

Inspector Ricci held up his hands in an apologetic gesture and leaned back in his chair, while Ryan paced around his office like a caged tiger.

"There has to be something," he argued. "Has anything else come through from the Parisian police? Surely they've gone through Bernard's flat with a fine-toothed comb for forensics, by now."

Ricci's face said it all.

"I'm sorry, my friend. They have a different policy in France. The authorities do not continue to investigate the disappearance of missing adults unless there is clear evidence of foul play or unless that person has shown signs of intending to commit suicide. The case of Luc Bernard does not fall into either category, so I heard from our colleagues today that they have now closed their investigation."

Ryan was silent for a full five seconds, during which time they could have sliced the tension in the room with a knife.

"You're telling me they've dropped it, just like *that*?" Ryan snapped his fingers angrily. "You're telling me they couldn't give a monkey's about that kid, who's probably rotting somewhere at the bottom of the Seine by now?"

Ricci pointed a finger.

"Calm down, Ryan. I am not your enemy."

"You're not much of a friend, either," Ryan snapped back. "Doesn't it rankle, even a bit, that Luc Bernard's life counts for nothing? What if he were your brother or your son? Would you care about it then?"

Ricci turned a slow shade of red and rose to his feet to plant the palms of his hands flat against the desktop.

"You are a guest in my city—"

"*Your* city?" Ryan queried.

"Yes! *My* city, not yours, for all you speak the language and know its streets. It doesn't give you the right to demand anything of me—"

"I'm not demanding anything of you that you shouldn't already be asking of yourself," Ryan snarled, snatching up the helmet for his scooter. "You call yourself a detective? Start detecting, for pity's sake."

He turned to leave, but Ricci's voice stopped him.

"Can't you see my hands are tied?" he said. "The police in Paris have closed the book on it and the Austrians are too scared—"

He broke off abruptly.

"Scared of what?" Ryan asked, silkily. "Scared because of who Riccardo Spatuzzi is, or of who his family are?"

Ricci's eyes flicked over to the door, which was ajar, and Ryan leaned across to push it fully shut.

"Start talking to me."

Before answering, the Italian moved across to one of his cabinets and retrieved a bottle of beer from a mini-fridge, shrugging when Ryan refused one for himself.

"The Spatuzzi family are notorious," he said, taking a long swig from his bottle. "Monica Spatuzzi is the head of the family, ever since her husband was assassinated three years ago. You might guess that we never found the culprit, although our sources indicate the Giordani family are most likely to have ordered the hit. That's a story for another day," he muttered.

"Go on," Ryan urged.

"Monica has three sons and a daughter, all of whom are active within the family operations except for her eldest son, Riccardo, who seems to have followed his own path. As you know, he is a lawyer and had worked for a leading Italian firm in Rome for over ten years, but he moved to Austria following his father's death, presumably because he did not want to be forced to take up the mantle."

Ricci paused to take another drink.

"Since we heard the news of Spatuzzi's disappearance, there has been a spate of organised crime. We think that Monica is searching for answers and believes one of the other families to be responsible."

"Do you think so?" Ryan asked.

Ricci muttered something in Italian.

"Until I heard from my colleague in Rome and until you arrived, yes, I believed one of the other families to be responsible. Punishment does not end at the Italian border," he said. "Even after I heard of the other missing person and of the...let's say the *coincidence* of Armstrong having met both men, I did not believe differently."

"But now?" Ryan prodded.

Ricci polished off his beer and dropped the empty bottle into a wastepaper basket with a heavy *thud*.

"Now...I do not know."

When Ryan would have argued again, Ricci held up a hand to stop him.

"I see what you see, my friend. I don't doubt what you have told me about Armstrong's history, especially after meeting him in the flesh today. He's a cold fish, that one."

"He's never been brought to justice," Ryan said urgently, willing him to listen. "That's why he's so complacent. He knows we don't have enough to charge him, so he can afford to be. But his ego is a fragile monster that needs constant feeding. If we continue to put pressure on him, continue to watch him, I believe he'll slip up."

Ricci made a clacking sound with his teeth, the only outward sign that he was conflicted.

"He is a famous man," he said. "We were given approval to question him and nothing more. If we go beyond that and are proven to be wrong, it would go very badly for you—and for me."

Ryan understood Ricci's concerns, but there were other people to consider, those whose lives mattered much, much more than any professional disgrace either man may suffer.

"Think of the families," he said, softly, and Ricci nodded.

"I am. It's the only reason we are still having this conversation. But I need to be clear, Ryan. We cannot approach him again without good cause. Leave it to me to try to find it and I'll do all I can, but I'm setting down a marker in the sand. Stay away from Armstrong, for now."

Ryan said nothing for a long, thrumming second.

"And if I happen to run into him at a public event?"

Ricci waggled his finger.

"The party on Saturday is a closed event," he said. "You cannot walk in from the street."

"You aren't the only one with connections," Ryan murmured, as he prepared to leave.

"If you're determined to unnerve the man, I can't stop you. But be careful," Ricci warned him. "Armstrong knows you are behind this; make no mistake about that."

Ryan nodded.

"I *want* him to know. I want him to worry."

"But he is the least of *your* worries, *signore*. Remember that."

When Ryan stepped outside the *Commissariato,* morning had given way to afternoon and the sun caressed the rooftops of Florence, backlighting its gentle curves and edges. As far as Tuscan landscapes went, it was the finest hour of the day, setting off the scenery with the kind of light artists craved the world over.

Ryan straddled his Vespa but, before starting the engine, he sat there for a moment and decided to put a call through to Anna, to let her know he'd be on his way back to the villa soon.

"I'm not at the villa," she surprised him by saying, when she answered the phone. "I'm around the corner, at a café in the *Piazza Santa Croce* waiting for you."

"You're—around the corner?"

"Magda's with me," she told him, so that he wouldn't worry. "Meet us at the Caffe Gelato and I'll order you a scoop of coffee ice cream."

Ryan hardly knew what to say, but there were few situations that couldn't be resolved by sugared cream.

"I'll be there in a minute," he replied, and a moment later he was drumming through the streets in search of his wife.

After meeting Anna and Magda in the square belonging to the church of Santa Croce, Ryan was brought up to speed with the results of Anna's meeting with Andrea Conti while he worked his way through an enormous ice cream cone. Though he wished he could have been with Anna while she met with Conti, he had to admire her approach, which had ultimately been very successful and had elicited information about the Spatuzzi family much more quickly than his roundabout method with Inspector Ricci.

"It strikes me that Monica Spatuzzi acted on her initial belief that a rival family took her son," he said. "Everything Conti and Ricci have told us would support that," he said. "But Riccardo still hasn't been found and the spate of crimes are still ongoing, which could mean she's still searching for answers. Sooner or later, Monica may turn her mind to the possibility of it having been someone else."

"Conti's 'little birds' include someone in the police," Anna said. "That seems obvious, and it also means he will be aware of who was interviewed earlier today. He's already made the connection with you."

Ryan nodded.

"It also seems obvious that, if Conti has found someone willing to talk, Monica Spatuzzi must have found several. Therefore, we have to assume she knows that we're here and that Nathan Armstrong was interviewed earlier today. That puts him at risk."

"And it puts you both at risk," Magda murmured.

Two dark heads turned towards her, both having almost forgotten she was sitting beside them.

"Yes," Anna agreed.

They sat there in the sunshine and watched the assortment of people passing by, idling away their afternoon, snapping pictures.

"I'll go and see her," Ryan said, quietly.

"Wh—?"

"Monica Spatuzzi," he clarified. "I'll pay her a visit."

Anna stared at him, her face a mixture of fear and fury.

"Over my dead body," she warned him.

"It is a very bad idea," Magda agreed, practically wringing her hands together.

"It's a pre-emptive strike," Ryan averred. "I don't want to wait for her to come to us, on the basis of misinformation. I'll explain to her that we pose no threat and aren't connected to her son's disappearance."

"Just like that?" Anna asked, dumbfounded.

"Yes," he murmured. "Just like that."

CHAPTER 17

After a pit-stop at the charcuterie in Boldon, Phillips and Yates made their way back across the River Tyne and towards the Quayside, on its northern bank. It was an area they knew very well, being less than a couple of miles from Police Headquarters and the setting for a series of bombs which had laid siege to the city only a week before. The pace at which their lives moved onward with each new file that landed on their desks meant it was easy to forget past cases, but as they drove along the road leading to the courthouse, they were afforded a stark reminder. The Millennium Bridge directly overlooking the courthouse was still in tatters and its metal construct was in the process of being safely dismantled to make way for a replacement. Further upstream, the mighty Tyne Bridge still stood proudly against the cityscape, its bottle-green painted steel girders already in the process of being repaired and repainted and its tarmac restored to its former glory by an army of volunteer tradesmen, who had given up their free time as a matter of civic duty.

"Makes you proud to see how people have pulled together," Phillips said, gruffly. "It'll take more than some fruitcake to kill off the community around these parts."

Yates nodded, thinking back to the widespread panic that had gripped the city.

"Sometimes, I can sort of understand why people do what they do," she said. "But bombing bridges and killing innocent people? It's the worst kind of madness."

They stopped at a set of traffic lights and Phillips wondered how to respond. Melanie was still so young... but then, he remembered he'd been the same age when he started out in the business. It was their chosen path and there was no shying away from it.

"There's worse than that," he said. "There's no end to the kind of madness driving people to kill or to maim, to strike fear into the hearts of their neighbours. It's human nature that some will be inhuman."

While Yates digested that, he pulled into a side street beside the courthouse and parked in one of the free bays.

"That was lucky," he said. "Better sort out a ticket, the inspectors are like bloody vultures 'round here."

A few minutes later, they made their way to one of the restored Victorian buildings lining the street. At one time, it might have been a shipping office or a storage warehouse but, now, it belonged to the shared offices of a group of barristers and called itself *Riverside Chambers*. The name of Edward Clarkson's former workplace had been carved into the stone lintel above the doorway and, alongside it, there was a painted sign listing all the barristers who worked there. They were ranked in order of seniority and, as she ran her finger down the list, Yates spotted Clarkson's name still listed on the entries.

"They haven't updated it since he left last year," she observed.

"Or maybe they thought he was coming back," Phillips said. "Howay, let's have a word with the clerks."

Once they were buzzed inside, they made their way up a narrow, plushly-carpeted flight of stairs and into a reception area where they were met by a young woman who had clearly been caught in the act of checking her social media accounts. After a brief word, she led them into a waiting room that reminded Phillips very much of a posh dental surgery he'd once been forced to attend after a particularly difficult encounter with a wisdom tooth. It was decorated with faux antique furniture and plants that were only just surviving, but the wallpaper was of expensively-striped silk and the carpet was a thick, ruby red, giving the overall impression of faded grandeur.

"You both coppers, then?"

They looked up at the unexpected sound of a broad Cockney accent and turned to see a man the size of a bear framing the doorway.

"You're about four hundred miles away from home, aren't you, son?" Phillips joked.

The man laughed good-naturedly and hulked into the room.

"Colombia Road, born and bred," he confessed, holding out his hand. "Stan Fowler, Head Clerk. Mind telling me who you are?"

"DS Phillips and trainee DC Yates," Frank replied, and once again retrieved his warrant card for inspection. "We need to have a word with you about Edward Clarkson."

"Ed? What's he gone and done now, then?"

Stan looked between them, as if he was expecting them to say the man had been caught streaking across a football pitch.

"Ah, do you have a private room where we could chat?"

Stan's jovial face fell instantly as he realised things were not what they seemed.

"Yeah, mate, no problem. This way."

He led them back out of the waiting room and up another narrow flight of stairs until they reached a large and well-appointed conference room with an enormous table in the centre of it, the kind Yates imagined navy admirals to have used when planning their strategies at sea.

"How's this?"

"It'll do," Phillips replied. "Look, I won't beat around the bush. Edward Clarkson was found dead yesterday morning and we're treating it as murder. We need to know all you can tell us about the man, professionally and privately, so we can try to find his killer."

Stan's ruddy face lost a bit of colour.

"I knew it," he said.

Phillips and Yates turned to one another in surprise.

"What do you mean?'"

"Well, it was bound to happen, sooner or later, wasn't it?" Stan said, with a touch of sympathy. "You can't go through life messing people around and not expect to have someone even the score. He always did fly too close to the sun, Eddie did."

"Are you saying he had a bad reputation, work-wise?" Yates asked.

"Naw, love, Eddie knew his onions. It was just that he didn't give a shit about anyone, that was his problem. You get some who know the law backwards and just don't care how it affects people. Eddie was one of those."

"What makes you say that?"

Stan looked uncomfortable.

"Look, I've been in this business all my working life. You get to know the different types."

Phillips left it, for now.

"I understood that he worked for the CPS? Don't they have their own offices?" he said.

"Yeah, the CPS have their own offices for their internal lawyers and support staff," Stan explained. "But they have an external advocate panel for court work—for most Crown Court trials, they'll instruct a self-employed barrister like Eddie."

"Wouldn't that be a conflict of interest, working in the same office space as the barristers who could be defending the person he was prosecuting?" Yates asked.

Stan was mortally offended.

"I don't think you understand," he said, very seriously. "Barristers are expected to have the highest standards of integrity. Just like in any law firm, they put Chinese Walls up—"

"Chinese Walls?" Yates interjected. "Sorry, what do you mean?"

"It's like an invisible wall. If we have two barristers working from the same chambers, one for either side of a case, they understand that they should never discuss it except through the proper channels. There are strict rules of confidentiality, the Bar Council's Code of Conduct and Ethics—"

"Aye, that's all very well and good," Phillips said, slicing through the bumf. "But an arsehole's still an arsehole, with or without a Chinese Wall."

One, two seconds ticked by and then Stan let out a roar of laughter that might have been heard back at the charcuterie.

"You're not wrong, there, mate," he said, knuckling a tear from the corner of his eye. "Look, I'll square with you: Eddie was a bit of a loose cannon."

Stan stole a glance over his shoulder, although the door was firmly shut.

"He always liked a drink," he confided. "And it got him well up shit creek, more than once."

"I didn't see anything on his criminal record," Yates put in.

Stan ran a nervous hand over his chin.

"Yeah…well, you wouldn't, darlin'. Eddie knew a few people, pulled a few strings…you know."

"What people? What strings?"

"I don't know all the ins and outs, but I know he was pally with some bloke in CID a few years back...the feller who was sent down for dancing around toadstools in his undies? You know, that Gregson feller?"

Phillips and Yates sighed in unison.

"Yeah, we know him."

"Right, well, I reckon he'd be able to tell you more about how he got Eddie off on all those speeding charges," he said. "Never went anywhere, so he must have had a word."

"Okay, thanks, we'll look into it," Phillips muttered, and mentally added it to the already burgeoning list of crimes and corrupt deeds that could be attributed to their former Detective Chief Superintendent Gregson, who was lounging behind bars at HMP Frankland, in Durham.

"Coming back to Eddie, we understand he left chambers back in March of last year—is that right?"

Stan scratched the top of his head, which was entirely bald and shone beneath the light of the central chandelier.

"Yeah, would've been around then," he said. "Dropped us right in the bloody shitter, n'all."

"How so?"

"Well, he never gave us any notice, did he? Eddie just pitched up one Monday morning and said to me, 'Stan, I'm packing it all in; cover all my cases and let me know what I owe for the ground rent.'"

"Did he say why?" Phillips asked.

"He clammed up like a bloody cat's arse," he replied. "All he said was, he wanted a fresh start. Thirty years I worked for him, thirty *bloody* years, and he gives me seven days' notice and pisses off into the sunset. Left me with a right headache, I can tell you."

"Do you believe him, when he said he wanted a 'fresh start'?"

"Do I look like I was born yesterday?" Stan said, jerking a thumb towards his burly chest. "I knew straight away he must have got himself in over his head. Thought it'd be some sort of pyramid scheme or investment gone bad. If there was one thing Eddie liked more than the drink, it was money."

Yates nodded.

"Can you be more specific? Did he ever mention anything that was worrying him?"

Stan shook his head and echoed what Jill had already told them.

"No, he wasn't that sort. Eddie liked you to think nothing was too big of a challenge, at least not for him, and, as far as worries went, he didn't have any. The most I ever got out of him was a mouthful, if a bundle of files hadn't arrived on time."

Phillips looked out the window at the river as it chugged slowly towards the sea, at the gulls crying loudly as they swooped down to dive into the water, and thought of the kind of man Edward Clarkson, latterly Charon, had been. A picture was starting to build up and it wasn't pretty. But, as Ryan would have said, every victim is equal in the eyes of the law and it wasn't their job to judge the kind of life he had led; only to help deliver justice, whatever that meant.

"Was he doing badly at work?" he asked, suddenly. "Had he had a run of bad cases?"

Stan shook his head.

"If anything, he was at the top of his game. Eddie kept himself trim and looked years younger than he was, not to mention that his brain was still sharp as a tack. Nobody even mentioned retirement because, honestly, I couldn't imagine anyone less likely to while away his days doing arse all, watching daytime telly."

Stan grinned at what he thought was an outlandish possibility, then asked the obvious question.

"Where'd you find him, anyway?"

"In Warkworth," Phillips replied. "Eddie was the boatman for the castle, giving ferry rides to tourists."

Stan let out another one of his roaring laughs.

"You've got to be kidding! Eddie 'Soft Top' Clarkson, giving boat rides? Not in a month of Sundays," he declared.

"Well, certainly not anymore," Phillips agreed, with a small grimace.

CHAPTER 18

If there was one thing Ryan had learned during his relationship with Anna, it was that words like, 'no, you can't come with me' and 'this might be dangerous' held very little sway. Consequently, he found himself hijacked on the back of his own scooter, clutching Anna's waist as she tootled through the backstreets of a city she hardly knew, in the general direction of the beautiful hilltop town of Fiesole, to the north of Florence.

"I love it!" she cried out, while he spat out a mouthful of her long hair that was blowing into his face. "I can't believe I've never ridden one of these before!"

"Watch the road! *Left*, take a left!"

"Right!"

Ryan's heart slammed against his chest in one hard motion as she swerved through a tiny gap in the traffic, pushing the scooter to its limits. They began to wind upward and into the verdant hills while the sun set behind them, casting wide arcs of pink and orange light over the city below.

"How far?" Anna called back.

"About another eight kilometres," he told her, and was surprised to find that he was enjoying himself.

"I love you."

"What?"

"*I love you!*"

"*What*?"

"Never mind," he laughed, and held on a little tighter as she rounded another hairpin bend, zooming past a wide truck overloaded with livestock as they climbed higher into the Etruscan hills. "Get us through this in one piece and I'll tell you again!"

Twilight had fallen by the time they reached Fiesole. Anna slowed the scooter to a crawl as they navigated unfamiliar roads, passing the outline of vast estates and ruined Roman walls and amphitheatres that had been built against the rock-face thousands of years before. The historian inside her cried out to explore, to understand everything there was to know about the elite little hillside commune that had once been a stronghold, then a summer residence for rich and famous Florentines and artists such as Leonardo da Vinci.

But there was no time for that.

"It's further along here, on the right, I think," Ryan told her. "Stop for a minute."

She pulled the scooter into a narrow lay-by and shut off the engine, giving Ryan a chance to dismount.

"There's a restaurant further along the road, in the town centre," he said. "You carry on and I'll meet you there in an hour. If I'm not back by then, call Ricci."

She didn't hesitate, but grabbed a fistful of his shirt.

"You're not going in there alone."

Ryan placed a gentle hand over hers.

"You've brought me this far but, Anna, you don't speak the language and I don't want them catching a glimpse of you. It's less risky this way."

Anna's heart sank because she knew he was right. She didn't speak the language and, besides, she wouldn't know the first thing to say, even if she did.

"Wait for me at the restaurant," he said. "I'll be there, I promise."

Anna felt a lump rise to her throat.

"What if anything…anything happens—"

"It won't," he said firmly. "It isn't in her interest to hurt me, not when I can help her."

Something about his tone and the set to his jaw convinced her that, in that moment, he could have done anything.

"Alright. An hour, tops, before I call Ricci."

She tugged on his shirt until she could take his face in her hands.

"Look after yourself," she warned him, and then bestowed a deep, heartfelt kiss to remind him of all he stood to lose.

Ryan waited until the red tail-lights of the scooter disappeared around the corner and then carried on walking for another hundred yards until he reached a set of tall, forbidding gates that had been twisted into a traditional Florentine style. He hadn't stepped within five feet of them before two guards appeared like apparitions on the other side and said something in Italian that was far from being a welcome.

Ryan held his hands out, palms open, and stood perfectly still.

"I'm alone and unarmed," he told them. "My name is Ryan."

"You are English?" one of them asked.

"Yes," Ryan replied. "I'd like to speak to Signora Spatuzzi, concerning her son, Riccardo."

At his mention of the man's name, the guards tensed visibly, and one moved to rest his hand on the butt of a weapon concealed inside his blazer jacket.

"Who are you?" they snarled, searching his face as if they might recognise him from past dealings. "Who do you work for?"

"I don't work for any of the families," Ryan said. "I'd like to speak to her and explain why I'm here."

Just then, a radio crackled into life and one of the shadowy figures reached for it. Their eyes never moved from Ryan's face while they replied in monosyllables, at first, then he heard them explaining who it was making a disturbance outside the front gates.

The men's eyes glinted in the light of the enormous lanterns hanging on either side of the gates, then one nodded to the other, who keyed in a security code.

"Walk slowly," they told him.

The gates swung open with hardly a sound and Ryan stepped inside, where he was ordered to spread his legs and arms while they frisked him.

"Easy on the goods," he muttered.

"This way," the man replied, giving him a hard shove.

As Ryan began to walk along the manicured driveway, he heard the gates clang shut behind him.

***

Monica Spatuzzi was not what Ryan might have expected.

If he'd imagined her to be an ageing matriarch with priceless jewellery dripping from her ears and fingers, he was dead wrong. The woman who awaited him inside a sumptuous library within the sprawling hilltop villa was understated in every respect; she was the epitome of a stylish Italian woman and, if he'd seen her on the street, he might have thought her to be an art or antiques dealer.

She wore all black, as was traditional for one in mourning.

When he stepped into the room, she gave him a slow and thorough assessment from his head to his toes, then nodded to the goons who had accompanied him from the gates.

"Leave us," she said quietly.

Music was being piped into the room from hidden speakers and the soft, painful strains of an Italian requiem washed around them.

"You favour your father," she said, in the same soft, cultivated voice. "I'm correct, am I not, that you are the son of David Ryan?"

Ryan nodded, and didn't bother to ask how she had known. It was her business to know everything about any person of interest in her city. He took a moment to be grateful that his father had never been posted in a diplomatic role in Italy; their experience of Florence might have been very different indeed.

"Yes. My name is Maxwell Finley-Ryan. I'm a police inspector, from England."

She nodded and, for the first time, looked him fully in the eye. Ryan felt a shiver run through him as he saw the emotions swirling in those dark, dark eyes; pain, anger and bitterness, all quickly veiled.

"And, Maxwell, are you in the habit of paying house calls to women you do not know?"

She moved across to one of the stylish easy chairs arranged around a fireplace, but did not invite him to sit.

"Nobody knows that I'm here, other than my wife."

"And your housekeeper," she murmured.

Ryan said nothing, but filed away the information for later.

"You know who I am?" she asked him, suddenly.

Again, he said nothing, which was the best possible response.

"You know my son?" her voice cracked, ever so slightly, on the last word and she reached across to take a long drink from the glass of iced water sitting on the table beside her.

"I never met Riccardo," Ryan replied, in an even tone. "I had never heard of him, until just over a week ago."

She continued to sip her water, then set it down again, very carefully.

"And yet, here you are in Florence, asking questions, visiting the *Gruppo* and visiting his mother. Why would you do that, *signore,* unless you knew my son?"

"Because I wish to find the person who…has taken him."

Instinctively, he refrained from using the word 'murder'.

"Enquiries have been made," she replied, in a business-like tone. "Why should you wish to be a part of this, unless your goal is to ingratiate yourself within my family?"

"I have no designs on your family," Ryan said, honestly. The ongoing fight against the mafia was a domestic problem that would be fought by others. "If…*enquiries* have been made but you are no closer to the truth, perhaps the truth lies elsewhere."

"And what would an English policeman know about that?"

"More than one person has been reported missing," he told her. That much was a matter of public record. "There may be a connection that will lead us to the person responsible."

"You have someone in mind," she said. "You will tell me who it is."

It was not a request.

"No," Ryan said, in the same tone of voice.

There was a terrible, tense silence in the room while she studied him, like a spider considering when best to pounce.

"You will tell me, or I will have my men extract the name from you. I have connections at the *Gruppo*."

Not as many as in years gone by, she lamented, and the prices were rising each year. That was inflation, she supposed.

"It would defeat the purpose," he said. "If the person I have in mind has taken more than just your son, it will deprive other families of rightful justice. I need time."

She rose from her chair in one fluid motion, her anger no longer contained.

"Why should I care? What are these people to me? *Nothing*! Riccardo is my son. My flesh. I owe the others nothing and you, *signore*, even less."

Ryan spoke gently.

"You may be many things, Monica, but you are a mother first."

Some undefinable emotion flitted across her face.

"There are other mothers, other families who deserve to know what has happened to their children. I'm asking you for a week. Just one week, where your men stand down and you agree to a temporary ceasefire. Do this, please, for your son, and for the children of other mothers."

She turned her back on him and put a hand on the edge of the mantelpiece, leaning heavily for support while she considered his words.

When she turned back, her face was so hard it might have been cut in stone.

"You think I am so stupid?" she spat. "You think that, even now, I am not aware that it is Nathan Armstrong who attended the station this morning? I am an old woman, *signore*, but do not make the mistake of underestimating me."

His stomach performed one slow flip but, outwardly, his face remained impassive.

"I assumed you would have contacts in the police," he said. "Therefore, I also assumed you knew the suspect I have in mind."

"And you have the audacity to come here and ask me to do nothing?"

She laughed, her knuckles turning white as they gripped the mantle.

"If you kill him, you'll never know what happened to Riccardo, or where to find him," Ryan said, forthrightly. "Don't you want to know where your boy is?"

"He will talk, believe me."

"No," Ryan took an involuntary step forward, compelling her to listen. "He isn't like all the others. I've dealt with him before."

She pushed away from the mantle and walked towards him. It was an odd sensation, Ryan thought, to feel intimidated by such a slight person but it had absolutely nothing to do with her physicality and everything to do with the waves of malice emanating from every pore of her skin.

"You have three days," she whispered. "No more."

"I need a favour," he said.

She laughed again, unsure what to make of the tall man with the face of an angel and the eyes of a soldier.

"Another? You astonish me."

"There's a masked ball being held for Armstrong at the Uffizi on Saturday. I'd like to be there, to watch him—"

"Is that all?" she said, wearily. "Consider it done."

"That was easy," he murmured.

"It should be," she drawled. "My family owns the majority share in his publishing house."

On that bombshell, she pressed a concealed button to the side of the fireplace and, seconds later, two different guards appeared.

"Show Signor Ryan out," she told them.

The walk Ryan made as he was escorted off the property would be remembered as one of the longest walks of his life. Even after the gates had closed behind him once more, he spent the remaining half-mile walk into the town centre of Fiesole wondering whether he would hear the echo of a rifle-shot sounding out into the night.

CHAPTER 19

Sunset fell over the county of Northumberland in a blaze of colour more beautiful than any painting, photograph or artsy filter that man could devise. Phillips locked his car and leaned back against the door to watch the sky for the final couple of minutes it took for the sun to sink below the horizon.

"You coming in or not? It's freezing out there!"

MacKenzie called to him from the front door of the little house they shared, then stepped outside to see what was holding his attention.

"Look at that," she breathed, as stars began to pop into the sky above the city like jewels. "It's usually too cloudy to see them."

"Aye, it's a clear night," he said, and wrapped an arm around her waist. "Let's get inside, though. It's freezing out here, you know."

"Really?" she muttered. "I hadn't noticed."

He grinned to himself as he toed off his work shoes and placed them neatly beside hers.

"You hungry?" she asked. "I was thinking of throwing together something like spaghetti and meatballs."

"I'll help," he said, and followed her into the small galley kitchen at the back of the house. At the mention of spaghetti, he instantly thought of his friend.

"Haven't heard from Ryan yet, today," he said, with a trace of worry. "Have you?"

MacKenzie rolled up her sleeves and reached for a knife to chop the garlic.

"Yes, Anna left me a voicemail around lunchtime, but I haven't had a chance to call her back. Apparently, all is well and they're making progress."

She didn't mention what Anna had told her of Ryan's family villa, for fear that Phillips might suffer a heart attack.

"She says the inspector in charge—Alessandro Ricci—seems decent. He let Ryan observe the interview with Armstrong this morning."

Phillips made a non-committal sound in the back of his throat and rolled a beef tomato in his hands, bruising the unsuspecting fruit as if it were a stress ball.

"It's not the same as having your own team with you," he said, mulishly. "Did they get anywhere with Armstrong?"

MacKenzie shook her head and dumped the chopped garlic into a shallow pan.

"It was always going to be a long shot," she reminded him, and held out a hand for the tomato before he reduced it to pulp.

"Speaking of long shots, we had a word with Edward Clarkson's former colleagues, today. I've got a list of barristers to interview over the next few days to see if they can shine a bit of light on why he suddenly turned his life upside down because, at the moment, it's about as clear as mud."

MacKenzie started to roll the meatballs between her hands while she thought of the case and Phillips' mind started to wander as he watched her, mesmerised by the motion of her palms.

"—Frank?"

"Eh? What's that?"

She tutted.

"You look tired, love. Maybe we need to get an early night, tonight."

His ruddy face took on a hopeful expression.

"You're probably right," he said.

"But getting back to Eddie Clarkson, or Charon, as he was calling himself…we need to dig deeper into the darker side of his life while he was a barrister. If he was willing to deal with Gregson to get himself off on minor charges, he obviously didn't have a conscience that was squeaky clean. That could be the tip of the iceberg—who knows what kind of favours Gregson might have demanded in exchange?"

Phillips nodded, turning back to the task of making a salad.

"Aye, we'll have a mammoth job on our hands. He had a thirty-year career and met thousands of people in that time, not to mention all the people connected to his cases that he never met. It could be absolutely anybody."

MacKenzie's heart sank.

"Let's hope that Faulkner comes up trumps with a DNA profile we can use. Without it, we're relying on hearsay and gossip."

"Not quite," Phillips sprinkled oregano over the salad he'd created with a deft sleight of hand. "We know something happened a year ago that forced his hand. Why last March? It must have been serious enough, must have frightened him enough, to make him change his name, his job and his address."

"And we know it wasn't above board, otherwise he would have approached the authorities," MacKenzie added. "What could have been so bad that he couldn't come to the police for protection?"

"That's the mystery," he said, then moved to slide his arms around her waist while she stirred the sauce. "You know, that could probably simmer for a while. Say, ten—no, twenty minutes?"

MacKenzie let out a husky laugh.

"You looking to be harassed, Frank?"

"By you? Always."

CHAPTER 20

It was after ten when Ryan received the call.

"Ricci?"

"A woman has been reported missing."

There was an infinitesimal pause.

"Who?" Ryan asked.

"Her name is Martina Calari. She works for the Uffizi Gallery as an events planner—"

"The Uffizi?" Ryan's mind immediately went into overdrive. "Another connection with Armstrong. For God's sake, let's stop wasting time and go over to his apartment *now*."

"She has only just been reported missing," Ricci said. "We can't jump to conclusions, especially if she turns up unharmed in a couple of hours. It's possible," he said, a bit desperately.

"What do I need to do to make you understand the man is a *killer*?" Ryan almost roared.

"I need more than another coincidence," the other man threw back. "I rang you as a professional courtesy and to let you know we will be monitoring the situation."

"If we act now, there may still be a chance," Ryan argued, feeling sick with frustration. "She may still be alive."

Inspector Ricci was distracted by the sound of another person entering his office.

"Just a moment," he said.

Ryan gripped the phone for long seconds as he tried to make out the conversation in rapid, colloquial Italian.

When Ricci's voice came back down the line, everything had changed.

"That was Banotti," he said quickly. "The switchboard just received an anonymous tip-off, within the last two minutes, from what sounded like a male caller."

"Yes?"

"The caller said he could hear a woman's screams coming from Apartment 12 of the *Palazzo Russo*. That's—"

"Armstrong's address," Ryan finished for him. "I knew it. I'm on my way."

Inside Apartment 12, Nathan Armstrong stood at the foot of his bed and surveyed the woman lying dead on its silk damask cover. With unhurried movements, he began to strip away his clothes, folding them in a neat pile to be destroyed at some later date, just in case. Luckily for him, the windows in the palazzo's biggest apartment were too high to be overlooked by anyone and its walls far too thick to be overheard by any nosy neighbours. Lucky, too, that the mess could be contained and dealt with efficiently, without any need to step outdoors.

He cocked his head to one side as he assessed the body, running his sharp gaze over the thin plastic cord still wrapped around the woman's throat, digging deeply into her skin. It had been taken from the small kettle in the kitchen.

"Probably broke her neck," he thought. "Nice, clean method."

Naked, he rooted around inside the bank of wardrobes and found a spare bedspread, not dissimilar to the one covering the bed. Easy enough to find a replacement to make up for the one he would lose, just as it was easy to replace the small kettle, so long as he was careful about it over the next couple of days.

Armstrong moved quickly around the bed, folding the ends of the silky fabric around the woman's wasted body, swaddling her in the yards of material until he no longer had to look into her empty, staring eyes.

His head reared back when he heard the first siren in the distance and he moved like lightning.

Ryan arrived at the *Palazzo Russo* less than five minutes after ending his call with Ricci. He'd driven the short distance across town with the kind of speed that put taxi drivers to shame, opting to take one of his father's cars rather than the scooter. As he slammed out of the vehicle, he heard long, wailing sirens approaching from two directions and swore viciously, knowing their sound would alert Armstrong. Precious seconds ticked away as he waited for Ricci to arrive and he watched the front entrance like a hawk, ready to intercept anybody trying to flee the building. After a full minute passed, he decided there was no more time to waste.

Ryan entered the building foyer and flashed his warrant card at the concierge, who stood up to chase after him as he made directly for the bank of lifts.

"*Scusi! Signore! Non ti e permesso lassu!*"

Ryan dodged him with ease and took the stairs three at a time, sprinting upward towards the fourth floor. He burst onto the landing, barely noticing its luxury furnishings as he jogged along the corridor searching for the right apartment. Finally, he came to a door at the end with a brass number '12' and an ornate doorbell beside it.

He didn't hesitate.

"Armstrong! Police! Open the door!"

He banged a fist on the sturdy oak panel and, when nothing happened, he took a step backwards, ready to ram his body into the wood to force entry.

But two pairs of strong arms caught him from behind.

"Ryan! *Porca merda*, stay back!"

Ricci hauled him away with the help of a breathless concierge and another police officer while Ryan fought like an angry wasp.

Just then, the door opened.

Armstrong stood in the doorway of his apartment with a towel wrapped around his lower body, revealing a muscular, hairless torso. His skin appeared to be wet from a recent shower and he held another towel in his hands, which he used to dab at his face.

"What the hell is going on?" he demanded.

"Sir, we apologise for the disturbance, but we've received a report—" Ricci began to explain, but was cut off when Armstrong caught sight of Ryan.

"I might have known!" he sneered. "You'll stop at nothing to destroy my reputation with your conspiracy theories. Harassing me in my own country not enough for you, eh, Ryan? You have to come to Italy, to spoil what should be one of the greatest moments of my career?"

Ryan had heard enough.

In one fluid motion, he reared away from the hapless concierge and elbowed Armstrong aside, storming into the apartment to search each of the rooms in turn before anyone could stop him.

"This is an outrage!" Armstrong yelled. "I'm calling my lawyer."

"Please, *signore*, there is no need—"

Ricci tried to placate him, but it was no use. The phone was already ringing.

"I'll have your job for this," Armstrong vowed.

Rapping out a series of orders to his sergeant concerning damage limitation, Ricci hurried after Ryan.

He found him in the bedroom, looking confused.

"She's not here," he said, staring at the wardrobes he'd pulled open and at the neatly-made bed in the centre of it all.

"I can see that!" Ricci shouted. "I want you to leave, or I will have you removed. Even now, Armstrong is calling his lawyer who will make a formal complaint on his behalf before the night is out. It was badly done," Ricci finished, and put a none-too-gentle hand into the small of Ryan's back to propel him out of the room.

"I don't understand," Ryan said, ignoring Ricci's diatribe. "Why would anyone make an anonymous call about a woman screaming in Apartment 12?"

"It was obviously a false tip-off. It happens all the time; you should know that."

Ricci frog-marched him through the apartment, but Ryan stopped when he reached Armstrong, who was standing beside the front door with a towelling robe draped over his shoulders while Banotti did her best to convince him not to make a complaint to their superiors.

When he looked up and saw Ryan again, his lip curled.

"You're finished," he said.

"On the contrary," Ryan told him. "I'm just getting started."

On the street outside, Inspector Ricci rounded on Ryan immediately.

"What the hell do you think you were doing back there?" he burst out, squaring up to him while passers-by slowed at the sound of raised voices.

"My job!" Ryan shot back. "Acting on information that was time-sensitive."

"We agreed at the start, this is *my* city, *my* investigation—"

"And you agreed to act," Ryan reminded him. "Instead, I was left standing out on the street, losing vital minutes as you took your time getting here. The police station is a couple of minutes' drive from here, no more."

"We came as quickly as we could," Ricci said, flushing a bit.

"Not quickly enough." Ryan was merciless. He had to be. "And the sirens? That gave Armstrong time to cover himself. I don't know how, yet, but I'll find out."

"A body does not vanish into thin air," Ricci laughed, shaking his head at what he thought was pig-headedness. "As for the tip-off, I told you before, it was obviously a hoax. Somebody looking to make trouble for Armstrong, for some reason, a competitor—"

"Bullshit. It wasn't a hoax."

"The woman was not there!"

Ryan stepped closer, lowering his voice.

"What did you think Armstrong had been doing, when he opened the door?"

"He had just come out of the shower or a bath. We interrupted him, obviously."

Ryan smiled grimly.

"I checked the bathroom," he said. "There wasn't a drop of water in the bath, or the shower. That's unusual, for a man whose hair was so wet."

Ricci's lips clamped shut and his eyes strayed upward, to the fourth floor of the grand old palace that was now a haven for its ultra-rich inhabitants. Taking her opportunity in a moment of calm, Sergeant Banotti stepped forward to speak quietly in his ear and Ricci nodded.

"Martina Calari's parents have arrived at the police station," he said, running tired hands through his hair. "I need to go back and speak to them."

"And say what?" Ryan asked. "Are you going to tell them what you told me? That she hasn't been missing long enough to cause concern; that it hasn't been anywhere near twenty-four hours and to come back tomorrow?"

Ricci sighed.

"She went missing after work, so I'm going to request the CCTV from the Uffizi to see if it can help us. I'm going to send in the sweepers to see if there are any traces at her apartment and we'll speak to her fiancé." He paused, lifting his eyes to meet Ryan's blazing ones. "At this stage, I do not have to do any of that, but I'm going to *act*. On one condition: that you do *not*."

He lifted a hand and swept it through the air.

"No more contact with Armstrong, no more observations, no more breaches of jurisdiction. In return, I will do all I can, but you must *trust* me."

There was a word that carried a wealth of meaning, Ryan thought.

"And what if I happen to meet Armstrong in a social setting?"

"There is no reason that you would."

"My wife and I will be at the party tomorrow night," he said. "It will be impossible to escape the acquaintance."

Ricci was surprised.

"It is an invitation-only event, how—?"

"You're not the only one with connections."

Ricci's face darkened, but he didn't enquire further.

"It doesn't matter. You will not be going, nor will your wife. You have caused enough trouble this evening and we cannot afford any more. This is a final warning, Ryan."

As Ricci headed back to his car, Ryan turned to look up at the palazzo towering behind him and locked eyes with the man who watched him from one of the higher windows. Anger washed over him as he saw Armstrong's smiling face, which bore the smug expression of a man who believed he was above the law.

Time, Ryan thought.

The most precious of all commodities; and his time was running out.

CHAPTER 21

Saturday, 24ᵗʰ February

Chief Constable Sandra Morrison was at her desk in Northumbria Police Headquarters before eight. She'd had a dreadful night's sleep, having spent most of it tossing and turning in her bed. Around four-thirty, she'd accepted defeat and resigned herself to a day filled with a higher-than-usual caffeine content.

It was all thanks to the late-night phone call she'd received from the Head of Police in Rome. Director General Jacopo Romano had explained that he was hearing less-than-glowing reports from his colleagues in Florence and that complaints were pouring in from important public figures concerning DCI Ryan's behaviour. He'd told her that, perhaps, it had been a bad idea to suggest they work together, after all. Their approaches were too different...*blah, blah*...he did not understand the hierarchy...*blah, blah*.

All of which made her smile, because he was describing Ryan to a tee.

How many times had her star detective frustrated her with his forthright methods and uncompromising view of policing?

Too many to count.

She leaned back in her desk chair while the sun rose in the window behind her, brightening the functional office with its taupe-coloured walls. She raised a third cup of coffee to her lips and thought about the Problem of Ryan.

If it was a problem, at all.

Yes, he was pig-headed at times. He could be stubborn, unyielding and it was an understatement to say that he did not suffer fools gladly. But he was always kind, he could be very charismatic—though her choice of word would have embarrassed him—and sensitive to the victims of crime. He was also highly perceptive, with an unrivalled understanding of what made the criminal mind tick. Above all else, Ryan was a complicated man with a simple moral compass, which distinguished 'right' from 'wrong' and seldom wavered. Because of it, he would never, ever, accept a second-rate approach to the ongoing fight against serious crime. It was, in part, due to the loss and trauma he had experienced first-hand but that alone wasn't responsible. It took a patchwork of life experiences to build up the fabric of a person and whatever it was that had contributed to the man Ryan was today had made him virtually incorruptible.

And hard to manage, she added, with a small smile.

Morrison had a reputation for being a fair woman but one who was not afraid of tackling difficult decisions or conversations, where necessary. If she felt the situation warranted her intervention, she would not hesitate to recall her man and give him a thorough dressing down for his behaviour; after all, Ryan was not in Italy as a private tourist, he was there in his capacity as a Chief Inspector of the Northumbria Police Constabulary, albeit unofficially.

She spent another couple of minutes mulling the situation over, then leaned across to place a call through to DI MacKenzie, who answered almost immediately.

There are, after all, two sides to every story.

"You wanted to see me, Ma'am?"

After a courteous tap on the Chief Constable's office door, MacKenzie stepped inside.

"Yes. Close the door, would you?"

MacKenzie did as she was bid and came to stand in front of Morrison's desk, which took up almost the full width of the room.

"Have a seat," the other woman offered.

MacKenzie took the same approach as Ryan as far as proffered seating was concerned and tended towards the presumption that, when a senior officer invited you to sit, it was because they were about to impart news that was either very good, or very bad.

"How's things?"

Subconsciously, MacKenzie's back straightened a bit in the uncomfortable visitor's chair as she prepared to deliver a progress report.

"I hope things have transitioned as smoothly as possible over the past couple of days," she said. "The staff seem happy enough and we're just about juggling workload."

"Quiet time of year, in comparison with the usual rounds of GBH and robbery leading up to Christmas," Morrison observed. "Same pattern, every year."

MacKenzie nodded.

"What about numbers? Anything taxing?"

"We caught a new one up at Warkworth on Thursday morning," MacKenzie said. "I wouldn't say it's taxing us, yet, but we're about to review the victim's work history to see if he was dealing with anything that triggers a connection with organised crime. That's likely to put a bit of strain on resources and, as you know, his death was reported on Wednesday's evening news so that adds a bit of public pressure. I'm waiting to hear from forensics to see if there's a lead there but, so far, we haven't been lucky."

"Pity," Morrison said. "Did I hear the victim was a ferryman for the castle?"

"Yes, although he had recently changed his name and relocated to Warkworth from Newcastle, where he had lived and worked as a successful prosecuting barrister for years."

Morrison frowned.

"His name was Charon?"

"No, ma'am—that was his new name. Previously, he was Edward Clarkson."

Morrison's sandy blonde eyebrows raised a bit.

"I know him," she said. "Or, rather, I knew him back in the days when I was building cases for trial. He was lethal in court but not very likeable on a personal level, I seem to recall."

MacKenzie was unsurprised, since that tallied with everything she had already heard.

"There's some suggestion he was connected with former DCS Gregson," she added, somewhat hesitantly. The Department was still dealing with the extensive fall-out following that man's wide-ranging and corrupt criminal activity, so it was always a touchy subject to raise.

"Another one," Morrison muttered.

"Possibly, yes."

MacKenzie felt a fleeting moment of sympathy for the other woman, who carried a heavy weight of responsibility on her shoulders. It gave her no pleasure to add to the existing burden.

"We'll look into it, ma'am, and update you if there's anything concerning on that score."

"Thank you," Morrison said.

There was a short, awkward silence and MacKenzie assumed that was the end of the meeting. She began to rise from her chair, then Morrison's voice had her plopping back down again.

"The thing is, Denise, you're needed elsewhere. I heard from my counterpart in Italy last night," she explained.

"It seems Ryan has been rubbing people up the wrong way, shaking things up…in other words, being himself."

MacKenzie's face broke into a huge grin.

"He has a tendency to do that."

Morrison gave a rueful smile, then became serious again.

"They want him out," she said. "They think he has a personal vendetta against Nathan Armstrong and he's a liability."

There was another short pause.

"You want me to go and bring him back?" MacKenzie asked, and her voice cooled, just a fraction.

"No," Morrison replied. "I want you to go and help him bring the bastard in." She'd made the mistake of doubting Ryan's instincts and abilities once before. It wasn't a mistake she planned to make again.

MacKenzie found a new level of respect for the woman sitting across the desk.

"When should I leave?"

"As soon as you've briefed a suitable replacement," Morrison replied.

"Phillips—?"

"No, take him with you. Those two are like peas in a bloody pod," she muttered, affectionately. "What about Lowerson?"

MacKenzie thought of the young detective constable, a man who had lost his way for a while but who would always remain their friend. Only the week before, he'd been through his own personal hell and was taking time off to recover himself.

It was too soon to ask him to come back, and she said as much.

"Agreed," Morrison said, then seemed to shrug it off. "Alright, leave that to me. You and Phillips concentrate on getting yourselves over there and find out what the hell has been going on. You can probably manage Operation Hotspur remotely, for the sake of a couple of days, but I'll keep an eye on it from this end."

"Thank you, ma'am."

As MacKenzie rose to leave, she paused.

"Can I ask you something?"

Morrison waited.

"Why not just tell him to come home, to stop rocking the boat?"

Morrison huffed out a laugh.

"Firstly, he'd never listen. Secondly, Ryan wasn't the only one to feel burned when Armstrong walked out of the foyer downstairs, free as a bird. I've looked back over the files, myself. It was a travesty and it needs to be corrected, morally and otherwise. Our first duty is to protect, and that's exactly what Ryan is trying to do." She shrugged. "Does that answer your question, DI MacKenzie?"

"Admirably, ma'am."

CHAPTER 22

Ryan had not slept particularly well, either, but it had nothing to do with his present standing in the eyes of the *Gruppo Investigativo Delitti Seriali* and everything to do with the mystery of what had happened the previous evening. All through the night, his mind grappled with the questions of *who* had placed a call to the *Gruppo* with their tip-off about Armstrong's apartment and *where* Armstrong had taken Martina Calari, the events planner at the Uffizi Gallery.

If he hadn't been aware of Armstrong's history and exploits, Ryan might have passed off a chance meeting with a Parisian waiter as coincidence. However, a second 'chance' meeting with an Italian lawyer and a third 'chance' association between Armstrong's forthcoming party at the Uffizi and the subsequent disappearance of the woman who was planning the event was too much to swallow.

The fact was, he needed more information: he needed to see the CCTV from the Uffizi Gallery; he needed to speak to those who had been last to see Martina Calari before she disappeared; he needed to know how far the police had traced the anonymous tip-off; and he needed to listen to the call himself.

He couldn't do any of those things without making his peace with Inspector Ricci.

Humble pie was not a favourite dish of Ryan's—in fact, he was hard-pressed to remember the last time he'd swallowed any—but he was prepared to make sacrifices for the greater good of the investigation.

"Ricci!"

He pushed away from where he'd been lounging on his scooter for the past forty minutes waiting for the inspector to emerge from his apartment building. It wasn't far from the Boboli Gardens, an impressive park located directly behind the imposing edifice of the Pitti Palace, which had been the main residence of the Medici grand dukes in the sixteenth century. As with much of 'Old Florence', Ricci's apartment building consisted of a period property that had been divided into numerous apartments with a central courtyard concealed behind a set of tall, heavy oak doors that opened directly onto the pavement.

"Ryan? I thought I made myself clear—"

Ricci eyed him with frank suspicion.

"Just listen," Ryan said, and dodged a man cycling at speed along the pavement. The road was entirely clear of traffic but that didn't seem to make any difference, so he counted himself lucky not to have sustained a broken ankle and focused on the task in hand.

"I've come to apologise."

Ricci gave him a searching look.

"For flouting procedure or for embarrassing my department?"

"Both," Ryan answered, without hesitation. "I was frustrated because things were moving more slowly than I'd like and, instead of waiting for your approval, I took matters into my own hands. It was presumptuous, and I apologise unreservedly."

Ricci scratched a thumbnail against his freshly-shaven jaw and then reached for his sunglasses to ease the early-morning glare of sunlight as it streamed through the streets and alleyways.

"I am not so stupid as to believe what you have just told me," he drawled. "You forget, my friend; you and I are the same. Do you imagine I have never made a similar speech?"

Ryan said nothing and fell into step beside Ricci as he began to walk slowly in the direction of the gardens and the centre of the city.

"You're hoping to remain a part of our investigation."

"Yes," Ryan said, deciding honesty was best.

Ricci sighed.

"You must understand that things are different here—"

"Murder is the same the world over," Ryan said, softly.

They were silent for a minute or two as they continued to walk along one of the long Florentine streets shielded from the sun by the tall buildings on either side, passing tiny shops that were little more than hatches out onto the street, selling coffee and pastries to early-morning commuters. As they came to the southern side of the Ponte Vecchio, Ryan realised that Ricci had steered them in the general direction of the Uffizi Gallery, which spread out along the northern bank of the River Arno, directly on the other side of the bridge. Ryan turned to look at him with a question in his eyes.

Ricci gave one of his little shrugs.

"Don't make me regret this decision," he said, and the two men crossed the bridge to go in search of CCTV footage.

While Ryan digested a generous portion of humble pie, Anna swallowed the last of a delicious breakfast served up by Magda on the terrace at the Villa Lucia.

"Have you ever considered emigrating to England?" she asked, hopefully.

The other woman laughed richly.

"You need feeding up," she said, in a motherly tone. "Too skinny."

After the meal she'd just enjoyed, Anna thought she may never be able to eat again.

"Do you have children, Magda?"

The housekeeper's hands stilled as she helped Anna to collect the plates, then busied themselves again.

"I did."

Anna looked up sharply, but Magda was already turning away and walking back inside. She followed her at a slower pace, wondering whether she should say anything further. She found Magda clattering around the sparkling marble kitchen loading a dishwasher with an assortment of crockery and leaned down to help.

"I'm sorry," she murmured. "I asked the wrong question."

Magda only shook her head, but turned away to look out of the window and across the gardens.

"My son died a long time ago."

With that, she turned and walked back outside to retrieve the remaining tableware and Anna left her to it, unwilling to press an already open wound. Perhaps, once they knew one another better, Magda would choose to confide in her.

Until that time, there was work to be done.

Anna made her way into one of the living rooms where she had already laid out a series of books about the history of Florence and several true-crime volumes about the so-called *Mostro* that had inspired Armstrong's book of the same name. She might not be a detective, she thought, but she knew how to research. While Ryan focused on gathering evidential facts, she would focus on learning about the terrain and its history, its people and the tunnels and passageways that made up the city, with particular reference to the area around the Uffizi Gallery.

Things were seldom as they appeared on the surface.

CHAPTER 23

The Uffizi Gallery was one of the largest and most famous art museums in the world, located in the historic centre of the city of Florence. It consisted of two enormous wings separated by a narrow courtyard looking out towards the River Arno through a screen of Doric columns, and had begun life as an office complex commissioned by Cosimo de' Medici in 1560. Now, it drew in over two million visitors each year to view its extensive collection and, as he stepped inside the courtyard, it seemed to Ryan that half of that annual number had turned up already, judging by the heaving mass of tourists waiting outside its front doors.

"There is a booking system to regulate the numbers who enter," Ricci said, catching sight of Ryan's expression. "You grow used to it."

Ryan thought of the quiet of Northumberland with its hills and seascapes, and felt a sharp pang of homesickness. He missed the mellow, misty fields and rugged coastline where he and Anna had been married the year before, and which suited his temperament so well. Florence was beautiful, undoubtedly, but it was not home.

"Which way?" was all he said.

"Follow me," Ricci replied. "Sergeant Banotti is speaking with the local authorities to gather footage from the street cameras to see where Martina went, after leaving her work at the museum. Let's see if we can find out what happened while she was here."

He led Ryan up a set of stairs towards the entrance. The route took them past a group of wide-eyed teenagers wearing identical green backpacks who, catching sight of the tall, good-looking stranger, proceeded to giggle uproariously.

Ricci glanced back at the look of confused horror on his new friend's face.

"Come quickly, before you're mobbed," he said, with a chuckle.

Ricci spoke with the museum's Head of Security and they found themselves ushered inside the Uffizi's hallowed walls fifteen minutes before its official opening time. The small, square-shouldered man introduced himself as Matteo Alfonsi and led them through a discreet doorway to the left of the main entrance and along a corridor to the security office. Although Ryan could have followed the conversation in Italian, he was impressed when Ricci indicated that they should speak in English.

It was a small enough gesture, but he noted it all the same.

"Thank you for your cooperation," Ricci said, as they entered an impressive, high-tech facility. Banks of gleaming screens were stacked three or four rows high and he counted five security guards manning them, presumably divided up into different zones of the museum.

"Martina is my daughter's age," Matteo replied, and didn't bother to elaborate. The hard look in his eye told them, more than words ever could, how he might act if somebody had taken his child. "What do you need from me?"

If only it were always this easy, Ryan thought.

"Martina was reported missing after six last night," Ricci said. "According to our contact at the publishing house who are hosting a party at the gallery tonight, two of their team were here with Martina until five-fifteen yesterday evening, discussing the final arrangements. They say that, when they left, she stayed on to lock up the event space and speak to suppliers. There's a gap in time, then her fiancé called to file a Missing Persons Report after she failed to pick up their toddler from the crèche after finishing work at six."

"What time did he call?"

Ricci looked uncomfortable.

"At around seven o'clock," he admitted. "He was told to wait a while longer by the Control Room, but he was adamant Martina would never have left their daughter that way."

And yet, Ricci hadn't told him the woman had been reported missing until just before the anonymous tip-off had come through, Ryan thought.

A full three hours later.

"It's a bad business," Matteo remarked, as if he'd heard Ryan's thoughts. "There must be something on the cameras. Let me see what I can do."

"The party is taking place in the Western Corridor on the second floor," Ryan pointed out. "It would make sense to check the cameras immediately around there, first."

Matteo nodded, then turned to the other security personnel in the room and clapped his hands.

"I need to see the footage from last night between, let's say, five o'clock and six-thirty. All sectors, starting with the Western Corridor, as quick as you can."

While Matteo moved off to walk along the line of screens, Ryan turned to Ricci and spoke in an undertone.

"What about the telephone companies? What efforts have been made to trace her mobile phone? Is it still transmitting?"

Ricci held up a hand to fend off further questions.

"I spoke to Martina's fiancé late last night and, before you ask, he was at work surrounded by dozens of people, until he received a call from his daughter's crèche to ask why nobody had collected her. He gave me Martina's number and we will be contacting the telephone company this morning," he paused to check his watch.

Eight-fifty.

"It may be too early in the day, but we are moving as quickly as we can on that score."

Ryan stuck his hands in the pockets of his lightweight trousers and told himself to stay calm. He knew from long experience it could be a tedious, bureaucratic task eliciting data from outside organisations; it was the same problem where he came from.

"I don't understand it!"

Both men turned at the sound of Matteo's anxious voice and the exchange of fast-flowing Italian that followed as several guards began to speak at once.

Ryan strode across the room and put a steadying hand on the older man's arm.

"*La questione*? What's the matter?"

"The recordings…the files, they are corrupted. There is nothing from last night, at all."

"What do you mean, 'nothing'?" Ricci asked.

"Nothing! *Nothing*!" The man made a gesture like sand falling through his fingers. "The recording is fine again after midnight and throughout this morning but there is nothing at all left of yesterday. It is a major incident."

Matteo looked as though he might keel over, so Ryan urged him into one of the chairs nearby and pulled up one for himself, so he could lean in and speak closely to the Head of Security.

"Tell us, Matteo, who was on shift yesterday?"

The man held a hand to his forehead.

"Ah—myself, Gabriella, Marco…I can get the full list for you, *signore*, but first we need to check the museum, in case anything has been taken. This happened before, many years ago, and valuable paintings were stolen…"

"I understand," Ryan told him. "Do what you have to do to make the area safe, then come back and speak to us. Alright?"

He looked up at Ricci, who nodded his agreement.

"*Grazie*," Matteo muttered, and heaved himself up again to instigate a room-by-room check of the premises.

While the others in the room talked animatedly about past security breaches and the possibility of foreign sabotage, Ryan and Ricci stood at the back of it all, surveying the empty screens.

"This is a breakthrough," Ryan decided.

"You can't be serious," Ricci scoffed. "This is a disaster. The artworks, the integrity of the museum…it will all come under public scrutiny, now. There are many private benefactors as well as the pieces donated by the Medici in perpetuity."

"I like art as much as the next person," Ryan snapped. "But I like people a lot more. I couldn't give a shit about the paintings, Alessandro. I'm talking about the fact that whoever took Martina Calari has *shown* themselves, now."

"How?" Ricci muttered. "They've shown us nothing."

"Firstly," Ryan ticked the points off on his fingers, "if there was any doubt before, it seems much more likely that Martina has been taken against her will, rather than simply going AWOL for a few hours. Secondly, tampering with a security system as sophisticated as this one tells us that whoever we're looking for is equally sophisticated."

He thought immediately of Armstrong's holiday home back in Northumberland, which was brimming with gadgetry and an expensive CCTV system that must have cost many thousands of pounds to install and operate remotely from his smartphone. Home security was one thing, but the man lived as though his address was Fort Knox.

"Thirdly," Ryan continued, "it tells us the action was premeditated. He or she had to have known about the kind of system likely to be in place before setting out to take Martina, who wasn't any random pick, either. They must have known where she would be and what her appointments schedule looked like."

Ricci's eyes strayed to the huddle of security personnel chatting amongst themselves.

"Yes," Ryan agreed. "We need to look at all of them, especially those who were on shift yesterday. That said, it's easy enough to hack into an integrated system remotely, once you know what you're dealing with. I'd want to know who's seen the inside of this room, or who's been asking questions about the level of security."

"All of Florentine society is coming to the event later this evening," Ricci told him. "Many have private security who will have liaised with the team here, ahead of time. It's usual procedure."

"Then I want their names," Ryan said. "A list of everybody who so much as asked what was behind this door."

Ricci nodded.

"Perhaps the street cameras will be able to give us something," he said. "Whoever took Martina may have been able to wipe the cameras inside the museum, but it would have been impossible to do the same with every CCTV camera in the city. There must have been a car or some form of transport waiting outside—"

"We need a map of the museum," Ryan cut in. "Showing all possible exits. It would have been dark after six but, all the same, there are people on the street to see if Martina had been taken against her will."

Ricci made a rocking motion with his hand.

"We have no way of knowing whether the woman was drugged, in which case she might have appeared the worse for wear after one too many glasses of wine. Nobody notices that sort of thing, except in passing."

Ryan had to admit that was true, but then thought of Armstrong's palazzo apartment, situated virtually around the corner.

"Ask Sergeant Banotti to request the CCTV from the south and western ends of the gallery," he said. "They're the most likely routes he'd have taken."

Ricci frowned.

"It may not have been Armstrong who did this. It seems fantastic to believe he would jeopardise his position in this way."

"Let's err on the side of history, shall we?" Ryan replied. "We're not dealing with an ordinary man."

"She may still be alive, my friend. It's possible."

Ryan remained silent and, as if he had conjured it, Ricci's phone began to ring. He heard snatches of the conversation that followed and watched the changing expression on the inspector's face, hardening his heart against the bad news that was to come.

Ricci ended the call with his sergeant and took his time slipping his phone back into his pocket before he looked up and into Ryan's shuttered face.

"That was Sergeant Banotti," he said, needlessly. "A body has been found, washed up on the riverbank near the *Passerella dell' Isolotto*. It is a pedestrian bridge connecting the Isolotto district of Florence with Cascine Park," he explained.

"Is it her?"

"There has been no formal identification yet," Ricci started to trill out the party line, then stopped himself. There was no need for pretence between them. "It matches the description of Martina, yes. Banotti is on her way there now and will oversee the transfer of the body to the mortuary within the hour."

"We'll meet her there," Ryan said.

Ricci nodded.

"If we presume the body is Martina and it was dumped into the river, we need to see the CCTV footage. The question is, how would a killer remove her from the Uffizi without being seen?"

How did Armstrong get her to his apartment without being seen? Ryan amended, privately.

It was the multi-million-dollar question.

CHAPTER 24

"Look, son. I don't think you understand what I mean when I say, 'stottie cake.'"

MacKenzie walked back into CID after her meeting with Chief Constable Morrison and came to an abrupt stop beside Phillips' desk. He appeared to be engaged in a heated debate with an unknown caller on the topic of baked goods, which had nothing whatsoever to do with murder or serious crime.

At least, she sincerely hoped not.

"No. No, it's not a cake, it's a bread. No, not like soda bread. Naht, it's not a scone, either. Imagine the King of all Breads. The fluffiest, lightest, tastiest…no, man, it's not a pitta. We're gannin' from bad to worse, here—"

MacKenzie tapped a finger against her watch and rolled her eyes.

"Alreet, listen. Just hold off on the stotties for now and I'll call you back later."

Phillips set the desk phone back into its holder with a little more force than was necessary, then made a raspberry sound with his lips.

"Trying to arrange a decent caterer for this wedding is like gannin' on a quest for the Holy Grail," he complained. "What kind of self-respecting chef doesn't know what a stottie cake is?"

"It's all soda bread and chowder, where I'm from," she reminded him, having decided to humour her soon-to-be husband for a couple of minutes. "Which reminds me, I had my auntie on the phone, earlier."

Phillips winced. MacKenzie's ageing Irish aunt was a strong-headed woman from County Kerry who was known throughout that land as being one of its most opinionated and outspoken residents.

"She had a list of complaints about our plans," MacKenzie continued. "She doesn't understand why I wouldn't want to marry in the church where I was baptised, rather than having a civil ceremony in the beautiful castle I've admired since I was a girl. I didn't bother telling her I haven't seen the inside of a Catholic church since I was investigating one of its holy men for murder."

Phillips chuckled.

"Aye, that wouldn't have gone down too well," he said, then reached across to touch her hand. "Would you like me to have a word with her? You shouldn't have to deal with all that nonsense, love. It's supposed to be a happy time, planning our special day."

MacKenzie squeezed his hand.

"Thanks, Frank, but there isn't really time just now. We have to shake a leg."

Assuming she was referring to the Warkworth case, Phillips reached for his notepad.

"Well, I've just heard back from Faulkner, who says he's having a devil of a time trying to find any useful DNA that doesn't belong to the victim. Yates has been liaising with the Crown Prosecution Service and the Courts Service to pull together a list of all the people he prosecuted—and sent down—while he was practising."

He didn't need to mention what a mammoth task that might be.

"Tell her to cross-check against prison releases between eighteen months and six months ago," MacKenzie suggested. "If our working theory is that Edward Clarkson was scared enough to leave his old life behind, maybe it was to do with him worrying that someone from his past would be coming for him."

Phillips nodded.

"I can give her a hand—"

"That all depends," MacKenzie said, very casually.

"—and I'm still waiting to hear back from the banks about his financial…eh? What's that?"

"It might be tricky to help when you'll be in Italy with me," she said.

Phillips sat up a bit straighter in his chair.

"What's happened? Is our lad in trouble?"

"Nothing Ryan can't handle," MacKenzie said. "But Morrison reckons he'll handle it a lot better if we're over there with him, to lend a hand. Besides, I told her you speak a dozen languages, that you'd blend in like Al Pacino and that, with any luck, we'd be home again by morning."

Phillips gave her a toothy grin.

"Does this mean you'll start calling me The Godfather?"

MacKenzie tapped a hand against his cheek and clucked her tongue.

"Ah, now. Let's not start delving into the realms of pure fantasy."

"Yes, ma'am."

CHAPTER 25

While Phillips brought his holiday civvies out of mothballs, Ryan stood beside a metal gurney at the Florence City Morgue and looked upon the ravaged body of Martina Calari. His face was carefully neutral and, to the casual observer, appeared entirely devoid of emotion.

But his eyes gave him away.

They had darkened in grief to a colour akin to the North Sea in winter and swirled with a stormy blend of anger and compassion.

"Has she been identified?" he asked, softly.

Ricci shook his head.

"Her fiancé will be coming in shortly," he answered. "It's just a formality, really."

Ryan understood what he meant. The woman's face, though wasted by an evening spent in the murky waters of the Arno, was still recognisable enough. She wore a ring on the third finger of her left hand that was a perfect match to the description given by her fiancé. Apparently, the cluster of sapphires and diamonds now caught between the bloated folds of the woman's finger had been in his family for years.

"The cause of death seems obvious," he said, but looked across at the police pathologist for confirmation. The woman was somewhere in her late thirties, with serious brown eyes and a quiet air of authority.

"Yes," she replied, reaching out a gloved hand to point towards the deep circular tear in the woman's neck. "She has been strangled, and with some force. Enough to tear the skin and crush her trachea, here."

"By what?" Ryan asked.

The pathologist made a murmuring sound while she thought.

"It's too early to say for certain, but I would think a slim cord of some kind, perhaps of a similar circumference as the cord of a hairdryer, or any household electrical device."

"We already have a reasonable idea of post mortem interval but is there any way to narrow it down?" Ricci asked.

The pathologist shook her head.

"She has been submerged for at least six to twelve hours, that much I can tell you by the condition of her skin. Her core temperature has been affected by the surrounding water, which was approximately six degrees Celsius overnight."

They nodded, casting sympathetic eyes towards the body.

"As for the time of death, I can't give you anything specific, but I can tell you that, if she went missing sometime after six last night, it would be consistent with the level of decomposition."

"What about defensive wounds?" Ryan asked.

"The water will probably have washed away any skin samples or fluids," she replied. "But her nails were torn, here," she pointed to the woman's hands. "It's possible this happened in the water, but it's more likely to have happened during a struggle. Unfortunately, I suspect the nails were torn against her own skin, as she tried to loosen whatever was cutting off her air supply; there are scratches down her neck that appear self-inflicted."

Ryan nodded his thanks.

"Is it the same?" Ricci turned to him and, for once, his face bore the evidence of stress. "Is this what you found before?"

Ryan didn't pretend to misunderstand.

"Armstrong's last victims—or, should I say, *alleged* victims—were stabbed and bludgeoned with the blunt end of a heavy copper pan, respectively. He has no known MO, other than being supremely careful with forensic matters. It makes our job harder, but it doesn't rule him out of having done this," he gestured mutely to the woman's remains, then turned away to face Ricci fully. "If you're asking me whether I believe Nathan Armstrong could be responsible for this, then my answer is 'yes'. I believe he has it in him to kill without mercy, with force and, what's more, he'd sleep like a baby afterwards."

Ricci swallowed and, for the first time, appeared out of his depth in the harsh light of the mortuary.

"I'm no inexperienced boy," he said. "I've seen what people are capable of, whether for love, for money or because they are mafia. But it has been a long time since Florence has seen anything like this. So long, that whoever was *Il Mostro* has become more of an urban legend; something the kids say to frighten one another at Hallowe'en, or the kind of gruesome story that authors use to inspire novels," he added, with a small smile. "I was one of those kids. I grew up years after the murders happened and never saw anything remotely like it during all the time I've been at the *Gruppo.*"

"You're fortunate," Ryan breathed.

Ricci nodded soberly.

"I heard…that is, I know what happened to your family. I was sorry to hear of it."

Ryan gave a short nod.

"You were unlucky, my friend. But, living through that kind of experience can change a man. Make him see shadows around every corner."

Something flickered in Ryan's eyes, something that might have been hurt, but was quickly extinguished.

"You're right," he said. "Losing your sister to a serial killer and almost being murdered yourself is something you don't tend to forget. I see his shadow around every corner. I see the lingering embers of what might be called 'evil' in Armstrong's eyes, just as I once saw them in the Hacker. But it doesn't make me a paranoid quack; no longer capable of distinguishing between reality and unreality, or between right and wrong. I see them both, very clearly, *my friend,* and it gives me a competitive advantage. You know why?"

Ryan asked, conversationally. "Because, when the wolf comes knocking at my door, I'll recognise him."

Without waiting for any response, Ryan turned and walked out of the mortuary and didn't stop until he reached the street, where he emerged like a drowning man to suck in massive gulps of warm air. People passed by, stepping around him as they carried on with their ordinary lives.

Never thinking, never imagining that they might be next.

The street seemed to contract, closing in around him as Ryan stood there gasping for breath. He stumbled back against the stone wall of the mortuary building, fumbling with the top button of his linen shirt but finding it already open at the neck.

He told himself to breathe.

Breathe.

In…out.

In…and out.

After a moment, the dizzying loss of control passed and the numb, pins-and-needles sensation in his fingertips began to fade. The street was whole once again, the same as it had been for centuries. Its walls had been tarnished and worn with time, battered and bruised, but they still stood tall.

As would he.

When Ryan arrived back at the villa, the clock on the mantel had just struck five. Light streamed through the enormous arched windows, but its rooms were silent.

His pace quickened as he moved from room to room and he fought back an overwhelming panic that gripped his heart and forced him to imagine every worst possible outcome.

"*Signore?*"

Ryan spun around at the sound of Magda's calm voice and found her framed in the kitchen doorway.

"Hello, Magda. I was looking for Anna?"

Magda noted the pallor of his skin with concern but, wisely, chose to say nothing.

"The *signora* is in your father's study," she answered. "Shall I bring some coffee through to you?"

As though she had spoken the magic word, Ryan's face transformed.

"That would be great, thanks. Oh, and Magda, I don't suppose you know where I can find a couple of decorative masks, at short notice?"

She gave him a smile not unlike Da Vinci's *Madonna*.

"I have already laid them out on your bed," she told him. "I had them delivered before lunchtime."

"You're one in a million," he declared, and surprised her with a quick peck on the cheek.

She watched him move off in search of his wife and thought of her own boy, lost to her now.

———

Ryan's father, David, was a methodical, traditional sort of man who had laid out his study very much like the one he had back home in Devon, save for the ornate touches that were to be expected of an old Florentine villa. He had resisted his wife's none-too-subtle hints that he might want to brighten the place up a bit and give it a lick of paint, preferring instead to retain a rustic, more simplistic space where he could focus on the difficult matters his job had entailed. In more recent years, the space had become a reading room where any of his family might retreat for a few hours to lounge in the comfortable leather desk chair or on one of the velvet-covered day beds.

It also happened to possess a long wall-space that was free of wall hangings or paintings, unlike most of the other rooms in the Villa Lucia, which had been the deciding factor for Anna.

"What's all this?" Ryan asked, as he stepped inside the musty room.

His wife stood in the centre of the room, arms folded, surveying her handiwork. She turned distractedly when he entered and, for a fraction of a second, Ryan saw the expression he so often wore reflected on his wife's face.

"Hi there," she said, and her face broke into a smile. "I missed you today."

He closed the space between them in three long strides.

"I missed you, too," he murmured, and kissed her deeply.

Long minutes later, Ryan turned back to the wall and took a closer look at what she'd created. On one side, she'd tacked up images of Duncan Gray and Kate Robson, two people who had died at the hands of Nathan Armstrong at Kielder, in Northumberland, but for whom justice had been elusive.

In the middle, she'd tacked up images of missing persons associated with Armstrong, alongside the dates they were reported. So far, she had Luc Bernard and Riccardo Spatuzzi, whose faces stared back at him in bold colour against the muted wall. A little further away, in her own space, there was a picture of Martina Calari, presumably taken from her social media account. A pretty young mother who smiled happily out at the camera, frozen in time forever. Ryan had a flash memory of how she'd looked only a couple of hours before, and bore down against a fresh wave of anger.

He turned to another part of the wall, where there was a detailed timeline stretching back to the events at Kielder last year, when they had first encountered Nathan Armstrong at his house on the lake, known as 'Scribe's End'. Above it all was a large, annotated paper map of Florence, similar to those found in guidebooks or given out as pamphlets with areas of interest drawn in tiny 3D form. Dotted around the map were what appeared to be schematic drawings of various buildings, alongside printed images of them taken from the web.

In other words, his wife had created a Murder Board.

It must have taken hours, systematically finding and researching areas and people of interest and setting it all out in the way she knew he liked to work. There was nothing she could have given him that would have meant more to him in that moment.

"Thank you," he said huskily, and turned to bestow one of the special smiles he reserved only for her. "You've saved me hours of precious time."

Anna smiled.

"I wanted to help," she said, simply. "I don't know if it's right—"

Ryan moved closer to study the wall, his eyes skimming over the handwritten details she'd added onto the map before moving to fall once again on the picture of Martina Calari. Wordlessly, he reached for her photograph and tugged it off the wall, only to move it a little further left, alongside the images of Duncan Gray and Kate Robson.

"She was found earlier today," he said, and stepped back again.

"I'm sorry," Anna murmured. "I know it's what you suspected but it doesn't make it any easier."

"No," he agreed. "It's one instance where it doesn't feel good to know you were right all along."

Just then, Magda arrived with a tray of coffee. They thanked her, and she disappeared soundlessly, her eyes glancing once at the wall before falling away again.

"She's discreet," Anna observed. "I wonder how she came to work for your family?"

"She was a friend of my mother," Ryan explained. "Has been for years. I think she needed the work and, as far as security goes, she passed the enhanced background checks."

His eye caught on a schematic drawing of the Uffizi Gallery and he pointed at it.

"The police and security teams searched the whole museum before its doors opened to the public," he explained. "Martina Calari went missing from there but, when the CCTV footage was requested this morning, we found it had all been wiped."

"Completely?"

Ryan nodded.

"Armstrong's home in Kielder is kitted out like a technological fortress. I wouldn't put it past him to know how to tamper with the cameras, even remotely."

"Do you know his schedule?" Anna asked.

"I have a rough idea," Ryan answered. "His public schedule is available online. He's been hopping between radio and television gigs for the past couple of days, plus book signings around the city. I don't know exact timings for all of them, but I can find out."

"It depends how long he had to himself, between events," Anna mused. "He's a recognisable face around these parts, so he couldn't just come and go as he pleases."

"That's the conundrum," Ryan admitted. "The street cameras outside the museum haven't recorded any sighting of Martina Calari—or Armstrong, for that matter—in the period she went missing. I don't understand how he managed to enter and leave, let alone take her with him, without being caught on camera."

"The Vasari Corridor," Anna said. "I've been looking into possibilities all day and it's the only one that fits."

Ryan frowned, trying to remember why the name rang a bell.

"It's an enclosed, elevated passageway," she explained. "It was built by Cosimo de' Medici in 1565 to allow his family and their guests to move freely between their residence at the Palazzo Pitti and the government palace at the Palazzo Vecchio without having to sully themselves on the street."

"Alright for some," Ryan said. "But I don't see how it helps us."

"The corridor runs south of the Palazzo Vecchio through the Uffizi Gallery," she explained, moving over to trace her index finger over the map to show him its route. "It then bears west, running parallel to the River Arno until it reaches the Ponte Vecchio. It crosses the bridge and continues south, over the church of Santa Felicita, until it reaches the Palazzo Pitti and ends in the Boboli Gardens. It's around a kilometre long, in total."

Ryan walked up to the map.

"You said it runs parallel to the river, here," he said. "Does it run through these buildings lining the river, or around them?"

"Mostly, it runs through them, but with the notable exception of the Mannelli Tower—the story goes that the family refused to allow Cosimo to hack through their palazzo and it seems he respected their gumption in refusing him, even though he was the most powerful man in Florence, even Italy, at that time. He built the corridor around the tower instead, supported by enormous brackets, but for the most part the Medici built directly through whichever buildings stood in the way."

"Including the *Palazzo Russo*?" Ryan asked, referring to the building containing Nathan Armstrong's apartment.

Anna nodded.

"Exactly."

All at once, everything seemed to fall into place.

"How do you access the Vasari Corridor from the Uffizi?" he asked, already scanning the schematic drawings to understand the route.

"Here," Anna explained, pointing to an access door. "Normally, that part of the corridor is open to the public, exhibiting a collection of self-portraits, but it's been closed for renovations for over a year."

"Is there an access point as it passes through the *Palazzo Russo*?" he asked, and Anna nodded.

"It took a lot of work to find that schematic; I rang a friend of mine back in Durham, who happens to be an architect, and he spoke to the head of the Museum of Architecture in Rome. The access door to the *Palazzo Russo* hasn't been open for over a hundred years, according to them, but it's located on the fourth floor."

Ryan's eyes flashed molten silver.

"Son of a bitch. The bastard must have hidden her in the corridor when he heard us coming."

Ryan walked away for a moment to look out of the window, drawing in the familiar scent of his father's study as he looked out across the gardens basking in the afternoon sunshine.

"That's why we never caught Armstrong on the street cameras," he said, once he could trust himself to speak. "He must have accessed the gallery using the corridor."

"In theory, yes," Anna said. "Because the corridor is mainly closed to the public, he could come and go virtually as he pleases."

"What about the workmen?" Ryan thought aloud. "Wouldn't the renovations team have seen him?"

"Not if it was after six o'clock," she said.

"Ricci will call this conjecture, unless we can show him there's a functioning access door right beside Armstrong's apartment," Ryan said. "I want to try to find it, while we're at the Uffizi later tonight."

Anna didn't bother to argue with him, because she'd known from the outset he would need to see it for himself.

"Armstrong will be busy at the party," she said. "You can slip away, and he won't be able to follow."

Ryan turned to face her again and the sun cast his face in shadow.

"There's just one other thing I don't understand," he said.

"What's that?"

"Ricci must have known about the Vasari Corridor. Hell, it's a tourist attraction. Why didn't he mention it, earlier today? He may not have known it runs directly through the *Palazzo Russo*, or that there's an access on the fourth floor, but he knew there was an access on the second floor of the Uffizi, which is the last place Martina Calari was seen alive."

"It might not have occurred to him," Anna said, but the words sounded weak. "Perhaps there's some reasonable explanation."

Ryan stepped away from the window and she could see his face properly again, but it was dark with anger.

"Secrets and lies," he growled. "This city is full of them."

CHAPTER 26

As the sun went down, the glitterati of Tuscany turned out to celebrate twenty years of Nathan Armstrong's literary genius. Enormous golden lanterns illuminated the Uffizi Gallery by night, shining a flattering glow on those who arrived at the entrance in a cavalcade of luxury cars and stepped out into the night wearing an array of sweeping gowns and spotless tuxedos. Faces were hidden by extraordinary, intricately carved masks depicting folklore and mythical creatures so that only a person's eyes remained visible.

Having made no plans to attend anything remotely like a masked ball, Anna and Ryan had relied upon the goodwill and good taste of Magda, and had not been disappointed. In a departure from her usual 'go to' Little Black Dress, Anna found herself swathed in a long column of jade green silk which clung in all the right places, or the wrong ones, depending upon the point of view.

"For goodness' sake," she muttered. "I feel half-naked in this thing."

"Terrible, isn't it," Ryan said, deadpan.

She gave him a withering look and tried tugging the fabric away from her hips.

"Nearly there," he said, and reached across the back seat of the taxi to take her hand. The lights of Florence flickered through the car windows as they passed through the city and made their way towards the Uffizi, polishing his hair to a deep, gleaming black. She allowed herself to imagine they were just like any other couple, heading out for an entertaining evening of good food and wine.

But nerves jangled as the car crawled along the riverfront and came to a halting stop, edging forward as the cars ahead divested themselves of passengers and moved on. Ryan raised her hand to his lips in silent support, then held it between both of his own to warm her cold fingers. He looked across at the beautiful woman who was his wife and wondered how he had stumbled through life for all the years before they had met. In his profession, he walked into the darkest corners and saw the product of the very worst that one person could do to another. Before Anna, he had walked into those corners and then returned to an empty flat on Newcastle's Quayside, maybe after a pint with Frank, to sit alone and brood about all that was bad in the world.

Lonely.

He could say it, now that he understood himself better. There had been other women, fleeting relationships without depth that managed to stave off the bitter feeling of isolation for months, sometimes years at a time. But there had been nobody who understood him and with whom he could be entirely himself, until now.

Until Anna.

It was not fashionable to admit to feeling lonely and, he supposed, it had not been expected of a man like him. If the magazines and daytime chat shows were to be believed, loneliness went hand in hand with old age. But what of all the twenty and thirty-somethings who walked through life unable to connect, unable to find just one person who could look into the depths of their soul and like what they found there?

Ryan had been one such person, walking through life putting one foot in front of the other, convincing himself he needed nothing and nobody. And, he supposed, he didn't. If he had never met her, his heart would continue to beat, and the sun would rise and fall each day. But it would have been a hollow existence, one where his senses were dulled, like food without flavour.

Anna turned to look at him.

"What are you thinking about?" she asked him.

"You," he answered honestly.

"Oh dear," she joked. "Nothing bad, I hope?"

Ryan almost laughed, but instead he leaned across to brush his lips against hers.

"Never," he said.

"Are you alright?"

His eyes warmed, fathoms deep with love for her.

"Never better," he said, crisply. "Here we are, time to put our masks on."

The Uffizi Gallery was lovely during the daytime but, by night, it was spectacular.

Clever lighting through its hallways and passages backlit smooth marble statues and priceless works of art, from Botticelli to Michelangelo, as guests were directed towards the main event space along the Western Corridor on the second floor. Anna and Ryan filed into their number, having found their names included on the guest list, which indicated that Monica Spatuzzi had kept her end of the bargain.

They followed the line of masked men and women into a long gallery area where a small podium and mic had been set up with the publisher's brand splashed all over it. Smartly-dressed waiters moved smoothly through the crowd with trays of canapes and fluted champagne, while music drifted on the air and over the heads of at least a hundred people, and counting.

"There's the door," Anna whispered.

Ryan followed Anna's line of sight and, just to the side of a more impressive set of wooden doors, he noted an unremarkable doorway cut into the wall and painted the same colour. He had walked through the gallery several times and had never noticed it before.

"Through that door, there should be a short flight of stairs," she told him. "That takes you to the corridor, which you follow for about a quarter of a mile. Stop just before you reach the Ponte Vecchio and, if there's an entrance to the *Palazzo Russo*, it should be on your right."

Ryan nodded.

"Just one problem," he murmured, and watched one of the security guards walk a slow circuit then come to a standstill right beside the door. "I don't know how many guards are on, tonight, but I'd rather not have to ask Ricci's permission—which he's unlikely to give—then seek out the security guards and ask them to stand away from the door. It'll cause a fuss and alert Armstrong."

Before they could think of a solution, they were approached by a woman wearing a tasteful, sweeping mask over her eyes, which complemented the simple black velvet dress she wore.

"I see you found your way here, Chief Inspector."

Even if he hadn't recognised her before, Ryan could not have mistaken the voice.

"Good evening, Signora Spatuzzi. Allow me to introduce my wife, Anna."

Anna was grateful she wore a mask to hide her face as she met the woman who was responsible, directly or indirectly, for countless mafia-related crimes.

"Good evening," she managed.

"You make a handsome couple," Monica remarked. "I trust you have met our guest of honour?"

Even Ryan's trained ear could detect no trace of the anger he had seen, so clearly, at her villa in Fiesole. If Monica

Spatuzzi believed Nathan Armstrong had killed her son, Riccardo, then he could detect nothing of it in her voice or demeanour. That ability to shut down emotion and display nothing of what she felt was more terrifying than if she'd held a gun to his head.

"Not yet," Anna said, in a tone that implied she had no wish to.

"Oh, but you *must*," Monica went on. "Follow me, and meet the man who is the toast of the city, tonight."

The crowds parted like the Red Sea for Monica Spatuzzi as she led them towards the centre of the room, where an ice sculpture had been carved into the shape of a giant book.

"Tasteful," Ryan muttered. "I'm surprised he didn't ask for it to be a giant effigy of himself."

"The sculpture is Nico's work," Monica replied. "He is an art dealer and his latest conquest is a young man with a flair for sculpture. So, we have mediocre ice and marble sculptures being commissioned throughout the city, in every gallery and department store. How Michelangelo must be turning in his grave."

Right on cue, a man of average height wearing a simple black mask almost collided with them whilst carrying two brimming flutes of bubbling liquid.

"*Mille scuse!*" he chuckled.

"I see you are already getting into the spirit of things, Nico," Monica said. "Be careful you do not fall into the sculpture, won't you?"

"I never do, *signora*, I never do," he said, switching into English. "Wh' don' you introduce me to your friends?"

"This is Maxwell Ryan and his wife, Doctor Taylor-Ryan. They have a villa here."

Ryan smiled, knowing she had deliberately left off his official title.

"Villa, eh? Need any sculptures to deck the place out a bit?"

"Sadly not," Ryan replied.

"Pity. Still, let me know what you're in the market for and I'll keep a look-out. Monica's got my number."

Nico sauntered off into the crowd, the drinks teetering precariously in his hands, while they continued onward in search of the man of the moment.

They found Nathan Armstrong holding court amongst a group of journalists and literary editors, wearing an elaborate gold and silver mask plumed with glossy black feathers.

"What I really wanted to convey in that book was the extraordinary sense of *fear*," he was saying. "People have used words like, 'ground-breaking' and 'revolutionary' to describe it over the years but I don't really care about all that," he scoffed, whilst simultaneously angling his head towards the flash of a nearby camera. "I was just happy to have captured the essence of the story of *Il Mostro* and, of course, to have portrayed the lives of victims as sensitively as possible."

"I think we can all agree, you've certainly done that," one of the men standing beside him chimed in and, for a worrying moment, Ryan thought he might be sick.

"There are some, are there not, who believe the book to be exploitative of the victims' families," one of the journalists pointed out and, with a sudden start, Anna realised it was Andrea Conti of the *Florence Daily News*. "What would you say to them?"

"There will always be those who fail to understand the subtleties of the book," Armstrong said, in much the same manner as he might have patted the head of a disabled person. "I'm sorry for them, of course, but it is only fiction inspired by true events, after all."

"Yes, and, as I'm sure you appreciate, Mr Armstrong has many people to thank this evening," his publisher put in, ever so smoothly. "Excuse us."

He began to steer Armstrong away, but one word from Monica stopped them.

"Gabriele? If we could have a moment of your time," she asked, in the same quiet tone she employed at all times.

"Monica," the man said, with a nervous laugh. "I'm sorry, I didn't recognise you at first. By all means, allow me to introduce you to Nathan Armstrong, the international bestselling author of *Il Mostro.*"

He swept a hand theatrically and ushered the man forward.

"Nathan, I have the great honour to present Signora Monica Spatuzzi, who sits on the board of Elato Publishing," he added, meaningfully.

Armstrong's face was covered by the preposterous silver and gold mask, so it was almost impossible to tell if he had registered any reaction to the name, or the familial connection to Riccardo Spatuzzi. He merely took her proffered hand and executed a tiny bow.

"*Signora*, a pleasure to meet you. If you're one of the trustees, I must have you to thank for this wonderful evening."

Monica had already withdrawn her hand, which was now fisted tightly at her side.

"*Non e niente*," she murmured.

Armstrong's gaze moved to the man and woman standing just behind her, watching him with unblinking eyes that stared through the gaps in their masks. Even without taking into account the man's height, his posture and even the cut of his suit, Armstrong would have been able to pick Ryan out of the crowd.

"Who are your friends?" he asked, with an edge.

"Ah, how rude of me," Monica said. "This is Maxwell Ryan and his wife, Anna. They're visiting us from England."

"We're already acquainted," Ryan said, but accepted the hand that the publisher stuck out as a matter of courtesy. "D' you know, I'm struggling to remember the last time we saw one another, Armstrong. Perhaps you can enlighten me?"

There was a humming pause while Ryan waited to see whether Armstrong would reveal the embarrassing circumstances in which they had last been in the same room back in the Interview Suite of Northumbria CID.

Armstrong took a slow sip of his drink, savouring the fizzing liquid as it rolled around his tongue.

"I'm afraid I can't remember," he said, apologetically. "I meet a lot of people, most of them utterly forgettable. I'm sure you understand."

With another small bow for Anna, he moved off to speak to the next group, his publisher in tow. In the remaining silence, Monica took a long drink of her champagne and then handed the empty glass to Ryan.

When she spoke again, her voice was hard.

"You have two days left."

With that, she walked in the direction of the exit. Two burly-looking bodyguards Anna hadn't even noticed mingling in the crowd behind them peeled away to join her, flanking the older woman on either side as she left.

CHAPTER 27

As Monica Spatuzzi left the Uffizi, Phillips and MacKenzie bundled themselves into a taxi outside Florence Airport.

"Where would you like to go?" the driver asked, in perfect English.

"I've got this, love," Phillips said, pulling out an Italian phrase book. "Portatchee dal macellayoo."

The driver looked between them, clearly confused as he worked through the terrible mispronunciation.

"You want to go to the...butcher?"

"Give me strength," MacKenzie muttered. "Can you take us to the Villa Lucia, please? It's on Viale Machiavelli."

The driver smiled, his eyes lingering a moment too long on MacKenzie's fall of Titian hair.

"Eyes forward, son," Phillips growled.

They were soon on the road leading into the centre of town.

"I spoke to the housekeeper before we got on the plane," MacKenzie said. "A woman called Magda. She looks after the place for Ryan's family—"

"A housekeeper? Always said he was a bloody posh southerner. Who needs a full-time housekeeper to take care of a little holiday flat?"

MacKenzie wondered how to prepare her fiancé for what was to come, then decided to let the place speak for itself. Her second thought was whether she should have put the local Accident and Emergency department on alert.

"Mmm. Anyway, she's expecting us. Ryan and Anna are out at a party, tonight."

"A party?" Phillips burst out. "I thought he was over here hunting down a killer, not gallivanting around the place hobnobbing with the locals."

MacKenzie grinned as she watched the passing scenery. Even in darkness, she could see the outline of towers and spires and her heart began to melt.

"It's not quite your average party," she explained. "It's Armstrong's party, thrown by his Italian publishing house. They're celebrating twenty years of it being one of their bestsellers."

"Aye, well, Ryan'll take him down a peg or two," Phillips said, with a gravelly laugh. "Wish I was there to see it."

Ryan and Anna found a relatively secluded spot on the edge of the crowded room which had the added benefit of affording them a clear view of the doorway leading to the Vasari Corridor. They remained there for a while until Ryan could be sure of the security guard's movements.

"He walks a circuit around the room every ten minutes," Ryan said, and recognised the man from the security room that morning.

He checked his watch.

Eight thirty-seven.

"If he's running to schedule, the guard will get up and walk around again at eight forty."

Sure enough, three minutes later, the guard heaved himself up from his chair and began a slow walk around the event space, in an anti-clockwise direction.

"As soon as he gets up at eight-fifty, we'll move across and I'll slip inside," Ryan decided. "Will you be okay waiting here? There's a roomful of people, so it should be fine for fifteen minutes, max."

"I'll be fine," Anna assured him. "If you wait much longer than that, the party might start to thin out and your absence will be noted."

Ryan nodded.

"Where's Armstrong now?"

They searched the sea of faces for any sign of his ostentatious gold and silver mask, then Anna clutched Ryan's arm.

"*Look!*"

As Ryan's head jerked around in the direction of the Vasari Corridor, he caught the tail end of a plumed gold and silver mask as it disappeared behind the doorway.

"I don't believe it," Ryan muttered, taking a step forward as if to follow him.

"Wait! You can't go in there now. Not while he's there too."

"Anna, for all we know, he's drugged someone and is taking them back to his apartment," Ryan said. "I can't sit back and wait for another person to die."

"Call Ricci and tell him to get down here," he said.

With that, he made for the doorway and, seconds later, he disappeared behind the wall.

"It's like Beverly Hills, 'round here," Phillips remarked, as the taxi began to climb the winding road upward along Viale Machiavelli.

"Hey, it'd be funny if Ryan's family had one of those, wouldn't it?" he laughed, pointing towards the Villa Lucia and nudging MacKenzie's ribs as if to share the joke.

"Ah, Frank—"

The taxi slowed to make a left turn.

"Villa Lucia," the driver pronounced. "Here we are."

As the taxi swept into the driveway and came to a stop, Magda stepped outside to greet them. MacKenzie, fearful that Phillips might be suffering some sort of low-grade cardiac episode, hurriedly paid the driver and pushed him out of the car.

"*Signorina*," Magda shook MacKenzie's hand and looked over her shoulder to where Phillips was still standing on the driveway, staring goggle-eyed at the magnificent eighteenth-century villa. "Ah, does your fiancé need any help?"

"Aye, he does, but not in the way you mean," MacKenzie said, and gestured for Phillips to pull himself together.

"C'mon Frank, the house won't bite," she said.

"It's…it's…very big."

"Small wonder I fell for your charms, with poetry like that," she quipped. "Come along now, it's getting chilly out here."

Phillips followed them inside the main entrance in a sort of trance.

"I spoke with Mrs Ryan soon after your telephone call," Magda said, directing her remarks towards MacKenzie who she deemed—rightly, as it happened—to be the only one possessed of their full capacities at that moment. "She is expecting you."

"And Ryan?"

Magda smiled.

"She told me to keep your arrival 'tucked up my sleeve', as a surprise."

MacKenzie looked across to where Phillips was turning full circles in the marble entranceway, trying to take it all in.

"Probably for the best," she said. "It'll give Frank a chance to screw his head back on the right way."

———

When Ryan stepped beyond the doorway of the Uffizi Gallery, he tugged off his mask and followed the short flight of stairs leading to the Vasari Corridor, which was in darkness save for the merest glimmer of light shining through a series of porthole-sized windows overlooking the streets below. He moved quietly and cautiously while his eyes adjusted to the lack of light, keeping to one side of the corridor. He could see the shadows and empty viewing boxes where artefacts and paintings had once hung but had been removed for safekeeping during the renovation works, and the detritus of paint cans and stepladders piled together further along. He was careful not to disturb any of it, treading softly as he moved further away from the distant sounds of party revellers towards the end of the long stretch that would lead him, eventually, to the Ponte Vecchio.

It was an eerie place, and Ryan found himself imagining the footsteps of so many others over the centuries since it had first been built. What had these walls seen and heard? How many others, like him, had found themselves here after dark?

How many had come back out again? his mind whispered.

Ryan shoved the thought aside and continued to move along the long corridor. He paused to look back and was surprised to see how far he had already come. The doorway leading back into the Uffizi seemed a long way away, now.

But he had come too far now to turn back.

There were other people to think of—and the possibility that, right now, somebody was suffering at Armstrong's hands. Just thinking of it, Ryan's pace quickened, and he moved swiftly along the corridor, his footsteps making little noise as he headed deeper into the shadows.

CHAPTER 28

Anna left the noise of the party and turned into one of the large, empty gallery rooms next door to place a call through to Inspector Ricci's office. She swore softly as the number rang out, then stabbed 'redial' to try once more.

This time, on the final ring, somebody answered.

"*Pronto*?"

"Can I speak to Inspector Ricci, please?"

"Who is calling?"

"This is Anna Ryan," she said. "My husband—"

"Ah, *si*, *si*. I am Sergeant Banotti," she explained. "What has happened, *signora*?"

"We're at the Uffizi Gallery, at a party for Nathan Armstrong. Ryan—that is, we think Armstrong has been using the Vasari Corridor to get around the city without being seen. We saw him—Armstrong—heading into the corridor and Ryan has followed him."

"He has followed?" Banotti repeated, incredulously.

"Can't you see? He's worried there might be another victim!"

"*Calmati*, stay calm," the sergeant replied. "You think your husband may be in danger?'

"Yes! Please, send somebody now," Anna said, trying not to panic. "He's in there alone with Armstrong."

"I will come myself," Banotti said. "Stay where you are, Mrs Ryan, and preferably amongst lots of people. Where are you now?"

Anna looked around the vast gallery room with its smooth marble effigies, then shivered. There were dark places here, shadowy corners where a person might hide.

"I'm—look, never mind about me! Just get here as quickly as you can."

She ended the call and made quickly for the door that led back towards the party, her high heels clicking against the tiled floor in a staccato rhythm. She had almost crossed the room when the outline of a masked man appeared in the doorway.

Anna came to a shuddering halt.

"Speak of the devil and he shall appear," Armstrong said softly. "The thing about old rooms like these is that voices tend to carry. Now, tell me, Mrs Ryan: if I'm supposed to be in the corridor with your husband, how is it that I'm standing here talking to you?"

———

Ryan reached the other end of the corridor without mishap, listening for any sight or sound to tell him that Armstrong might be near. But the only sound was the thud of his own racing heartbeat as it chased the blood around his body, thundering in his ears as he came to stand at the juncture where the corridor veered south over the Ponte Vecchio. The schematic drawings indicated an entrance to the *Palazzo Russo* must be roughly where he was standing, and he studied the empty wall on the north side of the corridor for signs of a doorway.

Ryan blinked against the darkness, hardly able to distinguish light and shadow from a crack in the wall, so he resorted to using his fingertips instead. He ran his hand lightly over the wall, back and forth, covering section by section until his fingers brushed against a long indent in the plasterwork.

He curled his fingers around the edge of the handle and tugged hard.

It opened smoothly, on hinges that had recently been oiled.

Beyond the doorway was a small inner corridor built into the wall cavity and, beyond that, the door leading into Apartment 12 stood ajar.

Anna was frozen, staring at Armstrong's masked face as though she had stepped back in time; back to Holy Island and the moment when a man wearing an animal mask had almost killed her three years before. The memory of it still plagued her nightmares, nipping at the edge of her daily life to remind her that, once, she had been so close to never seeing the dawn of a new day.

She grappled with the memories and he enjoyed watching her struggle, wondering what it might be like to feel so deeply. He looked at her as he might study a specimen he'd found in a garden pond, a jumble of flesh and bone that was his for the taking, if he wished.

Anna was angry with herself. She'd made a promise a long time ago never to allow another person ever to frighten her again but, here, she found she was only human, after all.

"It's a foolish man who leaves a prize like you all alone," he whispered. "Why don't I keep you company for a while, hmm?"

Anna's lip curled.

"Many people would give their right arm to spend an evening with me," he continued. "Why don't I give you a private tour? I can show you *so* many things."

"None of which I want to see," she snapped. "Excuse me."

"If he comes back alive, tell your husband to drop the investigation," Armstrong snarled, all the specious charm suddenly gone.

"Tell him yourself," she said, and tried to brush past him.

His hand shot out to clamp around her wrist in a bruising grip and Anna didn't think twice about driving the business end of her heel into the sensitive part of his foot.

"*Bitch*," he rasped.

She took her chance, running back into the party to await the arrival of the police.

Ryan listened at the open doorway of Apartment 12 but heard nothing. He hesitated, wondering whether to make a safe retreat or press on to find out why Armstrong had left his own party.

There had to be a reason.

He pushed the door open slowly, edging into the room with extreme caution, watching and listening for any sound of life.

But the person who awaited him had spent much longer practising silence, long into the dark hours of the night as the rest of the world had slept, days that had soon stretched into years. Ryan stepped into the room like a cat burglar, pausing beside the hidden doorway that led into Armstrong's sitting room, half concealed by a palm plant.

The figure slipped behind the door to the bedroom as Ryan's footsteps sounded softly against the thick-pile carpet, making hardly a sound in the quiet evening, but it was enough to gauge his distance.

One...

Two...

Three.

Ryan heard the *whoosh* of air a millisecond before the cord wrapped around his throat.

He threw up his hands, managing to curl a single index finger beneath the thick, plastic-coated electrical wire as it tightened around his neck, cutting off the blood supply.

Acting on instinct, he threw his body backwards, slamming his assailant against the line of wardrobes in Armstrong's bedroom with enough force to splinter the wood. He gasped for air, tugging against the cord with his finger, just enough to keep it from slicing into his neck.

At the same time, Ryan heaved his body backwards, trying and failing several times to crack his skull against his attacker's nose, waiting to feel the cord loosen in shock.

But it never did.

He was beginning to see stars as his mouth opened wide, desperately drawing in choking breaths as his body struggled, still writhing to break free, his other hand clawing at the air to try to find the other person's face but missing the mark.

In a monumental effort, Ryan used his body weight to fall forward, toppling them both to the ground and providing enough slack to draw in great gulps of air. He heard his own heaving breaths in the silent apartment, rivalled only by the surprised grunt of his attacker who was temporarily winded by the fall.

But not for long.

Ryan rolled away, the cord still wrapped around his neck, doubled over as he struggled to draw enough oxygen into his body.

Through his semi-conscious fog, he saw the shadow rise up again.

The fight had only just begun.

When Anna ran back into the party, she was met by a sea of strangers and, for a moment, the line between reality and unreality wavered. Their colourful masks, once so beautiful, melted like wax so that they appeared like mannequins, their fixed, glossy-eyed faces staring out at her from behind the façade.

With a sob, she searched for the doorway and the security guard sitting beside it, who looked the worse for wear after a long and tiring evening babysitting a group of fancy-dressed socialites.

"Please," she said. "I need to open the door."

She started to paw at the doorway, searching for a handle.

The man started to speak in rapid Italian, rising from his chair to block her path.

"I don't have *time* to argue," she almost shouted. "I need to go inside! There's a man in danger!"

The security guard gave her a hard, disapproving stare and she realised that he might imagine she was drunk, or worse.

She tried once again, this time speaking slowly and clearly.

"I don't want to argue," she said. "I just want you to let me pass. The police are on their way," she added.

When he said nothing, only continued to stare at her, she started to reach around for the door handle again. This time, he took hold of her arm—the second man to do so that evening—and sent her blood boiling.

"I said, I don't want to argue," she gritted out, and then took hold of his wrist, twisting it hard to release his grip on her sensitive flesh and he yelped at the unexpected shock of pain.

She had MacKenzie to thank for that particular move.

Still putting pressure on the guard's wrist, Anna reached out to grasp the door handle and tugged it open before racing inside.

CHAPTER 29

Ryan staggered to his feet, aware of a rushing sound as the blood recirculated around his head and he almost fell again as the pressure rose too quickly. Clutching one hand to his head, he drew painful gasps of air into his starving lungs and watched as the figure moved towards him once again, warier the second time around now that the element of surprise had been lost.

Ryan opened his mouth to speak, to try to convince them to stop, but no sound came out except a rasp which degenerated into a wheezing fit.

He held a hand out, as if to stop the shadow from coming any closer and—just for a second—it seemed to work. The figure paused, as if unsure.

Then lunged forward again.

A pair of strong hands went for Ryan's throat and he batted them away repeatedly, swinging out in the darkness to try to land a blow on their face or head, but still too weak to connect.

"*Stop*," he managed, though the sound was barely audible.

Suddenly, strong hands were around Ryan's throat, the fingers wrapping tightly around the cords of muscle and artery in his neck to finish the job.

***

"Ryan!"

Anna called out to her husband even as she heard thundering footsteps behind her, but didn't stop to turn around, instead kicking off her heels and lifting the long skirt of her dress to run faster down the darkened corridor. Her foot collided with something heavy and she almost fell as it clattered against the wall, but she recovered quickly and pushed herself onward.

"*Signora!*"

Voices rang out from the shadows but still she kept going, sprinting full pelt into the unknown until she reached the point where the corridor turned left to head south over the river. Panting a little, she scanned the wall for signs of an entrance and leapt forward when she spotted it, still half-open as Ryan had left it a few short minutes before.

She had hardly stepped inside the hollowed-out cavity when she heard the muffled sounds of a tussle from within.

***

Ryan had almost passed out, his lungs completely deprived of oxygen and, he was later to learn, if Anna had come even thirty seconds later he would have lost the fight.

But as soon as she ran into the sitting room, the pressure on his throat stopped completely as the strong hands snapped away and the figure stood up, moving quickly into position behind the bedroom door. Ryan watched as if in a dream, unable to think coherently, his brain having been deprived of oxygen, too.

The world was a haze of light and dark, of moving shadows and tears which fell like rain against his face. He smelled his wife's scent, the unmistakable aroma of Anna as she bent down beside him, ready to administer CPR. Through hooded eyes, Ryan watched the shadow slip away again, as if it had never been there at all, and his finger raised to warn her.

"There! Look! Turn around!" he wanted to say.

But no sound emerged from his mouth and his chest heaved as he fought to regain consciousness.

Her lips on his, breathing life back into his body.

Her gentle hands, running over his face, checking his airways.

Suddenly, there were more voices in the room, more light as the overhead chandelier was turned on. The sudden glare blinded him, and Ryan closed his eyes against the force of it, willing himself to recover, for his muddled brain to react.

"Ryan?"

Anna's voice crept inside his mind, urging him to float back to the surface.

"Ryan, please. Please, God…stay with me…"

Somebody tugged her away from him and Ryan's head jerked in reaction, seeking her out even as his body wanted to collapse again.

More voices, now. More people dressed in uniform, then a plastic mask around his face, pumping air back into his body.

Predictably, Ryan refused a stretcher.

It had taken ten minutes to bring him back to full consciousness, back from what he knew to have been the very brink of death. His throat burned with the effort of breathing, let alone talking, but he could still be understood by the sheer force of his steely-eyed glare.

Sergeant Banotti had been true to her word, arriving at the scene only moments behind Anna.

"You need to go to the hospital for a check-up," she told him, and Anna happened to agree. "Rest assured, we will find whoever did this to you."

"Know…did this…" Ryan managed.

Banotti strained to hear him, subconsciously raising a hand to her own neck as she caught sight of the angry red line against his throat and the deep finger marks that were already blooming into vivid bruises.

"I've got officers combing the building," she said. "We'll take a full statement from you, when you're ready."

"Arrest…him," Ryan tried again, unable to understand why Banotti hadn't already slapped Armstrong in handcuffs.

For their part, Anna and Sergeant Banotti knew it could not have been him, so failed to understand the urgency.

"Let's go to the hospital," Anna tried again to persuade him.

Ryan looked between the pair of them and shook his head, standing up suddenly to make for the door leading back into the corridor. A couple of police officers looked across in surprise and moved to stop him.

"Ryan, it's not a good idea for you to return there," Banotti told him. "There has been enough drama for one evening."

"Have you...checked?" he looked between them in frustration, wanting to know if they'd checked amongst the guests for any sign of Nathan Armstrong. Surely, somebody would have noticed his absence?

"Checked for what? The assailant? Yes, Inspector Ricci is on his way to the main entrance now, he will conduct discreet enquiries—"

Discreet? Ryan thought, incredulously. After what he'd just been through, he wanted Armstrong's head served up on a platter.

Anna watched him with worried eyes, noting the way Ryan gripped the edge of the door for support, his other hand rubbing the back of his neck to ease the pain that was growing more intense with every passing minute.

She turned to Banotti.

"We'll go home," she said, quietly. "I'll get a doctor to come out and check him over."

Banotti nodded.

"We'll keep looking and come by in the morning."

Physically and emotionally exhausted herself, Anna walked across the room and simply took Ryan's hand in hers.

"I nearly lost you, this evening," she said. "I won't lose you again."

Ryan needed no further bidding. Everything inside him screamed for vengeance, to find the man who had almost robbed him of life, but Anna was right. He was physically exhausted, his body still racked by shock and he could already feel the effects of the strong anti-inflammatory drugs on his addled mind.

Tomorrow was a new day and, besides, Armstrong would be ruined, after this.

Slowly, clutching his head, Ryan turned towards the front door of the apartment and saw a figure standing in the doorway.

Armstrong.

He had removed his mask and the gaudy gold and silver party piece dangled from his finger as he struck an affronted pose.

"How dare you?" he demanded, of the room at large. "The police require a warrant before entering a person's private residence!"

Ryan could hardly believe his ears.

Less than twenty minutes earlier, the man had almost killed him, almost choked the life out of him, and he had the audacity to return to the scene to front it out?

He saw red.

Illness and trauma pushed angrily aside, Ryan broke free of Anna's hand and crossed the room in seconds, hauling Armstrong up onto his tiptoes and slamming him against the nearest wall.

"You're…finished," he choked out, before two of Banotti's men pulled him away.

"I couldn't make that out," Armstrong said, tugging his tuxedo jacket back into place. "Got a frog in your throat, Ryan?"

Ryan bared his teeth, surging forward as if to go at him again.

"Well, sergeant, I think I will press charges, this time," Armstrong turned casually to address Banotti, who stood nearby. "I assume one of these officers can take down my statement and will bear witness to what just happened. As an innocent, law-abiding citizen, the last thing I expect when I return home is to be attacked by the very people one expects to *protect*."

Banotti opened her mouth to say something but Anna was quicker.

"On that topic, I wonder if one of your officers might be able to take down *my* statement," she said, very calmly. "As you can see from the bruising on my wrist, I was assaulted earlier this evening by Mr Armstrong and would like to press charges against him."

The look that passed over Armstrong's face was unpleasant.

"That's nothing more than a desperate, ridiculous lie," he shot back. "Nobody will believe it."

"Where did the alleged incident occur, Mrs Ryan?"

"In the Niobe Room of the Uffizi Gallery. I happened to notice at least one CCTV camera nearby, so I would be surprised if it didn't capture the incident in its entirety. It will be embarrassing for me, when the story is reported, but at least I'm just a humble university lecturer. It would be much worse if I were, let's say, a *minor* celebrity..."

Banotti turned back to Armstrong and stuck her tongue in her cheek.

"And, ah, you also wish to make a statement, Mr Armstrong?"

His eyes swept over Anna and she felt a jolt of fear that was purely primal, a recognition that there may be repercussions for the challenge she had just laid down.

"No," he drawled, at length. "I suppose we can put it down to a misunderstanding on both sides."

Anna gave Sergeant Banotti a short nod to indicate the matter was closed.

Ryan was released, and he walked across the room, past Armstrong, past his wife and the police, to stand beside the bed. At his feet, the end of a length of kettle cord was just visible.

"Bag this," he said, and, sweeping his gaze around the room, turned to look directly at Armstrong. "Swab everything."

With that, he reached for Anna's hand again.

CHAPTER 30

"I could get used to this."

Phillips was just polishing off his fifth *cannoli* of the evening as they sat around the marble breakfast bar in what was, to all intents and purposes, Magda's kitchen at the Villa Lucia.

"Don't get too comfortable," MacKenzie warned him. "The closest thing you'll be getting to homemade pastries is a multi-pack of rice cakes, from now on."

Phillips licked the sugar off his thumb.

"Wouldn't mind a dip in that pool tomorrow," he said, spinning around on the bar stool like a kid on the night before Christmas. "D' you think it's heated?"

"It doesn't matter, since we're not here to splash about sunbathing. I thought you said you hated sunshine holidays, anyway?"

MacKenzie gave him a searching look and Phillips cleared his throat.

"Aye, well, I do. But, since we're here, y' nah, we might as well make the best of it."

She glanced around the opulent kitchen.

"Right enough, Frank. Since we're in this *hell hole*, better make the best of a bad lot, eh?"

"Make do and mend," he agreed, massaging the back of his hand as she slapped it away from the platter of *cannoli*.

Just then, they heard a car pulling into the driveway outside and, a moment later, the sound of muted voices and footsteps in the hallway.

"*Magda?*"

"In the kitchen!" she called out, with a wink for Phillips and MacKenzie, who prepared to surprise their friend.

But their smiles fell into lines of shock and dismay when Ryan stepped into the kitchen, his skin almost the same shade as the marble floor against the black suit he still wore, and his neck battered and torn.

For his part, he took one look at the tableau and broke into a lopsided grin.

"Might have known you'd be enjoying yourselves, while I'm being strangled half to death," he wheezed.

Phillips was the first to recover.

"Aye, and I might have known you'd be getting yourself into scrapes without me here to keep you on the straight and narrow."

He slipped off his stool and walked over to greet his friend, pausing awkwardly for a second before pulling the younger man into his bear-like embrace.

"Com' 'ere, y' daft bugger," he muttered, blinking away sudden, unexpected tears before anybody should see them. "Looks like we landed in the nick of time."

It was almost midnight by the time they settled in the drawing room, where Phillips built a fire. The heatwave that had swept through most of mainland Europe had finally retreated, making way for more usual wintry Mediterranean temperatures.

"Looks like we brought the weather with us," he joked.

"It's still warmer than Northumberland," MacKenzie said, wriggling her toes in the hope of a foot rub. "But we didn't come to talk about the weather. We came to see how you're getting on."

Ryan sank onto the sofa opposite, having changed into a high-necked sweater to hide the worst of the damage, including the brace the doctor had insisted he wear.

"You mean, Morrison sent you?"

"She sent in the cavalry to help, that's all," Phillips wanted that to be clear from the start. "Seems some bigwig in the Rome office got in touch with her and started making noises about reining you in."

"Oh?" Ryan was amused by the thought. "I must be making them nervous. I wonder why."

"Could be something to do with the fact you barged into Armstrong's place without a warrant and started making noises about him being a deranged killer," Phillips said, scratching the side of his nose. "Just because it happens to be true, doesn't mean everybody's convinced. The bloke's a bloody celebrity and he's using it."

"The fact is, there's no way that the person who tried to strangle you in Armstrong's apartment could actually have been Armstrong," Anna said, tucking her legs up onto the sofa as she settled beside Ryan. "The timings are all wrong."

He watched the flames flickering in the grate and then nodded his agreement.

"Whoever it was had a similar build, wore a black tuxedo—although, so did every man in the room—and wore the same ridiculous mask."

"Are you sure?" MacKenzie had to ask.

"We both saw him—or her—slip inside the corridor through the Uffizi doorway," Anna said. "I saw the mask, too."

"If the person inside Armstrong's apartment was somebody else, it changes everything," Ryan said, reaching for the cup of soothing honeyed tea Magda had left for him, to ease his throat.

He took a long sip, then chose his words with care.

"To gain access to the apartment, they'd have to know there was a link to the Vasari Corridor, and that Armstrong was using it."

"Armstrong knew it was in use," Anna agreed. "He almost said as much, when he cornered me in the gallery."

"So, this second person needed to know that Armstrong was using it," Ryan said. "They also needed to know the mask Armstrong planned to wear tonight, either to buy a second one or have it copied, to look like him. All of this suggests long-term planning, well ahead of the party. This isn't a last-minute, opportunistic grab."

"But, if that's the case, how could they have known you would follow them down the corridor?" Phillips asked.

Ryan's lips twisted.

"They knew I would follow Armstrong and that we would make the link with the Vasari Corridor. That leads me onto another important point: the postcards. What if—just *if*—Armstrong didn't send them after all? What if somebody else did? The fact Armstrong was arrested months ago was reported in the national press, although his lawyer managed to get a gagging order pretty quickly. Still, word travels. What if this second person found out about Armstrong and the fact he hadn't been charged? Easy enough to find out the name of the investigating team, or to find out that I hadn't let the matter drop, if you talk to the right people."

Ryan looked amongst their faces, swallowing the pain in his throat.

"Sending me those postcards was a taunting gesture, one I mistook as coming from Armstrong, but they might have come from somebody who wanted me to follow the trail of breadcrumbs. They wanted me here, on this day, in this city."

"What about the DNA on the postcards?" MacKenzie said. "How would they manage it?"

"Just because Armstrong is a killer, doesn't mean *he* killed *those* people," Anna murmured, taking the words out of

Ryan's mouth. "It could be that somebody else is responsible for Luc Bernard and Riccardo Spatuzzi going missing."

"It never really struck me as Armstrong's style," Phillips admitted. "Y' know, sending postcards. Oh, I know he sent that one to Duncan Gray's mother, but that was years ago, to cover his tracks. It isn't like him to send postcards to the man he knows wants his arse in jail. If anything, he'd want to protect himself and put distance between you. He cares about his reputation."

"Nothing is more important to him," Ryan agreed. "So, somebody else brought me in. The question is, *why*?"

"Why try to kill you in Armstrong's apartment?" MacKenzie said. "Why set it up so that it looks like Armstrong's responsible?"

"To frame him," Anna said, and the other woman nodded.

"It's the second time," Phillips said. "The first time with that Italian lass—"

"Martina," Ryan murmured.

"Aye, Martina. What if that was done for the same reason—to set Armstrong up?"

"If our theory is right, then it goes back further than that," Ryan said. "Luc, Riccardo and whoever else we haven't found yet, all of them might have been attempts to stage a murder implicating Armstrong."

"Why wouldn't he report it?" Anna asked. "Why wouldn't he call the police and report a body found in his place? Why would he hide it and pretend to know nothing about it?"

Firelight danced in Ryan's eyes as he looked around the room at the small collection of people he could trust.

"He didn't report it because he has something to hide, something that implicates him. We already know what he's capable of," Ryan said. "What if this other person knows it, too, and wants to unmask him? It's much easier to plant a body than to wait around trying to catch Armstrong in the act. They wouldn't have any idea when he might strike next, and he's careful—unlike them," he tagged on.

"It's the same MO," Phillips said, suddenly.

"What's that?"

"They used a kettle cord to try to strangle you this evening and you told us Martina Calari was strangled in a similar way. That seems quite a specific choice," he said. "There are plenty of easier ways to do somebody in."

"You're right," MacKenzie said. "The murders up at Kielder were committed in a variety of ways, by reference to what Armstrong had at hand, whereas that's two for two. I wonder why they like a kettle cord, so much?"

"Who knows what drives these fruitcakes," Phillips said, with his usual sage wisdom. "Probably has a grudge against kettles, as well as people."

That gave them a much-needed laugh.

"What we really need to know is, why do they hate Armstrong so much?" Anna said, after a pause. "What's driving them to do all of this? It doesn't seem as simple as showing him to be a killer because if they have any dirt on him, they could just come to the police, again.

This seems like something more deep-rooted, like a vendetta."

"Why else choose the twentieth anniversary of his most famous work, unless the object is to cause maximum damage to Armstrong's reputation?" Ryan said. "It must be personal."

"It's a killer hunting a killer," Phillips said, casting concerned eyes over his friend. "And you're caught up in it all."

"Better me than another young mother," Ryan said softly, thinking of the baby girl who would now grow up without one of her parents.

There was another long pause while the four people in the room watched the orange flames licking at the logs on the fire, considering what might drive a man to murder and how to catch him when he did.

"The biggest task now is finding out who this unknown person is," Ryan said, breaking the silence. "Armstrong will never tell us, even presuming he knows himself."

"Must have been a right pain in the backside for him, coming home to find bodies lying around," Phillips remarked, in a flash of dark humour. "Must have really put his nose out of joint."

Ryan didn't answer directly.

"I wonder if he's running scared, or whether it's just one more person to find and put down?" he said. "Nathan Armstrong doesn't feel emotions the same way we do; he doesn't experience fear like we do, or feel scared of what the consequences might be if he's discovered. He only cares about his persona, the careful ideal he's woven for the past forty-odd years."

"I think the only person who understood Armstrong's motivations before us, was the person who's trying to ruin him," MacKenzie put in. "They understood, long before we did, that the best way to bring him down was to attack the only thing he cares about, which is himself."

There were nods around the room.

"But who is Kaiser Sose?" Phillips said, earning himself an eye-roll from his future wife. "What?" he shrugged. "It's from that movie, *The Usual Suspects*. I've waited years for the opportunity to say that during an investigation."

"What's next on the list?" Ryan asked.

"*I'm going to make him an offer he can't refuse.*"

Ryan slapped a palm against his own face.

"For God's sake, I didn't mean, 'what's the next movie line', Frank. I meant, what's next on our list of things to do?"

Phillips glanced covertly at their smiling faces and was glad his ploy had worked.

"Oh, aye. Well, I think it's bedtime, for starters. Been a long day and it'll be another long one tomorrow, if I'm any judge."

After the fire was guarded and their cups returned to the kitchen, Ryan put a hand on his friend's shoulder.

"Thanks, Frank. To both of you."

"Don't mention it, son. What else is family for?"

As Phillips climbed into a bed not much smaller than the square footage of his entire house back home, another man stared at the television screen in his apartment. The room was in darkness, otherwise, with only the glare from the screen bouncing off Armstrong's unmoving figure seated directly in front of it. His eyes bored into the face of an Italian newsreader, who was delivering a report that was, by now, a few hours old.

It had been recorded outside the Uffizi Gallery as the party guests had departed the building just after midnight, the local *Who's Who* of Florence pausing to wave to the cameras. He was amongst them and had given an interview, hitting just the right note somewhere between modesty and affability. But the interview had been superseded, cut short since the story of Ryan's attack had reached the news desk. Images of Ryan taken from old press reels portrayed him as the handsome hero; the detective with an unrivalled reputation for getting his man and championing the victims of crime.

"*Almost killed at the Palazzo Russo,*" they said.

"*The same address as Nathan Armstrong,*" they said.

And the public were left to draw any inference they liked from that.

Unable to stand any more, he turned the television off but remained seated in the darkness for a while afterwards. It gave him no trouble to sleep on the same bed where he'd found Martina Calari—the sheets had been changed, after all—but he was too immobilised by rage to think of sleep.

How *dare* they come here, to the apartment he owned, and invade his domain? How dare they threaten all that was his, by rights?

He knew who it was—of course he did.

It had taken a little while to understand, but after the first three bodies turned up—each of them with an electrical cord wrapped around their neck—it hadn't taken too much of a leap to figure out who was stalking him across Europe. He had a name, a name Armstrong barely recognised and hadn't heard in many years, but he was undoubtedly using an alias now and would likely have changed his appearance.

If the situation were reversed, he would have done the same thing, himself.

But the situation could not be allowed to continue, especially now that Ryan was in Florence. The forensic team had been inside his apartment for hours, swabbing everything. Ryan's attack had afforded them the perfect excuse to gather samples from his home, samples they could now compare with Martina Calari's DNA to form a link.

Of course, he'd simply say this unknown assailant must have been using his apartment for his own reprehensible ends, but there was only so many times a person could deny their involvement without some of the dirt beginning to stick.

He had Ryan to thank for that. If the man had only let things lie, if he hadn't kept digging, always *digging,* then things might have continued happily for the rest of his days and nobody would be any the wiser.

What did it matter, anyway?

What difference would Duncan Gray have made to the world? Why did Ryan care? He was just nobody. Nothing.

And everybody had loved him, the voice inside his head whispered. *Everybody liked Duncan.*

Not you.

Never you.

Armstrong stood up to pace around in the darkness, remembering his childhood holidays at Kielder in Northumberland, thinking of all the times he'd wanted to be accepted, to be part of the gang. They'd let him in, of course, especially since his family had money enough to buy cans of lager and as many packets of crisps as their greedy little hands could hold.

He'd been one of them, but only just.

After Duncan…it was like he'd been reborn. The world seemed insignificant, somehow, and everybody in it just pawns to play with. He couldn't even remember who the next had been, or where, only that they'd served a purpose at the time. Perhaps they'd insulted him or taken something that should have been his. It hardly mattered now.

But he remembered one person in graphic detail.

He would never forget that one.

CHAPTER 31

Sunday, 25th February

Divide and conquer was the order of the following day.

Ryan had awoken to blistering pain around his throat but, thankfully, none of the tell-tale signs that his cervical spine had been damaged during his assault the previous evening. He hadn't held out much hope of sleep but, in the end, he fell into an exhausted slumber with his arm curled protectively around his wife. Anna had moved at some point during the night, restlessly shifting this way and that until, unable to chase away the nightmares, she'd risen at first light to swim a quick thirty lengths in the pool outside.

He watched her completing the final laps from the terrace, admiring the way she cut through the water, back and forth until she had exhausted her body and emptied her mind. It was early yet, and the morning fog that had rolled in from the surrounding hillsides overnight lingered, bringing with it a cold wind which swept over the high cypress trees lining the garden's perimeter.

"Water's chilly, today," Anna said, bundling herself into the towelling robe he'd laid out for her. "Feels good to get the blood flowing, though."

Ryan smiled, knowing that she was used to swimming in far colder waters than the heated outdoor pool could boast.

"Rather you than me," he said, although he might have liked to swim a few lengths, if his neck would have allowed it. "Coffee?"

He poured a cup for her and she sat down beside him on the terrace, content to sit in silence as they looked out across the city vista stretching far below.

"I thought I'd take Phillips down to the *Commissariato San Giovanni*," Ryan said. "Banotti told me they'd made appointments with various people who attended the party last night so that, rather than disturbing the event, they could come down to the station today and give a statement. I have to know who it was. Somebody must have looked out of place, somebody mustn't have been on the guest list," he muttered.

"I can show MacKenzie around," Anna offered. "Take her around the main points of interest, so she can understand the route of the Vasari Corridor."

Ryan nodded.

"Stay together," was all he said.

Anna stretched her hand across the table to squeeze his, very briefly.

"It's me who should be warning *you* not to venture out alone," she said, in mild reproof. "I can't stand another scare like last night, Ryan."

He tried to laugh, but the sound came out as a cough.

"Trust me, I can't either."

Anna grew serious.

"If…whoever this person is, wants to damage Armstrong, they singled you out as the conduit. Just because you survived the first attempt doesn't mean they won't try again. Be careful."

Ryan was serious too.

"I was careful last night, that's the damning thing about it. I didn't forget my training, I entered with caution and was still surprised. That takes a certain amount of cunning, or skill."

"You think they're military trained?" she asked.

"Or police," he muttered, and his thoughts strayed to Ricci, who had been notably absent the evening before.

"Are you sure it was a man?"

"I thought so, yes. But, the more I think about it, the more uncertain I am. Physical strength is a factor in face-to-face combat, where things like height and muscle mass can make a real difference. But once you have a noose around somebody's throat, it doesn't take too much strength to hold on for as long as possible. It just takes sheer, bloody willpower."

"So you're saying they might have been female, after all?"

"At a push, yes. The main determinant would be height and breadth to appear similar to Armstrong. He's a man of around six feet and he's trim, around average size—but toned, as you might expect of a raging narcissist," he said, pausing to take another sip of coffee. "The marks on my neck show the angle of the noose was low, suggesting the assailant was shorter than me. That doesn't necessarily tell us much, since I'm a couple of inches over six feet in my socks."

Anna thought of the marks on his neck and something must have shown on her face, because he tugged the top of his jumper up, to hide it again.

"The marks will fade," he said, gently.

She merely shook her head, battling sudden tears.

"I thought—I thought you were gone," she said, huskily. "I found you there on the floor and, even in the darkness, you were so pale. You weren't moving, and I couldn't hear you breathing. I've never been so terrified."

Ryan listened, his chest tightening with emotion.

"I thought I'd failed us," he confessed. "I'd been careless with my own life, enough to deprive us of a future. I could feel myself fading and I remember thinking of you, of *us*, and it was the only thing that kept me alive. I'm certain of it."

Without a word, she stood up and walked across to him, sliding onto his lap. His arms held her tightly to him and she let all the stress and worry pour out as they clung together.

"I'm sorry," he said quietly.

"For what?" she asked, with a sniff. "Being who you were born to be? I fell in love with you because you're a fighter and because you go the extra mile, when others would abandon their ideals. I could never ask you to change, to become less than you are."

Ryan closed his eyes, rubbing his cheek against her wet hair.

"You'd have a quieter life," he said.

"Who needs quiet?" she argued. "I'll have enough quiet when I'm dead."

"I love you."

"Same goes, Chief Inspector."

Meanwhile, Phillips found himself in the throes of ecstasy.

"That was incredible," he said. "The best I've ever had."

"I'm so glad you think so," Magda replied. "I've never had any complaints."

"You'll get none from me, pet."

MacKenzie walked into the kitchen and took one look at Phillips' guilty face.

"I swear, I didn't mean to," he told her.

Her eyes strayed to the crumbs on his plate, then across to the housekeeper, who gave the motion that her lips were sealed.

"Was that…a stottie cake?"

"Aye," Phillips said, with a daft grin. "And it was delicious. I've half a mind to ask Magda to come and do the catering for the wedding."

"Frank, there are no words," MacKenzie said, and found herself laughing. Where in the world had she found this charming, funny man with his silly sense of humour that could melt even the hardest of hearts?

"Breakfast is the most important meal of the day," he declared. "Got to keep my strength up."

"I'll bear it in mind," she muttered. "I think Ryan's looking for you. I've just had a message from Melanie Yates, back in the office, about the Warkworth case. I'll stay behind and deal with that, then take a look around the city with Anna while you're with Ryan."

"Be interesting to see how they do things, over here," he said.

"Catching criminals is a fine art," MacKenzie replied. "Given their pedigree in that department, I'd say they probably turn their hand to criminal detection with the same eye for detail."

"Aye, well, I was never much of an artist at school, but I can spot a duffer at fifty paces."

"They'll write books about you, in years to come."

"They'd better," he sniffed.

CHAPTER 32

Inspector Ricci and Sergeant Banotti were already sipping strong coffee in Ricci's office at the *Gruppo* when Ryan tapped on the door, just after eight-thirty. Their eyes skimmed past him and widened at the sight of a new arrival; specifically, at his choice of apparel. It was true that the Italians were known for a superior sense of fashion but, all the same, it took a lot to elicit the kind of surprise they exhibited upon seeing what DS Phillips liked to call his 'Holiday Civvies'. They consisted of a pair of linen trousers he'd bought in the early-nineties and which had, he was convinced, been shrunk sometime during the intervening years. He'd paired them with one of several multi-coloured shirts he'd acquired over the years, this one with a fetching print of miniature palm trees and pink flamingos which glowed in the dark. His thinning hair was protected from the sun by an oversized Panama hat and the pièce de résistance was a pair of leather, open-toed sandals he had picked up from a bazaar.

"Bon-jorno!" he said.

When their faces remained blank, Ryan stepped in.

"Ricci, Banotti, this is my sergeant and good friend from Northumbria CID, Detective Sergeant Frank Phillips."

They mumbled greetings and indicated he should pull up a chair beside them.

"Thank you for joining us, sergeant. I'm afraid we had no warning of your arrival," Ricci said, with a hint of irritation.

"Aye, well, you know us Brits love a bit of foreign travel," Phillips said. "I think our Chief Constable had a word with your Director General."

"I see. And, at the risk of sounding unwelcoming, are we to expect any more of your team?"

This last question was directed towards Ryan, who gave him a blithe smile.

"We missed you last night, Ricci."

The inspector's eyes frittered away.

"It seems I missed all the action," Ricci agreed. "I was needed elsewhere, I regret to say. A personal matter."

Ryan gave him a level look.

"I'm sorry to hear that," he said. "Hopefully, the matter has resolved itself now."

Ricci fiddled with the pen he held in his hand.

"I—yes, yes. But, on to more important concerns—I was shocked to hear what happened to you, my friend. How are you feeling, now?"

The truth was, Ryan was feeling dreadful, but he wasn't about to divulge that.

"Better than I was," he said, because at least that much was true. "It'll take more than that to kill me off," he added.

Ricci raised his eyebrow at the tone, but said nothing.

"We went over Armstrong's apartment at the *Palazzo Russo*," Banotti said. "We bagged up the cord that was used and will test it for fingerprints and so forth. We will do all we can to find whoever did this to you, you may rely upon that. We may be from different countries, but we are on the same team," she said.

Phillips smiled his approval.

"That's the ticket. Now, what about getting our hands on a bit of CCTV?"

"Already done," Ricci was pleased to say. "The cameras are top of the range at the Palazzo and their security team was very helpful. I've had a couple of my officers going over the footage this morning and it seems as though our culprit walked out of the Palazzo with his mask back on, posing as Armstrong, once again. The concierge even said 'good evening' to him as he left, but was surprised since he couldn't remember Mr Armstrong having passed through the foyer on his way in."

"I bet he was," Ryan murmured. "He'd have been even more surprised to see the man—the real Armstrong, that is—coming back inside the Palazzo twenty minutes later."

"Indeed," Ricci said. "It seems our imposter left the Palazzo and returned to the party, dressed as Armstrong. The footage from the CCTV cameras on the street and at the Uffizi confirm it."

"He's a cool one," Phillips remarked. "Having just fled the scene of an attempted murder, he kept a steady pair of hands, didn't he?"

"He's fortunate he didn't pass the 'real' Armstrong, on the way," Ryan said. "That might have made for an interesting exchange."

"Hard to say who'd come out of it on top," Phillips mumbled.

"Chiara and I were discussing theories," Ricci said. "We are struggling to understand why anybody would wish to pose as Armstrong, or to attack you. It makes no sense."

"It makes perfect sense," Ryan confounded them by saying. "As long as you begin to understand that Armstrong is not the man you think he is. The whole time I've been here in Italy, I've sensed your reluctance to accept what I've been telling you—what anybody in Northumbria CID will tell you—which is that Nathan Armstrong *is the killer who got away*. When you start believing that, it's much less difficult to imagine why somebody would want to frame him for murder and see him put behind bars, where he belongs."

Ricci and Banotti exchanged a glance.

"If we accept what you say, if we set aside what the world knows about Armstrong, you're asking us to believe that somebody has been planning a campaign against him for months...possibly, years. For what? Vengeance?"

"Got it in one, son," Phillips said, cheerfully.

Ricci's lips twitched.

"But, who? Who could hate him so much?"

"That's where you come in," Ryan said, enigmatically. "Logic tells us this person knew something of Armstrong's plans, about his address on every calling point of his book tour, and even about the details of the mask he planned to wear last night. It must be somebody with access to that kind of information, added to which, they're technologically savvy. We know that already from their tampering with the CCTV at the Uffizi."

"They have to be somebody unthreatening, too," Phillips put in. "Recognisable, or at least known to Martina Calari, otherwise she'd never have let down her guard."

"On that point, we heard back from the pathologist," Banotti said. "They ran tests on her blood and hair and found no trace of drugs in her system or, at least, none that showed up."

"Okay, assuming they didn't need to drug her, it stands to reason that this person lured Martina away from the events space at the Uffizi and into the Vasari Corridor on strength of character alone."

"What about the workmen, wouldn't they have seen her?" Phillips asked. "I thought there were renovations going on?"

"Not on a Friday afternoon," Ricci said. "Our master craftsmen like their early finishes at the end of the week as much as yours, my friend."

Phillips nodded. Who didn't like a pint down at their local after work on a Friday? It was the only civilised way to live.

"Maybe they told her they'd found a new entrance, or maybe they wanted to show her their concerns about security access for the party?" Ryan thought aloud. "If they already had Martina's trust, they could have told her any number of lies to get her away from the communal areas."

"Poor lass," Phillips said, gruffly.

"I agree that it must have been somebody who was already a guest at the party, or who managed to gain entry," Ricci said, steering them back towards the facts. "Anybody who was registered to attend could reasonably have discussed security arrangements to find out how things run at the gallery. As for Armstrong himself, his public engagements are listed on his website—"

"Does he have an assistant?" Phillips asked. "Somebody to arrange things for him? He looks the type."

"He certainly looks the type," Banotti agreed, with a grin. "But no, he prefers to manage his own affairs."

Never a truer word spoken, Ryan thought. Men like Armstrong wouldn't like third parties looking too closely into their lives.

"How about his publisher?" he said. "I met somebody by the name of Gabriele last night who appeared to know Armstrong well."

And they were of the same height and build, he added to himself.

"Gabriele Marchesa," Ricci confirmed. "He is the Chief Executive of *Elato,* Armstrong's Italian publisher and a patron of the arts in Florence. Publishing has been in his family for generations, although he only recently took up the position after his brother passed away, last year. We have an appointment to speak to him, first, at nine o'clock."

Four pairs of eyes swung up to check the clock on the wall, which read five to the hour.

"Any minute now," Ryan murmured.

CHAPTER 33

A bracing wind circled the Florentine valley, humming through the tall trees and sweeping around the elegant old villa. MacKenzie was seated at the desk in the study with her laptop open, scrolling through a mind-boggling list of cases the late Edward Clarkson had prosecuted during his active years as a barrister, sent through by trainee DC Melanie Yates. She narrowed her eyes as she studied the list, recognising several cases she'd worked on over the years, tutting now and then as she thought of the memorable ones.

You could never win them all, but it was remarkable how many Clarkson *had* won during his time with the Crown Prosecution Service.

Perhaps too remarkable.

The law was there to provide checks and balances and, despite all she saw during her day job, she was firmly of the opinion that a person was innocent until proven guilty. She was not of the Old Guard, who sometimes believed that a conviction should be obtained at all costs, even if it meant bending the law. She believed in the process, which relied on them providing enough evidence to remove all reasonable doubt in the minds of a jury. If their case fell short…well, that was where the Defence came in.

There must be a balance on both sides, or justice meant nothing.

Unfortunately, that meant there were times when guilty ones walked free. But, from what she could see of Clarkson's work record, he had been a man who liked to win. That kind of ambition was a double-edged sword, she'd always found, for where did it end? There was always the next conquest to strive for, the next notch on his legal belt.

Helpfully, Yates had taken the trouble to cross-check all the cases Clarkson had prosecuted against a list of prisoners who had recently been released, over an eighteen-month period. She'd highlighted those rows and, when MacKenzie clicked on their names, a separate summary note popped up giving pertinent details of each. A quick scroll down the spreadsheet threw up around a hundred different names.

"Okay," MacKenzie said, clicking on the first highlighted name. "Here goes."

An hour passed quickly and MacKenzie hardly looked up when Anna stuck her head around the door.

"Mac?"

"Mm hmm?"

"Brought you a cuppa," her friend said, setting a cup and saucer down beside her. "How's it going?"

"Slowly," MacKenzie replied, rolling her shoulders to ease the tension. "When I look at these case summaries, there's nothing obvious that jumps out at me. Yes, all these people had reason to dislike Edward Clarkson since he contributed to their guilty verdict. But, on the other hand, he was just a cog in the wheel, part of a wider system of justice. Although it's a bit of a stereotype about ex-cons chasing down the people who put them away, it hardly ever happens in real life."

Anna decided not to mention an obvious recent exception to that; it had only been a year since MacKenzie's own ordeal with the Hacker, after he'd broken free from prison. It did no good to rake up the past, especially such painful memories.

"What kind of people are they? The ones who got out recently, I mean."

MacKenzie decided they were too far gone to worry about breaching confidentiality; sometimes, it was a case of picking your battles.

"I've already discarded the ones who served a minor jail term," she said, turning the laptop screen around so Anna could see the magnitude of her task. "It's not outside the realms of possibility that somebody who was handed a two-year jail term held a grudge, but it's much more likely that somebody who was put away for a good chunk of time would have hated Clarkson enough to kill him."

Anna made a murmuring sound of agreement as her eye scanned the names.

"It's more interesting that this guy—Clarkson, I mean—was the one to run away. He must have known somebody dangerous was about to be released and made preparations to sell up and change his name and address. He needed advance warning, to give himself time to do all that."

MacKenzie smiled, thinking that her friend had a knack for detection.

"Yes, that's what I thought, too. So, I'm prioritising serious cases where the prisoner completed their sentence up to six months before Edward Clarkson moved into Warkworth, last March. That takes us back to September 2016, potentially, but if nothing turns up I can always go further back in the records."

"Narrowing down the timescale and looking at the nature of their crimes is good, but can't you just find the leak?"

MacKenzie gave her a quizzical look and Anna shrugged.

"You know, his contact. The person who must have told Edward Clarkson when this dangerous person was due to get out?"

"If only," MacKenzie sighed. "That sort of information could be found quite easily, through the proper channels, especially since Clarkson worked in the same sort of field. He probably knew loads of people who could have kept him up to date on this person's movements."

Anna pulled a face.

"Back to the spreadsheet it is, then," she said.

"I'm afraid so," MacKenzie said, and took a grateful sip of tea. "What about you? Ryan tells me you put together the Murder Board."

She nodded towards the study wall, now heaving with information.

"I guess I've seen him do it so many times, at home, it seemed like the thing to do," Anna said, a bit embarrassed. "I wonder how the interviews are coming along. Unless there's some kind of breakthrough, I don't know how they're going to crack this one."

MacKenzie toasted her teacup.

"If there's a Ryan, there's a way," she said.

CHAPTER 34

"I can't understand a bloody thing they're saying."

Phillips made his pronouncement from the observation area overlooking one of the interview rooms at the *Gruppo,* where he and Ryan had been permitted to stay and watch. Unfortunately, his Italian phrasebook just wasn't cutting the mustard.

Not so for Ryan, who found himself stepping into the shoes of a translator for the duration.

"Ricci is asking a few warm-up questions of Gabriele Marchesa," he said, his eyes never moving from the glass. "He's saying that somebody with malicious intent is trying to damage Armstrong's reputation—*ha ha*—and he's wondering if Marchesa can help them to understand why. He's asking how he first met Armstrong."

Phillips turned to watch a smart, slightly red-faced man in his fifties gesticulate with his left hand, which sported a gold pinkie ring.

"He replied that he only met Armstrong about a year ago, at a dinner in London with Armstrong's UK publishing house…" Ryan murmured. "He's rambling on about the meal they had…Ricci is asking if that meeting coincided with him taking over the family business and Marchesa agrees. He's saying his brother managed Elato Publishing for the past thirty years. He doesn't go into the details, but says he returned from living abroad when his brother died, and the business had an uncertain future. He didn't want to see it go under."

"Wonder what he was doing with himself before," Phillips thought aloud, mirroring the question Ricci had just asked in rapid Italian.

"He says he was a man of leisure, having inherited a trust from his maternal grandmother. He was also bought out of the publishing house when he was a younger man, allowing him to live freely. He only manages operations now, he doesn't own any significant shares."

"We already know Spatuzzi's hoovered up most of those," Phillips put in.

Ryan nodded.

"Ricci's asking him whether he saw anyone resembling Armstrong, or wearing the same mask, during the party," he continued. "Marchesa says he didn't, he was with Armstrong for most of the first half of the evening, introducing him to all the guests, then he gave a speech at around eight o'clock and Armstrong was standing near the front of the crowd. He came onto the podium and gave an impromptu speech and it was not an imposter. He says that, in the second half of the evening, people just mingled."

"Bet that speech was scintillating," Phillips said, with a chuckle.

"It was interminable," Ryan muttered. He and Anna had found themselves near the front of the crowd, too, and had therefore been unable to beat a hasty retreat. "Banotti is asking him whether he left the Uffizi at any time during the night and Marchesa says he didn't leave the room other than to use the facilities. Most people left at around midnight and he was among the last of them."

They fell silent for a moment while those in the interview room paused to take a collective sip of water or coffee, before resuming their conversation.

"Ricci wants to know who liaised with the events planner at the Uffizi," Ryan said, with approval. "Marchesa says he liaised with her himself, alongside one of their publishing assistants—a woman called Sienna—as well as several other parties who were contributing to the event, including private security teams and Nico Bellucci, a local art dealer who was also providing a bespoke ice sculpture."

"Ice sculpture?" Phillips queried.

"That's what the man said," Ryan grinned, then rubbed absently at his throat. He'd taken the executive decision, against doctor's orders, to remove his neck brace; primarily because it irritated him but also because there had been no adverse effects on his back or spine, at least none that weren't to be expected.

Phillips reached for the warm camomile tea that was cooling on the table behind him and pressed it into his friend's hand.

"Thanks," Ryan murmured, taking a long slug of the soothing liquid before turning back to the interview that was playing out in front of them. "He looks relaxed, doesn't he?"

"Doesn't seem worried," Phillips agreed. "Either he's got nothing to hide, he knows nothing, or he's used to being inside a police station."

"Maybe all of the above," Ryan murmured.

"It's called prosecutorial bias."

By lunchtime, Anna and MacKenzie had relocated to the more salubrious surroundings of the terrace and were nibbling the fresh pasta that Magda had placed before them.

"God, this is delicious," Anna said, and scooped up another forkful. "What were you saying about bias?"

"Prosecutorial bias," MacKenzie said again. "It refers to when members of the prosecuting team, including the barrister for the CPS, withhold evidence or act without the appropriate level of integrity just to get a conviction. It's caused some massive scandals in the past, because so many cases were found to have been worthy of retrial or dismissed altogether on appeal thanks to their actions. It doesn't help anybody, in the long-run, and undermines public confidence in the system."

"You're thinking Edward Clarkson might have dabbled a bit?"

MacKenzie chewed thoughtfully, then nodded.

"It's certainly a possibility. The cases we've identified so far all concern convictions from the late nineties or early noughties, which was Clarkson's heyday. We're still dealing with the fall-out of numerous appeals from that period."

"So your theory is that somebody was sent down for the wrong reasons? Maybe they were innocent altogether?" Anna said.

"It would certainly fit the bill but…" She paused, shaking her head. "An innocent man doesn't get out and commit murder. That would make him guilty, after all."

It was a moral minefield.

"If this person, whoever they are, has been in prison for twenty-odd years they might have changed," Anna pointed out. "They wouldn't be the same person as before."

MacKenzie looked across the table at her friend and nodded.

"You're right," she said. "This wouldn't be an innocent person, any more. It could be a broken, damaged human being who had lost all faith in the society that had thrown him behind bars. And it's people like that who tend to commit the most dangerous acts because they think, 'I've been in prison before and I've already served a long sentence—I'm not afraid to do it again'."

They fell silent for a moment, the food forgotten as their appetite vanished.

"Let's look at that list again," MacKenzie said. "We have no forensic leads, no recent assaults, no history of threats being made or large payments to any one individual. It has to be somebody on that list, or we've nowhere else to turn."

CHAPTER 35

The interview suite at the *Gruppo's* headquarters had been a revolving door of Uffizi staff and guests, each suffering from varying degrees of hangover but none quite so much as Nico Bellucci. Through the glass partition, Ryan watched as the man wove into the room, clearly still inebriated from the night before, and plonked down heavily on one of the chairs.

"Looks like somebody enjoyed himself, at least," Phillips laughed.

"I think he's got a reputation for it," Ryan said. "He was pretty far gone when Anna and I saw him last night."

"Got to know your own limits," Phillips said, sadly.

His own father had been a functioning alcoholic and it had caused them years of worry and heartbreak, before he'd passed away prematurely at the age of fifty-nine. Only a few years older than Frank was now, or than the man sitting in the room beyond.

He watched Bellucci clutch his hands together to stop them trembling and sighed, thinking that it was just another tell-tale sign.

"It'll be a miracle if he remembers much," Ryan said, without any unkindness. There were many kinds of people in the world, but he could safely say that none of them was infallible, least of all himself. "Ricci's asking him how he came to know Armstrong. He says he only met him for the first time at the party last night. He knew of him but had never met him before then."

Phillips scrubbed a hand over his face and yawned.

"What's he saying now?"

"Banotti's asking who hired him to procure the ice sculpture…he says he was contacted by the events planner, Martina Calari. He's saying how sorry he was to hear about what happened to her, she seemed like a nice girl…" Ryan trailed off, deeming the remainder more of the same. "He says he met with her twice. The first time was two months ago, to discuss the plans for the design, and the second time was on the day she went missing. He met her with Gabriele Marchesa, another publishing assistant whose name he can't remember, and the Head of Security for the Uffizi. Matteo something or other."

"At least he corroborates what Gabriele Marchesa said earlier," Phillips said.

Ryan held up a hand so he could hear the next part, frowning as he focused on the discussion before relaxing again.

"Banotti asked whether he could remember who was the last to leave the meeting with Martina," he said. "Nico says he can't remember for certain, but it might have been Matteo because he left around the same time as the publishers."

There was a short pause, then Phillips said what they were both thinking.

"When's Matteo due to come in?"

Ryan smiled in the semi-darkness of the observation room.

"This afternoon," he replied. "Apparently, he's procuring the rest of the footage from last night, so we can track the movements of Armstrong's imposter."

"Let's hope nothing gets corrupted, this time, eh?"

"You took the words right out of my mouth, Frank."

"Look at this," MacKenzie called out.

Anna moved across to the desk where Denise was hunched over her computer, the same position she'd occupied for the past forty minutes.

"What've you found?"

"This guy, Antonio "Tony" Manetti—"

"Italian?" Anna said, in surprise.

"He was convicted in 1999 of killing his boyfriend, Andrew Wharton, in late 1998. Manetti was a local journalist working for *The Enquirer* and Wharton worked as a shop assistant. Wharton was found dead in the flat they shared—Manetti was the one to call it in but always maintained his innocence. He claims there was a witness who would have confirmed his alibi, but it was never disclosed by the prosecution. He was released after numerous failed appeals in October 2016; that's shortly after Edward Clarkson set up his new life in Warkworth."

"How much notice do you think he would have had that Manetti was planning to appeal again? Surely if he'd appealed before, and been unsuccessful, Clarkson would've had nothing to worry about."

"Manetti wasn't released on appeal," MacKenzie told her. "He'd served almost twenty years and was deemed to be no danger to society."

"They might have been wrong," Anna muttered.

"I'll ask Yates to send through the complete file and to request his prison records," MacKenzie said, shifting excitedly. "I get a funny feeling about this one."

Matteo Alfonsi arrived precisely on time for his interview with the *Gruppo,* clutching a flash drive in his hand which contained the footage of the party. Ryan had heard something before about Greeks bearing gifts but was prepared to keep an open mind, especially since they hadn't been able to ascertain how the cameras had been temporarily compromised.

"*Grazie mille*, Signor Alfonsi…"

Inspector Ricci began with his usual patter, asking a series of starter questions to put the interviewee at their ease.

"Now, this one looks nervous," Phillips said, and popped an olive into his mouth.

Ryan was about to agree with him, then did a double-take.

"Where in hell did they come from?" he asked, pointing at the small jar of black olives.

"The supermarket, o' course," came the easy reply. "Want one?"

Ryan popped an olive into his mouth and then refocused his attention on the interview. Phillips was right about one thing: the Head of Security looked nervous. Sweat was beading on his forehead and running in shiny rivulets down his rounded face.

"He must be used to talking to the police," Phillips went on. "Must chat to them all the time. Can't be first-time nerves, can it?"

Ryan gave a slight shake of his head.

"I want to see his bank accounts," he said, quietly. "He's a strong bribery risk and I want to see whether he, or his wife, have made any large deposits in the last three months."

"Aye, seems sensible," Phillips said. He could always spot the ones on the take. "Could be somebody slipped him some pocket money in exchange for him wiping the footage for an hour or two. Must have been a fair wad of cash, to tempt him."

"We don't know that's what happened, yet, but it would explain a lot."

"Ricci will get to the bottom of that. Seems a decent bloke."

"He's a stranger," Ryan said. *And therefore could not be trusted*, he added silently.

"What's he asking now?"

"He wants to know whether anybody asked to see the security room, anybody out of the ordinary. Matteo says everybody wanted to see their operations; representatives of the Spatuzzi family, the head of the publishing house and several private security staff belonging to local television celebrities."

"*Real Housewives of Florence*? Is that the kind of thing?"

"Pretty much," Ryan agreed, reaching out for another olive. "Can't say I keep up with it as much as you."

"Hey, man. Nowt wrong with a bit of mindless telly, to wind down at the end of the day."

"A book is better," Ryan argued. "Hang on a sec."

He paused chewing as he watched Banotti reach for a file of papers.

"She's asking him about a complaint made about him almost a year ago, by Martina Calari. She accused him of sexual harassment and her fiancé got into a fight with him about it. He says she made it up."

Ryan listened for a few minutes, then turned to his sergeant.

"When I spoke to him yesterday morning, Matteo Alfonsi waxed lyrical about the lovely young woman who reminded him of his daughter. Never once did he mention the real relationship they must have had."

Phillips did a funny little jig and rubbed his hands together.

"Ooh, the skeletons are all flying out of the closet now."

CHAPTER 36

While they waited for Yates to send through the remaining files on Tony Manetti, MacKenzie and Anna decided to take a walk into the centre of town. If not exactly happy about it, Magda was appeased when she learned they would be travelling together, and there were still a couple of hours of daylight left. Indeed, it was the most pleasant hour of the day, the wind having died down to a light breeze that whipped the crusted leaves from the ground and sent them dancing on the air.

"It's lovely here," MacKenzie said. "I wonder why Ryan never mentioned it before?"

"He's embarrassed, I think. He never really felt part of the world he was born into and finds it unequal, when compared with the kind of poverty he sometimes comes across."

MacKenzie thought of her own tough upbringing. There had been few pennies to rub together back at the tiny cottage where she'd grown up, one of seven children. Looking back now, she could admire the landscape of her homeland but regretted that there had been no work for a young woman who…well, who'd needed to get away.

It reminded her of the wedding, which was becoming a bigger headache than she'd ever anticipated.

"Frank's doing his best to arrange the perfect wedding," she said, pleased to talk about something other than murder. "But we're being thwarted at every turn. I keep telling him, I don't need a big wedding, but it isn't just that. My family are being so difficult, it doesn't matter how many guests we have."

"I'm sorry to hear that," Anna said. "Is there anything I can do?"

"Not really, it's just the way they are. If I say we're having fish, they want meat. If I say we're having a civil service, they want traditional Catholic. Then, there's the predictable complaints about the age gap between Frank and me—"

"I never notice it," Anna said, and made her friend smile.

"Neither do I," MacKenzie replied. "That's what love does to a person. He could be James Dean or Quasimodo, and I wouldn't notice the difference."

She paused.

"Well, I might notice if he was Paul Newman."

Anna laughed.

"Anyway, the band cancelled last-minute, the caterers are useless, and we're trying to arrange a wedding in Ireland from our base in Newcastle. I'm almost tempted to elope!"

Anna merely smiled.

"And if you could elope, where would you go?"

MacKenzie scuffed her toes through the leaves as they followed the pathway down Viale Machiavelli and allowed herself to imagine the perfect setting.

"I think, after all the hassle, I'd just have our closest friends," she said. "You and Ryan, obviously. Melanie and, of course, Jack Lowerson. I hope he's feeling a bit better," she added.

"He'll come through it," Anna said, thinking of their friend who had lost so much, lately.

"I'd like somewhere small and picturesque," MacKenzie said. "Somewhere I'll remember for the rest of my life."

"You've got your dress already," Anna said.

"The dressmaker ruined it," MacKenzie replied, glumly. "That's another thing for me to sort out, when I get home."

"Should be easy enough to find a similar style," Anna said, half to herself.

MacKenzie let out a shuddering sigh.

"Anyway, listen to me, ranting on about a wedding while there's a job to be done. C'mon," she said, quickening her pace. "Show me where everything is."

Anna matched her pace as they headed into the centre, two attractive women with a purpose.

"What's our first calling point?" MacKenzie asked.

"First stop, gelato," Anna said. "It's been at least ten minutes since we last ate."

"I'm surprised I haven't passed out, by now."

"In that case, better get a double scoop."

The last interviewee of the day was the journalist, Andrea Conti. He was a self-assured man, well respected around Florence, and he wore his reputation with a certain flair.

"Bit of a Flash Harry, this one," Phillips decided. "Is this the guy Anna spoke to?"

Ryan nodded.

"He has a reputation for knowing all about the underbelly of the city," Ryan said. "He worked out that I was over here investigating Armstrong in connection with Riccardo Spatuzzi's disappearance and warned us about the Spatuzzi family, in general."

"He's one of the good guys, then?"

"I wouldn't go that far," Ryan said. "He wants his pound of flesh—in exchange for not reporting everything he knows, he gets first scoop, when this is all over."

"Aye, some things are the same all around the world," Phillips declared.

"Ricci wants to know when he first met Armstrong," Ryan said, then took a step closer to the glass to listen more closely.

Phillips looked between his friend and the interview room in confusion.

"What?"

"Conti says he first met Armstrong about fifteen years ago. Apparently, Armstrong was researching some extra details around the real *Il Mostro*. He says it was a surprise, considering he hadn't been in touch during his research for the original story. Conti assumed he was writing a follow-up."

"Would have thought Conti was too young to have been around for *Il Mostro*," Phillips said. "Those murders happened way back in the sixties and seventies, didn't they?"

"Yes, but he's a bit of an expert on the subject," Ryan said. "Conti learned his trade from the guy who worked the crime beat back when it all happened, so he's pretty close to it all."

"In that case, I agree, it's a bit odd that Armstrong didn't look him up when he was researching his book," Phillips said, using the brim of his Panama hat to fan his face. They'd been inside the observation room for hours with only a short break to snaffle a sandwich, and things were heating up.

"Maybe," Ryan said. "He might have relied on other people to do that for him."

There was a short pause while they watched the people seated around a table in the next room, like characters in a film.

"Keeps coming back to that book, doesn't it?" Phillips said, suddenly. "The reason Armstrong is here, the reason for the party, it's all because of that book."

His words chimed like the bells of the Duomo.

"You're right, Frank. I think the book is the key to all of this. I only wish I knew *why*, or how."

CHAPTER 37

Late in the afternoon, the foursome met at a small café overlooking the Arno where, Ricci had told them, you could find the finest *osso bucco* in all of Florence. The atmosphere was convivial, and nobody paid any attention to the four visitors who settled themselves in a quiet corner of the restaurant, far away from prying ears.

"We're following a lead on the Warkworth case," MacKenzie said, smiling at the waiter who brought them a carafe of Tuscan wine.

"Oh, aye?" Phillips was intrigued. "That wasn't looking too promising, when we left."

"Yates sent through a list of people who were released from prison around the time Edward Clarkson changed his name and moved away. I've asked for the full files on one in particular—a man called Tony Manetti."

Ryan looked up at that.

"Italian? Quite a coincidence."

"You always say there's no such thing," Anna murmured.

"So I do," he smiled. "Tell us more about this Mr Manetti. Why did he stand out?"

"Well, he was the only one on the list who served an almost full life sentence. I don't know very much except that he was convicted of the murder of his boyfriend in '98—"

"1998?" Ryan interrupted her.

"Yeah, why?"

"Same year *Il Mostro* was published," he muttered. "Phillips and I were only just saying that, in one way or another, everything seems to lead back to that book."

"I can't see how the murder of a barrister-turned-ferryman could possibly relate to what's happening here," MacKenzie said. "They're two different worlds."

Ryan said nothing.

"There's something else we haven't really thought of," Phillips said. "We already know that Gregson was active around the time Eddie Clarkson was practising and that he probably bribed Gregson to get out of fines and things like that. Stands to reason, if Clarkson wasn't above bribery in general, he might have got himself embroiled in some of the heavier stuff. Maybe he was part of the Circle," he suggested, referring to the corrupt and murderous cult Gregson had been a part of throughout his time as a senior police officer.

"It would explain why Clarkson had such an extreme reaction," MacKenzie agreed. "The Circle was punishing anyone who renounced them during that time, so it would have been a real concern if he thought Gregson was sending someone after him."

Ryan nodded, but his mind circled back to Manetti.

"We could speak to Gregson, but he was no help to us the last time we tried. The man has very little remorse for what he did, so I don't think he'd feel any special inclination to be helpful now."

The others nodded their agreement.

"It still leaves us with Tony Manetti or, if not him, whoever was responsible for putting the fear of God into Edward Clarkson. What else do you know about Manetti?" he asked.

"Only that he was working as a journalist for *The Enquirer,* at the time he was arrested," MacKenzie said.

"Might be worth giving the paper a call," he suggested. "They may keep employment records, or there may be people still working there who remember what he was like. Did you find anything reported online about the murder?"

They paused while their food was delivered, then resumed after the first couple of bites.

"Back in the late nineties, some of the smaller regional news outlets were still figuring out the digital side of news reporting and they haven't uploaded their archived pieces, but I found something from a couple of the broadsheets," she said. "The story goes that Tony Manetti was an Italian national living in Newcastle on a work visa. He was living with a man called Andrew Wharton, who was from the area and worked as a shop assistant. In the early hours of an autumn morning, the police were called out to the flat they shared in Fenham and found Manetti clutching

Wharton's body. Apparently, it looked like they'd had a violent row which culminated in Manetti strangling Wharton."

Ryan looked up again, very slowly.

"Wharton was strangled?" he said. "With what?"

MacKenzie shook her head.

"The news reports didn't say, but I'll find out when the case files come through from Yates. Why does it matter?"

"It's just another coincidence," Ryan said. "How old would Manetti be now?"

"Somewhere in his late forties or early fifties, from what I can gather."

"Just like Armstrong," Phillips said.

"Yeah, just like Armstrong," Ryan muttered.

CHAPTER 38

With no further information available on Tony Manetti, the talk turned to the men and women who had been interviewed by the *Gruppo* throughout the day.

"Of the people we saw, there are only four who could possibly tick all the boxes," Ryan was saying. "If we're looking for someone who could pass for Nathan Armstrong in general build and height, that number reduces to three."

"Alright, lay it out for us," Anna said, as their plates were cleared.

"First, we have Gabriele Marchesa. He's the CEO of Elato Publishing which is financed, for the most part, by Monica Spatuzzi."

"I'm sure she's just a great reader," MacKenzie rolled her eyes.

"As it happens, she has an enormous library...but that's another story. The financial health of that publishing house will be a matter for the Italian CONSOB—"

"The what-ty?" Phillips asked.

"That's the *Commissione Nazionale per le Societa e la Borsa*," Ryan explained. "They regulate financial activities in Italy, other than insurance. If Spatuzzi is laundering money through the publishing house, that'll be a matter for them. As far as we're concerned, I want to know if its CEO is all he's cracked up to be."

"Did he give you reason to suspect otherwise?" Anna asked, curiously. "He seemed happy enough, when he was showing Armstrong around the party last night."

"People can be wonderful actors," Ryan said. "In terms of hard facts, we know this: he's the right age, height and build to impersonate Armstrong. He had full access to the Uffizi and to Martina Calari, before she died. He knows the city and its corridors and passageways. He only recently returned from abroad, where he was living the life of Riley, by all accounts, but we need to investigate his movements further. He was estranged from his family until his brother's death, which is very convenient—if he happened to have been in prison rather than on a luxury yacht, somewhere."

"It still doesn't tell us why he would want to ruin Armstrong."

"We don't know the answer to that, yet," Ryan agreed.

"Okay, who's the second on your list?"

"A man called Nico Bellucci," Ryan said. "He's an art dealer who was involved in planning the party and he supplied that hideous ice sculpture. He's about the same height and build as Armstrong, perhaps a little shorter. He knows everyone who matters, and yet, he's new on the social scene in Florence and he was vague about where he was before."

"He doesn't strike me as the type," Anna was bound to say. "For one thing, I'm not sure he would have had the capacity to overpower you, given the state he was in last night."

"That's true," Ryan admitted. "And I don't remember smelling alcohol during the struggle, although I was hardly making notes at the time."

"Do any of them feel like the right one?" Phillips interjected.

Ryan shrugged, wishing he knew the answer to that himself.

"I wish I knew," he replied. "I was watching them in that interview, trying to pick out mannerisms, trying to see their hands and gauge their size."

Ryan laughed at himself.

"It was a useful lesson today," he said. "I know from reading all the textbooks that victims of serious crime tend to overstate their aggressor's size, imagining them to be monsters rather than ordinary, average people like you and me. Somehow, I thought having that knowledge would make me immune; that I'd be able to give a full, detailed account."

He took a sip of water to ease his dry throat, before continuing.

"But I realised, I'm no different. When I close my eyes, I think of a shadow, a superhuman force I couldn't overcome. But in the end, it was just a man—though I can't say for certain which one. I might have shaken his hand and never known it was the same hand that had been around my throat."

Phillips clapped a manly hand around Ryan's shoulder.

"Don't beat yourself up, lad. None of us would have been able to give chapter and verse on somebody they hardly saw, let alone in the dark with a bloody cord strangling the life out of us."

"Who was the third option?" MacKenzie asked.

"That would be the journalist, Andrea Conti. He looks the part and knows everyone in Florence, and likely everything going on in the city. He didn't seem overly enamoured by Armstrong, given the direction of his questions last night but, on the other hand, it's his job to weed out answers to hard questions."

"It couldn't really be him, could it? Conti's based permanently in Florence, so he couldn't have really followed Armstrong around Europe, assuming that's what's been happening," Anna pointed out.

"I wondered about that, but he travels around Italy a lot and works freelance, these days, mostly from home. It'd be different if he was clocking into the offices of the *Florence Daily News* from nine till five each day, needing to account for his whereabouts. To be on the safe side, I've asked Ricci to check the movements of all of these people but that'll take time waiting for the Italian passport service to come back with the data."

"Okay, so who's the fourth reserve?" MacKenzie asked.

"The Head of Security at the Uffizi Gallery, a chap called Matteo Alfonsi. He's ex-Carabinieri, so he knows how to look after himself and he knows how the police system works. He had full access to the camera and security systems at the Uffizi and could have found out how to access Armstrong's apartment from the Vasari Corridor whenever he liked. Added to all that, he was pulled up on sexual harassment charges raised by Martina Calari before she died."

"On paper, he looks the most likely, but I sense a 'but' coming," MacKenzie said, and Ryan nodded.

"He's the least likely in terms of physical type and he was a bundle of nerves in the interview room. I'd peg him for taking a backhander to wipe the cameras, but he doesn't have the steady hands it took to kill Martina Calari or to attack me."

"Ricci's going to look into the financials," Phillips told them. "And he says he'll bring Alfonsi back in to sweat him a bit more tomorrow. Man after my own heart."

"While all this is going on, what's Armstrong doing with himself? Aside from managing to paint himself as the victim," Anna said.

"That's the worry," Ryan muttered. "The minute you take your eye off a cobra, it'll strike. Let's not forget the real reason I came here, in the first place. Just because Armstrong didn't kill those people, doesn't mean he hasn't killed others."

CHAPTER 39

Ryan had been right in his observation about snakes.

While the police teams tried desperately to join the dots, Nathan Armstrong took matters into his own hands and went about the business of removing the man who had been a scourge on his life for months, maybe even years. If he had been some unknown, a vagrant in the street, Armstrong would have had no qualms about seeing to it himself.

It wouldn't be the first time.

However, the man was wily. Armstrong would allow him that much, and it was probably the closest he would ever come to paying a compliment to another living soul. The man had created a new persona for himself, one that came with a certain protective armour which made it difficult for Armstrong to penetrate without being discovered. Until the heat died down and the press stopped reporting the drama, he could feel Ryan's eyes boring into the back of his head, watching and waiting for him to slip up.

There was no denying it had been a restless few months, a time of upheaval and uncertainty when he'd almost been afraid to open the door in case he found a new deposit in his home or hotel, awaiting disposal. The man had been voracious, like a cat who went out hunting at night and brought home the kill for its master.

His Master. Yes, he liked the sound of that.

Yet, even the best pets sometimes needed to be put down. The novelty value of the campaign against him had long since worn off and Armstrong had absolutely no intention of ending his days in a cell. But it was becoming harder and harder to get rid of the bodies at short notice and he was not a magician, after all. The inconvenience alone was enough to send him into a rage and it was imperative he stayed in complete control, at least until Ryan moved on and the eye of the law turned elsewhere.

And so, he'd come to the most logical place.

It had taken some smooth talking to get past the gates of the Spatuzzi villa and, needless to say, he was unaccustomed to the kind of rough welcome he'd received from the guards—two rifles aimed at his head.

Luckily, Armstrong was not a man who was easily put off and, considering the sensitive information he held in his possession, it was in the interests of all concerned that those rifles were lowered, and he was admitted to meet with the woman whose son was now buried in a landfill site on the edge of Vienna.

Not that he had any intention of telling her *that*.

He admired the *objets d'art* as he moved through the hallway and paused to look at a painting, until one of the guards muttered something rude and shoved him towards one of the doorways.

"*Ecco il bastardo*," they said, announcing his arrival to the mistress of the house, whom he'd met briefly the evening before.

"*Restare*," she murmured, and the two guards remained standing just inside the doorway to an enormous living space.

"Beautiful room," he said, oozing the kind of charm that usually softened up old ladies. "Your taste is faultless, *signora*."

She lit a slim cigarette and took a drag, dark eyes fixed on his face as she blew out a long tendril of smoke.

"This is the second time in a week that I've received an unexpected gentleman caller," she said, in the quiet tone she was known for. "I am surprised you found the courage to knock on my door, *signore*. I can only assume you have come to confess your sins to the mother whose son you have taken."

The words were clipped and cold; so cold that Armstrong could almost feel the temperature dropping inside the room.

"I fear you're mistaken on that score," he said, conversationally.

"*Non giocare con me*," she snarled. "Do not play with me. There will be only one winner, here."

"I wouldn't dream of it," he said, spreading his hands in an open gesture. "I understand you're labouring under the misapprehension that I have killed your son, Riccardo—an idea that was probably planted by that idiot, Ryan."

She said nothing, but continued to smoke rhythmically.

"The man is a fanatic," he said, with a trace of pity. "He's got the idea into his head that I'm all kinds of evil genius but, I ask you, would a killer come and speak to the mother of one of his victims? Especially when that mother is somebody of your…calibre, *signora*."

She stubbed out the cigarette in a nearby ashtray.

"These sound like the ramblings of a desperate man."

"On the contrary, I'm here because I want to help you find the *right* man. Neither of us is, let's say, whiter than white." His voice grew dark. "But in this instance, I was not involved in the disappearance of your son. There is a man with a grudge against me, something from years ago, and he hoped to implicate me in a series of murders."

"That you committed."

"No—that I knew nothing about! These people were chosen at random and killed to vilify me and draw the attention of the police. But it was not I who was responsible."

"More lies," she spat. "More arrogant lies, concocted by a man who knows the net is closing around him."

"There is no net." He shrugged. "I've gone from being a suspect to being a victim, thanks to this poor, insane fool. The police are searching for him right now."

Spatuzzi walked across the plush carpet and sank into one of the leather sofas. Armstrong was about to do the same but one icy look from her stopped him.

He had not been invited to sit.

"If you are lying to me now, *cafone,* it will be the last words you speak."

Armstrong was almost turned on. There was plenty of life in the old girl yet.

"His name," she breathed.

Armstrong gave the man's name—at least, the one he was using at the moment—and she surprised him by laughing.

"Impossible," she scoffed.

"Improbable," he corrected her. "But true, nonetheless. May I sit?"

She made no objection, this time, so he helped himself to a chair and settled down to relay a curated version of the facts. Spatuzzi remained silent throughout, looking at him with dark, unblinking eyes filled with hate.

In the end, she asked him one question.

"Where is my son?"

He held a hand to his heart.

"I wish I knew. Truly, signora."

She looked away, into the embers of the fire.

"Get out," she said, so softly he strained to hear.

Armstrong had no wish to outstay his welcome, so he rose quickly and gave a small, unnecessary bow before he turned to saunter out.

But the doors were barred.

"Signora—"

She murmured an instruction to her guards and they unslung their rifles, propping them against the door before removing their jackets.

"I thought you would be grateful," Armstrong cried.

"For what, *stronzo*? That you were not the one to end my son's life?" She rose suddenly, teeth bared. "It is still because of *you*, because of your past mistakes, that my son was killed."

Her eyes flicked past him to the guards and then she returned to her seat to enjoy the show.

Much later, Armstrong found himself outside the front gates of the Spatuzzi villa. Everything hurt, especially his ribs and torso but, blessedly, they'd avoided his face. He supposed that was a professional courtesy, of sorts.

He stumbled back to his rental car, grunting with the effort, and didn't relax until he'd collapsed inside the driver's seat with the doors locked. He checked his face in the rear-view mirror and was relieved to find he'd been right on that score.

Hardly a scratch.

The same could not be said for the rest of him, but he was sure he could find some discreet back-street doctor who would be willing to check over the damage for the right price. All in all, he considered it another job well done.

Whistling, he started up the engine and drove slowly back to Florence.

CHAPTER 40

Darkness cloaked the Villa Lucia, cocooning those who gathered inside in its velvety fold to hunt a killer. There was a stillness to the air; a calm before the storm which had been gathering all day and still permeated the night air so that it swirled heavily through the old rooms.

"It's so humid, it feels like an old-fashioned pea-souper," Phillips said, peering out into the cloudy night where the blurry lights of Florence were only just visible.

"It'll pass by morning," Ryan said, stepping into the drawing room. "Anna's having a shower and MacKenzie's just had a message come through from Yates. She's hoping it's the files."

"That'd be good." Phillips turned away from the window to study his friend's face, where the signs of strain were visible to anybody who looked closely. "How's your neck feeling?"

It was on the tip of Ryan's tongue to downplay the pain, to give some trite, superficial answer, but Phillips would not accept anything less than the truth.

"Hurts like hell," he replied. "I've taken as much ibuprofen as I dare."

"You should have it checked over again," Phillips said.

"I will, just as soon as this is over," Ryan said, and his friend sighed. "Don't worry about me, Frank. It hurts where the bastard had his hands around my neck, that's all—no permanent damage."

"You know best," Phillips said, in a fatherly tone.

Ryan walked over to join him at the window, keeping a weather eye on the doorway.

"Ah, since I've got you alone for a minute, there's something I wanted to chat to you about."

"Oh aye? Nothing serious, is it?"

"No, nothing like that. In fact, it's entirely positive."

Phillips' eyebrows raised as he listened to Ryan's suggestion, then deepened to a frown, finally settling on an expression somewhere between excitement and trepidation.

"You think she'll go for it?" he worried.

"Go for what?" MacKenzie asked, interrupting their *tête-à-tête*.

From the guilty looks on their faces, she assumed they'd been discussing the details of Phillips' stag do and pursed her lips.

"Well, *whatever it was*, can just wait. Mel's sent the files through on Tony Manetti. I used the printer in the study, so we don't have to huddle around a computer. I know it's old-fashioned, but—"

"It gets the job done," Ryan said. "What have we got?"

MacKenzie handed him the prison records and divided the remaining case and court files between herself and Phillips.

"Let's dive in and find out."

Anna joined them a short while later and then beat a silent retreat, understanding that there were some areas of their business that she was not privy to, nor would she want to be. It was true that she dabbled in research and her expertise had been useful to Ryan's team from time to time over the years. But the truth was, she had no desire to read over the gory details of human destruction, even if the rules allowed it. Mapping the Vasari Corridor was one thing but spending her days uncovering the darkest side of human nature was quite another.

Instead, she settled down to read the thriller of the moment, *Il Mostro*. They said that an author left shadows of themselves on the pages of the books they wrote, so she accepted a cup of Magda's excellent tea and prepared to see what Nathan Armstrong had chosen to reveal on the pages of his magnum opus.

Next door, all was quiet save for the occasional rustling of a page, or the crackle of a log in the fireplace.

"He looks so ordinary," Phillips said, as he studied the most recent picture taken of Tony Manetti. "Aged forty-nine, brown eyes, greying hair, average build. We might have passed him twenty times on the street and never known it."

Ryan was studying Manetti's picture, too, assessing the shape of the face and the line of the jaw. But he knew it was in the eyes that he'd recognise the man; people could buy coloured contact lenses and change their appearance with prosthetics or make-up but there was a certain individuality to a person's eyes that seldom changed.

And there was something in Manetti's eyes that he recognised as being a gateway to the man's soul.

"Here's the original statement Tony Manetti gave to the police on Friday, September 25th, 1998," MacKenzie said, skim-reading its contents. "He says he and his long-term boyfriend, Andrew Wharton, had a disagreement which caused him to leave the house and spend most of the evening away from home. He states he was at a gay bar in Newcastle until just after midnight, after which he decided to return home and resolve things with Andrew."

"Things escalated further?" Phillips asked, but MacKenzie shook her head.

"Not according to Manetti. He says he let himself back into the flat at roughly 12:45 on the morning of Friday 25th and found the place in disarray. Lamps were broken in the hallway and a mirror was cracked. He was immediately concerned that his boyfriend had been hurt and searched the house. He says he found Andrew in the kitchen, clearly having been strangled."

Ryan's eyes narrowed, and he propped his head on his hand, spearing his fingers into his hair as he considered the implications of that minor detail.

"The kitchen? What was the murder weapon—or was it manual strangulation?"

"He says there was an electrical cord lying on the floor," MacKenzie said, flicking the page with the edge of her finger. "Just like the cord that was used on you, last night."

Bingo, Ryan thought.

"Go on," he said.

"Manetti says he ran over to remove the cord from around Andrew's neck and to check whether he was still breathing, but he was obviously dead and seemed cold to the touch. He called the ambulance service and requested the police, too, reporting that a murder had been committed."

"I've got a police note here which says they found a suitcase half-filled with Andrew's clothing and the rest strewn on the floor, giving the strong impression Andrew had been on the verge of leaving Manetti. They theorised that was what caused Manetti to fly into a rage and, ultimately, to murder him."

"What about forensic evidence?" Ryan asked. "A recording of his 999 call?"

MacKenzie looked at the scanty paperwork and shook her head.

"No transcript of his call or reference to a recording," she said. "As for forensics, I've got a two-page report which states that Manetti's prints and DNA were found all over the flat."

"Of course they were, he lived there," Ryan said.

"What about the cord?" Phillips asked. "Surely that's the most telling bit of evidence."

"The report says they found Manetti's fingerprints on that, too."

"Which they would do, since he removed it from Andrew's neck," Ryan said, softly. "Did they confiscate his clothing and test that? It sounds a bit thin on the ground."

"There's no record of his clothing having been tested," MacKenzie said, double checking the paperwork.

"That was one of the grounds Manetti used to seek leave to appeal, ten days after he was convicted in early 1999," Phillips chimed in, thumbing through his own stack of documents. "Leave to appeal was denied, taking into account the Prosecutor's Response to the application, which was drafted by...well, look-ee here. Our very own Edward Clarkson, Esq."

"He was there at every turn," MacKenzie murmured.

"There's another application for leave to appeal on the grounds that the prosecution failed to disclose a witness statement obtained during the course of their investigation from a bartender at the gay bar," Phillips said. "It alleges homophobic bias in the handling of the case."

Ryan kneaded the tension working its way up the back of his neck.

"None of us in this room are under any illusions that there was widespread, systemic bias in police services throughout the nineties—and, if some recent cases are anything to go by, it can still happen with bad management. It only takes a couple of bad apples to rot the whole barrel."

"Couldn't have put it better myself," Phillips said. "Back when I started out, there were one or two who were known for being racist or homophobic, and yet they were never pulled up and they're probably still drawing down their pensions now."

"The question is, was Manetti right? Were the police biased in their handling of his case?" Ryan asked them. "If the answer is 'yes', then there's a very real possibility that Manetti was an innocent man who ended up serving nearly twenty years of his life behind bars."

He paused to flip open the file on his lap.

"Manetti's prison records are a mixed bag. In the early years, he kept to himself then, presumably after the appeal applications were dismissed, he tried to socialise for a while but ended up getting into fights. During the last seven or eight years, he kept to himself and completed numerous courses, including a PhD in Italian Literature."

"He was a journalist by profession," MacKenzie reminded them. "He probably already had a degree. Does it say anything else of interest? Any connections with Gregson, or any further dealings with Edward Clarkson?"

"None that I can see," Ryan replied. "Manetti was a quiet, intelligent man who helped to run the prison library service. He was released on 31st October 2016 on compassionate grounds."

"Not what I was expecting," MacKenzie remarked, with a frown. "Does it give details?"

"It does better than that," Ryan said. "There's a full medical report included with the record of the final decision. He was suffering from Parkinson's disease that had entered an advanced stage. The report is dated 1st September 2016 and predicts that Manetti will have succumbed to dementia within a twelve to eighteen-month period."

"Compassionate grounds, my arse," Phillips muttered. "They didn't want to pay for the nursing care, so they kicked him out into the wide world again."

"Well, it looks like Tony Manetti had other plans than finding himself a suitable nursing home," Ryan said, setting the file on the coffee table. "This is all useful information, but it brings us no closer to finding out who Tony Manetti is *now*, especially since there's nobody resident in Florence going by that name, according to the online records Yates has been able to access."

"It'd take weeks to go through every Antonio Manetti across the whole of Italy, if he's even based over here," Phillips said.

"Well, Yates came back with some data from the Italian passport authority that might help," MacKenzie said. "We know that Tony Manetti left the UK on the same day he was released, back in October 2016. There's a record of him landing at the airport in Rome but, after then, it's just sporadic travel across Europe and to the UK."

"Didn't hang around, did he?" Phillips said.

"The most telling thing is when I cross reference the dates of his travel with the dates of Edward Charon's murder in Warkworth," MacKenzie said. "He flew into Edinburgh

Airport from Frankfurt the day before Clarkson was killed and flew out again the day after."

"Where'd he go?"

"Three guesses," MacKenzie said, with a small smile.

"Rome or Florence?" Phillips tried, but MacKenzie shook her head.

"Pisa?" Ryan suggested. "It's a forty-minute drive from here and the security is less stringent than at Florence Airport."

"You get the prize," she said. "He flew into Pisa."

"Where was he when Luc Bernard went missing, or when Riccardo Spatuzzi disappeared?" Ryan asked.

"The dates roughly match," MacKenzie said. "Same pattern as before. He flies in a couple of days before he plans to strike, then flies out again almost immediately afterwards."

She looked up from the spreadsheet.

"It looks like we found our man," she said.

"He's still missing." Ryan was serious. "We still don't know who Manetti is, what alias he's using, and it would take weeks to check with pharmacies for records of Parkinson's prescriptions being ordered; it's a common illness, unfortunately."

"There's one thing we do know," Phillips said, with a valiant attempt at levity. "When in doubt, look to home. The Warkworth case was the key to finding the missing link here, after all."

"You could be right, Frank."

The answer came to him in the middle of the night.

Ryan sat bolt upright in bed, wrenching his neck in the process.

"Shit," he muttered softly, and slid out of bed to find a pair of pants and go in search of more tablets.

"Are you okay?" Anna called out, her voice heavy with sleep.

"Fine," Ryan reassured her, and pressed a kiss to her bare shoulder before padding into the adjoining bathroom to seek out some more anti-inflammatories.

After he'd swallowed a couple, Ryan sat on the edge of the bath and let the epiphany circulate around his mind. It was a tenuous link, in some ways, but it would explain everything. He was only surprised he hadn't thought of it earlier.

Surprise at the lengths the man would go to, to protect his new identity, swiftly gave way to anger. Ryan could now put a face to the shadow that had almost killed him, and he gripped the edge of the bath, bearing down against the memory.

He took a deep, shuddering breath and headed back into the bedroom to check the time on his smartphone, which rested atop one of the antique bedside tables.

Four-fifteen.

In another few hours, the city would come alive again. He wanted to get dressed and make an arrest, right now, but some small sense of grief for the person Manetti had once been stayed Ryan's hand. There had been a time when

Manetti had been wronged; when men in uniform had failed him, but that time had now passed.

Though he was conflicted, Ryan came to a decision.

He would allow Tony Manetti these last few hours as a free man; for morning was not far away and, with it, would come the long arm of the law.

CHAPTER 41

The morning sun had barely caressed the rooftops of Florence by the time Ryan, Phillips and MacKenzie made the short journey into the centre. They'd opted to walk, following a slightly longer route through the Boboli Gardens to enjoy a moment's calm before re-joining the road that would lead them across the Ponte Vecchio. From there, they would cut through the narrow streets towards the *Cattedrale di Santa Maria del Fiore*, known colloquially as the Duomo, a magnificent fifteenth-century cathedral, whose towering green and white marble dome was once the largest in the world.

For the most part, they walked in silence, questions of culpability swirling around their minds as their footsteps drew closer to their destination.

By mutual accord, they paused in the centre of the Ponte Vecchio to admire the view. Beside them, a group of tourists struck a variety of poses as their friends captured the moment.

"I read somewhere that Hitler once visited this bridge," Ryan said. "Mussolini took him for a tour along the Vasari Corridor and, apparently, he admired the view so much, he ordered that the bridge should never be bombed during the war."

"Big of him," Phillips snorted, looking up at the second level of the bridge where the corridor ran overhead.

"A small concession, in the grand scheme of things," Ryan agreed. "He didn't mind so much about the rest of the city, or its people. It's an interesting question, isn't it; the value of long-lasting art over human life. Somebody like Armstrong would probably say his so-called 'art' is more important than any single human life."

"He's pushing it, if he thinks those thrillers constitute art," MacKenzie said, in her no-nonsense sort of way. "But I agree, I'd never put bricks and mortar above the value of a life, however transient."

"Aye, the Ponte Vecchio's nice enough," Phillips conceded, watching the sky begin to bloom in shades of rich amber light. "But it's no Tyne Bridge."

Ryan put a hand on his friend's shoulder and flashed a smile. "It sure ain't."

Ryan checked the address he had written on a small scrap of paper and looked up at the apartment building nestled beside the Florence Library, a stone's throw from the Duomo.

"This is the place," he said.

He tried the buzzer several times but there was no answer from the intercom. In the end, he tried a neighbour's apartment instead, and the door buzzed open.

The neighbour turned out to be an American postgraduate student, and an affluent one, if her digs were anything to go by. She had long, sun-bleached hair and wore the tiniest shorts Phillips had ever seen, paired with a sweatshirt emblazoned with an embroidered logo which read, 'UNIVERSITY OF ARIZONA.'

"Mind your eyes don't fall out of your head, Frank," MacKenzie muttered, beneath her breath. "Think of your blood pressure."

"Thanks for your help," Ryan said, and let her scrutinise his warrant card. "We were hoping to have a word with your neighbour."

"Oh, if he's not at home, he'll be down at Caffe Duomo, right on the square opposite the cathedral. He goes there every morning."

MacKenzie tried the door for good measure.

When she shook her head, Ryan came to a decision.

"You two stay here, in case he's still inside or comes back. I'll call Ricci and tell him to try the office, in case he's there. In the meantime, I'll head over to the café."

The storm that had raced through the city's streets overnight seemed to have washed away the oppressive fog, carrying with it the mixed perfume of exhaust fumes, river water and the earthen scent of the soil of Tuscany.

The man sitting alone at the Caffe Duomo slipped on a pair of glasses and raised his face to the early-morning sun, breathing deeply of the fresh wind he would always associate with home. He had been born here, in a nearby state hospital, to loving parents who had passed away months before he was released—within days of each other.

He'd heard about that somewhere before; about couples who had loved one another for a lifetime and who could not bear to be parted, even in death. The one who was left behind simply...gave up—especially when there was nobody else to live for, certainly not their son.

The murderer.

He balanced his cup carefully in both hands and raised the lukewarm coffee to his lips. He would have preferred it hot, but it was safer this way.

If the heart, when broken, simply gave out, then why had his own continued to beat for twenty years? How had he continued in spite of it all, without Andrew by his side? There had been no peaceful release from his torment, no sweet oblivion. Days had rolled into weeks, then weeks into years.

He had considered suicide for a while—he would die a 'murderer' in the eyes of all who knew him and, worst of all, he thought he would never know who had killed Andrew. He'd spent years trying to find the missing clue, going over the details of what happened like a record stuck forever on repeat.

It was the library that had saved him, but not in the usual way.

He remembered the day vividly: a gloomy, grey day in March of 2001. The library trolley had replenished itself with books that were only slightly out of date, which was a rare treat, and he had been one of the first to have his pick. He'd seen the new thriller by Nathan Armstrong on top of the pile and it had brought back the memories again, of Andrew and his dream. His talent. He'd taken the book and turned it over in his hands, not even attempting to read it, not able to concentrate on more than one sentence at a time without wishing for death to claim him.

And then he'd seen it.

The picture of Armstrong inside the book cover; an artsy, black and white portrait of him sitting at his desk beside the tools of his trade. Pens, paper, notepad.

And Andrew's typewriter.

As the truth had come tumbling down, suddenly, there had been a reason for living again. No longer did he consider suicide and instead began to think of homicide; a testament to his grandfather who had taught him the motto, 'an eye for an eye.' All his life, he'd railed against it, thinking that it surely led to the whole world ending up blind, but those paltry reservations were nothing in comparison with his need for revenge. Soon enough, it was the only thing that occupied his mind.

What did he have to lose? What more could the world take from him that he hadn't already lost?

The answer was nothing.

CHAPTER 42

It took Ryan less than two minutes to reach the Piazza Duomo, skirting the perimeter of its gigantic cathedral walls with long strides while his eyes scanned the names of the numerous small cafes overlooking it. He scanned the faces of the crowd, too, sure now of who he needed to find.

It didn't take long.

Ryan slowed his stride, assessing the man's posture and taking note of possible escape routes. He looked lost in thought, a million miles away from the little plastic-coated table where he sat, alone.

He looked up as Ryan's shadow blocked the sun. There was a brief internal battle; part of him wanted to carry on with the persona, the clever pretence he'd created to get the job done. But the other part of him wanted to unburden himself of the dreadful truth, at least to one other living soul before it was all too late.

Before he forgot what the truth was.

"Mind if I join you, Tony?"

The man more recently known as Nico Bellucci, art dealer, cast a quick glance around the square and wondered whether he should run or put up a token protest. There were still places he could go, connections he could use.

But what was the use? It was over—he had failed.

"*Prego*," he murmured.

Ryan signalled the waiter for two more espressos, then sat down opposite the man who had almost killed him. Even now, even *knowing* he was right, he found it hard to imagine that the mild-eyed man with the curly grey hair and sculpted beard, the tailored suit and manicured nails, could have been the same shadow who had sought to choke the life out of him.

"You're wondering if you've made a mistake, aren't you?" Tony said quietly, clasping his hands on his lap. "You're asking yourself whether I could have been the one to commit those atrocities, to kill those people in cold blood. You're wanting to know why I don't look more the part, why you can't see the hatred in my eyes. Aren't you?"

Ryan searched the other man's face, then shook his head.

"No, Tony. I was thinking about what it must have cost you, every year you spent behind bars. Then I realised the answer was simple. It cost you your conscience, your soul... the thing that made Tony Manetti the man he was."

Manetti looked away and up at the Duomo, as if he hadn't heard him.

"I like to sit here because it's where Andrew and I met," he said softly. "I saw him one day, taking pictures. I think I fell

313

for him straight away." He made a sound that was half-laugh, half-sob. "He was such a beautiful man, inside and out."

He lifted his sunglasses to scrub away the tears which had, somehow, started to flow again. All these years and the memories hadn't dimmed.

"I can still see his face, from that first time. I dream about him almost every night, happy dreams where he's still alive and we've grown old together," Manetti whispered. "But each morning I wake up and find my mind has betrayed me again."

Ryan remained silent. He wasn't sure he knew the right words to say.

"I lost everything the night Andrew died. The night he was *murdered* by Nathan Armstrong," Manetti said, very clearly. "You say I lost my conscience, my very soul? You are right about that, but it did not take years for it to happen. It took only a few short months. When I knew that the police, the lawyers, everyone who had ever had a hand in the case didn't care about finding the truth, I think the last part of Tony Manetti slipped away."

"What remains?" Ryan asked.

Manetti laughed but it was a sad, painful sound.

"This…this shell," he said, gesturing to his body. "This collection of skin and bones that I feed and water. But there is nothing left of me, or soon there won't be. That's how you found me, isn't it? It has to be."

Ryan's eyes swept down to the other man's hands, which trembled against the table top.

"Tremors are a common symptom of Parkinson's disease," he said. "But your idea of feigning alcoholism was an excellent ruse. We bought it—hook, line and sinker."

Manetti lifted a shoulder.

"When you're diagnosed, you're given a choice. Either take the drugs that'll make the trembling stop alongside the other physical symptoms but be prepared for a mental decline. Or, vice versa. Put up with the physical symptoms but keep your mind intact for longer. I chose to preserve my mind, such as it is."

"You had a plan to execute," Ryan prompted him, and Manetti nodded.

"Yes. You have no idea how long I'd been waiting, never knowing if I'd ever be given the opportunity to try."

"Why go after Armstrong yourself?" Ryan asked. "If you knew he'd killed Andrew, why didn't you tell the police? There's no mention of it—"

"I didn't know until years later," Manetti said, and Ryan watched his hands begin to tremble more violently; so badly he folded his arms and tucked them beneath his own body. "I went to prison never knowing who had taken Andrew from me, only that it hadn't been me. I kept thinking that somebody new would come along and look at the files and give me another chance. When I read about the Circle and about all the people, in all walks, who'd been a part of it...I started to wonder whether Edward Clarkson was protected, if he knew people in high places. It isn't so different from the mafia in my country."

He shrugged, but it was an angry gesture rather than a dismissal.

"The police didn't want to find out, anyway. It was easier to imagine we'd argued and I'd killed him in some sort of mindless, jealous rage. As if I would ever have hurt him..." Manetti swallowed back tears before continuing. "There are some who hate the gay community. They try to hide it, to pretend, but it shows itself at times like that. They just didn't care enough to search for the truth and, even if they did, back in '98 there were corrupt forces beneath the surface. I didn't stand a chance."

"I read in the paperwork that there was a witness," Ryan said.

Manetti nodded, watching a pigeon swoop down and land nearby to peck at crumbs.

"There was a bartender at the club in Newcastle. I never knew his name, but I was at the bar almost all night—he was the only one who could confirm the exact time I left to go home."

Ryan nodded, thinking of what that must have felt like. In his business, he was more often the sword and not the shield, though he tried where he could. He caught the bad guys and left the wheels of justice to finish the job. But he knew that mistakes could be made—thankfully, not on his watch, so far—but he was only human and the possibility of overlooking a crucial fact or drawing the wrong conclusion from the evidence was something he never forgot. Listening to Manetti's story, it was a sombre reminder of the very real consequences of getting it wrong.

"You haven't told me how you worked out it was Armstrong," he said, coldly.

He would not pity this man. No matter the injustice, the indignity of prison, the freedoms he'd been forced to forego—it was never acceptable to kill.

But he could not help but pity him, and therein lay the moral dilemma.

"It was entirely by chance, a couple of years after I was incarcerated," Manetti said. "I took a book off the library trolley and it was Armstrong's new thriller, the first or second he'd published after *Il Mostro.* I knew his name, of course."

"You'd read his books?"

Manetti frowned, then his face cleared.

"Of course, you wouldn't know," he murmured. "It wouldn't be in the case files."

"What wouldn't?" Ryan asked, leaning forward.

"I'd never met Nathan Armstrong, but I knew him by association. You see, Andrew worked as an assistant in a sports shop in Newcastle but that was only temporary. He was an amazing writer," Manetti explained. "When I met him here in Florence, he'd been visiting the city to research a book he was hoping to write. A couple of years later, he did."

Manetti nodded, watching the dawning realisation on Ryan's face.

"The book was called *Il Mostro.*"

CHAPTER 43

Ryan felt the small hairs on the back of his neck begin to prickle as everything fell into place.

"It was the first book Andrew had written and he didn't have a lot of confidence, as it turned out," Manetti continued, thinking of the modest man he had loved.

"He'd met Armstrong at a book signing, one time, and asked if he could write to him for some advice about his book. Armstrong told him to contact his agent in London and they'd pass the message on. Anyway, he sent his manuscript and a covering letter to Armstrong's agent, who must have forwarded it on. Months later, he got a reply."

"Saying what?"

"A condescending letter from Armstrong saying that his work had *promise*," Manetti spat. "Saying that Andrew would have more of a chance of breaking into the mainstream if he tried ghost-writing, first. Armstrong offered him a deal. He'd give him ten thousand pounds for all rights to the manuscript and he'd recommend Andrew to his agent and everyone who mattered, if the book went on to do well."

Manetti paused to gather himself together.

"It came with a strict gagging clause," he continued. "Andrew was never, ever to reveal that he was the book's true author, or Armstrong would sue. You have to understand, ten thousand pounds was a lot of money, back then, and neither of us had any to begin with."

"So Andrew took the deal?"

Manetti nodded.

"The letter was so persuasive," he said. "It promised him a new life, if he just gave up this first 'effort'. We both reasoned that it didn't matter, since Andrew was so talented he could write a hundred other books in the future, in his own name."

"I guess he wasn't able to self-publish, back then?" Ryan said, with the ghost of a smile.

"Sadly not. The world is more advanced, now," Manetti replied. "But, back in those days, it was a case of finding a traditional publishing house."

"So what happened?"

Manetti waved away a street vendor touting keyrings in the shape of a miniature Duomo, then called him back. To Ryan's surprise, he handed over a few coins in exchange for one of them, which he turned over and over in his hand like a stress ball.

"What happened?" Manetti repeated. "We used the money to enrol Andrew on a creative writing course at the university. We forgot about it, until Andrew spotted the book in a window display at one of the bookshops in Newcastle. Soon enough, *Il Mostro* was everywhere. It was top of the charts in the UK and, within a month, it was worldwide. Things just took off, while Andrew was forced to look on from the sidelines.

"Do you know what the worst part was?" Manetti asked, not really expecting a response. "The bastard hadn't even changed a word of it, except the name at the front. He'd written a gushing foreword, thanking everyone who'd helped him write the book, without thanking the one person he had to thank for his reflected success. Everything he's ever written since has been tawdry, by comparison."

Over his shoulder, Ryan caught sight of Phillips and MacKenzie approaching them across the square and gave a tiny, almost imperceptible shake of his head to hold them back. He needed to hear all that Manetti had to tell him and, if they were interrupted now, the man might lose his nerve. Phillips raised a hand to acknowledge 'message understood' and they settled at a table several feet away, within sight, in case their help was required.

"Andrew couldn't stand it," Manetti said, picking up the story. "Every day, he was getting angrier and angrier about what was happening. When Armstrong got a film deal and won his first award, he was like a wild thing," he murmured.

"Did Andrew do anything about it?"

"He sent letters," Manetti said. "He got no reply, of course. It was like he didn't exist. After a while, Andrew stopped talking about it or telling me what was happening because it was starting to come between us. It's why we were arguing the night he died. I wanted to put it behind us and move back to Italy, to get away from it all for a while, but Andrew was adamant about staying put."

He sighed, presumably at his former self.

"But you must understand, back then, it never seemed plausible that somebody like Armstrong would kill. Not for something so trivial as money, or status. The prospect never entered my mind, not even remotely. Even trying to imagine Nathan Armstrong inside the little flat we had…as I say, I never dreamed of it. It wasn't until I saw the cover of his book in prison that I realised I'd been wrong."

"What was so special about the cover?"

"It was the typewriter," he said. "Some fancy photographer had taken Armstrong's portrait picture sitting beside Andrew's typewriter."

Ryan's heart sank. How could everything rest on a typewriter? That wasn't enough to pull Armstrong in.

Sensing his disbelief, Manetti smiled.

"You want to know how I'm sure it belonged to Andrew? Several things," he said. "Firstly, I was the one to buy it for him, here in Italy. I can even show you the shop. Look closely at the picture and you'll see the typewriter has the Italian-style keys, slightly different from the usual 'QWERTY' format, as in the United Kingdom or America."

"He could have come by a similar model," Ryan was forced to point out.

"But he didn't," Manetti said, and his eyes dared Ryan to argue. "I didn't notice when I came home that night—all I could see was Andrew. And the police never took a proper inventory of the house, never listed everything belonging to Andrew. But the typewriter wasn't there, and the only possible reason is because Armstrong took it, along with any other paperwork that would incriminate him, while he was in the house."

Ryan could imagine it. Dear God, he could imagine it.

"Did Andrew keep a copy of the book on a computer, any other physical copies?"

Manetti shook his head.

"We didn't own a computer. He used one from time to time at the internet cafes, but he wrote everything in notebooks or typed it out. That was the world back then," he said. "He kept a master copy of *Il Mostro* at home and sent a photocopied version to Armstrong. The master must be long gone by now," he said, sadly.

But Ryan remembered something important, something Gabriele Marchesa had told him at the Uffizi party. He'd said that Armstrong's UK publisher kept a copy of the original manuscript at their offices in London, for posterity.

Find the manuscript, find the typewriter, and he might just find Andrew Wharton's DNA alongside Nathan Armstrong's. That, at least, was something the police had stored on their database and was a coincidence too far for any jury to ignore.

He looked back into Tony Manetti's face, which seemed as though it had aged during the course of their conversation.

Sudden frustration overwhelmed him; impotent anger at the waste of life and the wasted opportunity.

"Why didn't you tell the police about this theory?" he demanded. "They would have looked into it!"

He hoped.

Manetti's eyes flashed with his own share of anger.

"I went through all the proper channels, time and again I tried. I begged them to listen, to hear my story, but nobody was interested. I might as well have been dead already. I strung it out a bit with Clarkson; sent him a few threatening letters so that he knew his days were numbered. From what I heard inside, any number of people wanted him dead. I expect that's why he changed his name and tried to hide. It didn't take me long to find him."

His eyes shone at the remembered thrill of finally catching up with Clarkson at the hermitage.

"But Clarkson was just an appetiser. I spent long hours imagining what would be the worst punishment for Armstrong—and death was not enough. I needed Armstrong to know how it felt to be publicly shamed, to have his reputation in tatters, and to know how it felt to come home and find death. Besides," he said, "prison is too good for him."

Ryan listened to him and then looked away as he thought about the best way forward. He prided himself on being an honest man and he could not say for certain what he would do if he came home to find Anna left in the same condition as Andrew Wharton. If he'd been imprisoned for years, left only to his own thoughts, tormented by the past. What might he do, if put in the same position?

He had faced death countless times and had even lost those he loved to the hands of men who were little more than animals. But, when faced with the opportunity to take his revenge, the will to take another life had not been there. It had not been in him.

And that was the difference between them.

Feeling suddenly hot, Ryan unbuttoned the top of his shirt and began to roll up his sleeves.

"I'm sorry for that," Manetti said quietly, nodding towards the marks on Ryan's neck before raising his gaze to look his victim in the eye. "You were not a person to me, then, but a means to an end. You were right when you said I have lost my soul."

His voice cracked on the last word and his lip quivered. He looked away, unable to face the cool, blue-eyed gaze any longer. The two men were silent for a moment, surrounded by the sounds of the city coming to life; the babble of the growing crowds of tourists, punctuated by the sound of a motorbike revving its engine along one of the many side streets between the high buildings that surrounded the square.

"Come to the station and tell Inspector Ricci everything you have just told me," was all Ryan said. "Turn yourself in and help us to bring in the man who killed Andrew, as well as others. Tell us what happened with the others and how many there are."

Ryan swallowed revulsion at the thought of how many had been sacrificed as a 'means to an end'.

Manetti scrubbed the heels of his hands over his eyes, then replaced his sunglasses to hide them.

"I'll come now," he said. "I'll help however I can."

After Ryan slapped some cash on the table, the two men stood up. Behind Manetti, Ryan saw that Phillips and MacKenzie followed suit and prepared to walk across to join them. Before they left, Manetti stopped.

"Take this, as a talisman," he said, offering the little keyring to Ryan. "Whenever you think of it, don't think of a lost man, a murderer. Please think of this beautiful place and of innocence. Think of how far a man can fall, if he allows it."

Ryan hesitated, then reached out to hold the little Duomo tightly in the palm of his hand.

The sound of the gunshot ricocheted around the square and suddenly Manetti's body jerked, his blood spattering over Ryan's face, and then his body fell forward against the little plastic table before slumping to the floor.

CHAPTER 44

The world seemed to move in slow motion.

Ryan watched it happen as if from a place somewhere outside his own body, with a kind of numb detachment. His arms flew out to catch Manetti, but he was too late; the man fell heavily to the ground, dead long before he reached it. Birds scattered into the air, their panicked cries echoed by the people below. It happened in the blink of an eye, then Ryan spun around to seek out the source of the gunfire.

And found himself staring down the barrel of a handgun.

The man wore a mask to conceal his face and was seated atop a motorcycle he'd pulled to a screeching halt a short distance away with its engine running. Ryan told himself to dive for cover, to move.

Move!

The next thing he heard was the crashing of tables being thrust aside and then something hit him hard from behind, sending him tumbling to the floor not far from where Manetti lay in a pool of his own blood. Over his head, more shots pinged off the tables.

"Shots fired!" he heard someone shout. "Get down! Get down!"

Satisfied that Ryan was out of the direct line of fire, Phillips heaved himself up again and grabbed one of the glass bottles which had fallen to the floor as tables were upturned. He grasped the neck and then stood up, lobbing it towards the masked gunman before ducking down again. The bottle hit its target, connecting with the handgun and sending it flying across the cobbled stones.

Meanwhile, Ryan recovered himself quickly, scrambling to his feet to grasp Phillips' arm, just once, to let him know he was grateful. Then, he turned to see the gunman already spinning the back wheel of his motorcycle to beat a hasty retreat, his job done.

"Ricci!" Ryan shouted. "Get Ricci!"

A short distance away, a woman on her morning commute was cowering behind the wheel of her car and Ryan ran across, reaching for his warrant card.

"*Polizia!*" he shouted. "*Ho bisogno della tua macchina!*"

He wrenched open the driver's side door and helped her out—with more speed than finesse, it had to be said— before taking over the wheel.

A moment later, he'd put the car in gear and was in pursuit.

The motorcycle's engine echoed through the streets and Ryan followed its sound, racing away from the Duomo and past the *Piazza della Republica*. Up ahead, the motorcycle wove through pedestrians who dived out of its path, their shopping bags spilling onto the floor as they rushed to safety.

Ryan had completed his Advanced Police Driving Course, but he was far away from home, in a strange car and only a sketchy memory of the road network, at best.

"Get out of the way!"

He thumped the horn on the old Fiat to give himself a clear path ahead and then pushed the car forward, flying past the café where Anna had met Conti, only days before, to join the road running parallel to the river.

The motorcycle came into sight again, weaving further along the road as if its driver was drunk. Ryan tried to figure out where its driver was headed but, in Florence, that could have been anywhere. A tiny little garage, tucked away somewhere, or to a different city entirely if he managed to join the motorway half a mile further west.

He slammed his foot on the brake as an old woman stumbled and half-fell into the street, missing his bonnet by a hair's breadth. Passers-by stopped to help her, calling out obscenities at the motorcycle's retreating back and Ryan felt a sense of defeat. Through his windshield, he watched the motorcycle gain valuable ground, putting more and more distance between them. A car was no match for a high-end motorcycle in a city that had never been designed for larger vehicles and he thumped the wheel again, this time in sheer frustration.

Then, eased his foot off the accelerator and brought the car to a complete stop.

Up ahead, there was a sudden *crash* and a cloud of smoke, like a bag of flour exploding as the motorcycle and its driver collided headlong with the front-end of a lorry on the crossroads in front of him.

Ryan sat there for long minutes, registering the long wail of police vehicles as they swarmed in from several directions. A moment later, his door flew open and another gun was pointed at his face; this time it belonged to the Carabinieri, the military police who kept order in the city.

Ryan raised his hands slowly and stepped out of the car.

CHAPTER 45

"You are a hero, Sergeant Phillips."

Phillips turned a deep shade of puce as several sets of police eyes turned on him, then he waved away the compliment with a broad hand.

"Ah, get away. I only did what anyone else would have done."

"I think not," Ricci said, nodding towards the television screen in his office at the *Gruppo's* headquarters, where a recording of Phillips' bravery had been taken by one of the tourists in the Piazza Duomo and was now being replayed on the local and national news. "You are to be congratulated."

"Why, I've seen worse than that on a frisky night out in the Bigg Market," Phillips said.

"The Bigg Market?" Ricci enquired.

"Don't ask," MacKenzie said, and Ricci gave one of his shrugs.

"Nico Bellucci died instantly," he said. "But you tell me that was not his real name?"

"No, it was—"

Phillips cut off when as the door opened again and his friend stepped inside.

"You are like a cat with nine lives," Ricci declared, and then gave Ryan a very continental embrace which left him taken aback. "We are glad to see you."

Ryan gave the inspector an awkward pat and then, uncaring of who might see, walked straight across to Phillips.

"Frank, I don't know how to—"

"Howay man, don't you start n'all."

Ryan held out his hand to shake his friend's and then did some embracing of his own, pulling Phillips in for a manly hug.

"You're the best there is," he said gruffly. "I'm in your debt."

"There's no debt," Phillips muttered, clearing his throat.

Ryan nodded, then stepped away again to face the room.

"The gunman has been taken to hospital," he said. "It's not looking good."

"Banotti is there," Ricci said. "She'll keep us informed of any change on that front, but she says he's already been identified as an associate of the Spatuzzi family."

They had suspected as much.

"There's only one person who could have told them about Nico Bellucci's real identity," Ryan said. "Armstrong is the only other person who could possibly have known."

"There is no way to prove that," Ricci said, though it gave him little pleasure. "Nobody in the Spatuzzi family will talk;

nor will the gunman, if he survives to talk at all. We are at another dead end."

"Before he died, Nico—real name, Tony Manetti—confessed to killing several people in a wider campaign of vengeance against Nathan Armstrong. Unfortunately, he died before telling me the full list of those he murdered. But he did tell me all about Armstrong."

Ryan spent the next few minutes briefing the assembled police staff on all that Manetti had shared, during their brief acquaintance.

"*Merda*," Ricci said, sinking into his desk chair. "The most we could do is charge Armstrong with the illegal disposal of a body…except, there is still no proof that he is the one to have disposed of the people Manetti left waiting for him. If we were to ask him about it, Armstrong would surely deny all knowledge."

"What about the DNA sampling in Armstrong's apartment, after my attack?" Ryan asked. "Did you find any unusual samples?"

"There were dozens," Ricci said. "Some belonging to Armstrong—others belonging to Manetti, we may now find. There were also several blood samples belonging to Martina Calari but Armstrong is sure to say it was all Manetti's work."

"And we still don't have anything to pin on Armstrong and take to the Crown Prosecution Service, back home," MacKenzie pointed out. "He'll walk, again."

Just then, Ryan's phone began to vibrate in his pocket.

Anna, the display read.

"Give me a minute," he said, and stepped outside into the corridor.

"Ryan, are you alright? I saw the news—"

Anna clutched one of the telephones at the Villa Lucia, telling herself to stay calm.

"I'm fine," he said, and it was true. He felt instantly better, simply hearing her voice.

"I had a meeting with Manetti and he told me his story but, as I was about to bring him in, the mafia hit him. We think they were tipped off by Armstrong."

"He was shot?"

"Right in front of me," Ryan murmured. He still had blood spattered down the front of his shirt, although he'd stopped by the gents to rinse off his face and hands.

"That's awful," she muttered. "What happens now?"

Ryan rubbed his forehead with the back of his hand.

"I don't know," he said, struggling to see a way forward. "Manetti said that Armstrong has things in his possession— or at least he *had* them—belonging to Andrew Wharton, Manetti's boyfriend who was killed back in 1998. He told me Wharton wrote *Il Mostro* and took a deal Armstrong offered him to sell all his rights and to keep schtum about the fact he'd been the one to write it."

There was a short silence.

"That explains it," Anna said. "The quality of his writing in *Il Mostro* is significantly better than in some of his other books. It seems obvious now that someone else must have written it."

"Ghost-writing is fairly common," Ryan said. "But Armstrong has built a reputation off the back of his *genius*. The last thing he would ever want is word getting out that he's a fraud. It sounds like Andrew Wharton might have written to him, maybe threatened him, and Armstrong paid him a personal visit to shut him up, once and for all."

"If you'd told me this last year, before Kielder and before Duncan Gray, I'd never have believed it," she said. "But now I do; I believe Armstrong is capable of that."

"I do, too. And we have to imagine Armstrong twenty years ago. His career was really sky-rocketing, thanks to Andrew's book. He'd been offered a film deal, all kinds of prestige, and that was only the beginning. No way a psychopath like him would give it all up, not when he'd had a taste of the Big Time."

"This needs to be put right," Anna said. "For the sake of the man's memory, the world needs to know."

"That's how Manetti felt," Ryan said. "But how the hell am I supposed to track down a twenty-year-old typewriter? It could be anywhere."

"The one in Armstrong's photograph?" Anna said, joining the dots without a pause.

"Yeah, Manetti said it has Italian keys and Wharton's DNA might still be on it, if we're lucky. I just don't know where to find it."

"Kielder," Anna said, immediately. "Armstrong has his house at Scribe's End locked up tight. You only do that if there's something valuable inside, or if you have something to hide, because the crime rate is so low in that area he could practically leave his door open and nobody would think to walk inside."

Ryan nodded, the light of battle beginning to shine once again in his eyes.

"Anna?"

"Yep?"

"What would I do without you?"

"Lord only knows," she said. "Now, get your arse in gear and bring home the bacon."

Ryan laughed but asked one last question.

"By the way, did you manage to get everything sorted out today?"

Her voice lowered conspiratorially.

"Everything's on track."

When Ryan stepped back into Ricci's office, he looked amongst their expectant faces and they recognised his expression as being one of total focus, signalling he had come to a decision.

"I have an idea," he said. "It's risky and time-sensitive, but it just might work. Ricci, what's Armstrong's last public engagement in the city?"

"A book signing at a shop on the *Piazza della Republica*," the other man replied. "He is scheduled to appear from two o'clock this afternoon until around three-thirty, following which he will travel to his next destination."

"Do you know where he plans to go?"

Ricci nodded.

"I looked into it," he said. "His book tour will have finished but it seems he plans to stay in Italy—he's due to catch the seven-thirty train to Naples."

"I need him on UK soil," Ryan said bluntly. "Where I can make an arrest without all the added hoopla."

Ricci weighed things up in the seconds it took him to come to his own decision. They could argue over jurisdiction later and, ultimately, Ryan's team had a prior claim that was much bigger than anything he might be able to pin on Armstrong.

"What do you need?" he asked.

"I need Armstrong to show his hand but, to make that happen, all I need right now is a telephone."

CHAPTER 46

At two o'clock exactly, Nathan Armstrong took his seat at a table brimming with copies of the twentieth-anniversary edition of *Il Mostro* and wondered idly whether his book-to-film agent had managed to secure a decent offer for the proposed remake, starring some of the most popular names in the film industry of the day. It would top off what was already shaping up to be an excellent day, since he'd already caught the morning news reporting the mafia assassination of Nico Bellucci, a respected Florentine art dealer.

Since nothing had been mentioned of the man's real name, he could only assume one of two things: either that the police had failed to uncover it, or that they were keeping it under wraps while they investigated further.

But what could they investigate? The man was dead and would no longer exist on the fringe of Armstrong's otherwise perfect life. There would be no more bodies turning up to deal with, no more sneaking about or covering his tracks.

He'd get a full night's sleep, for a change—and that would do wonders for his skin.

Armstrong continued to sign books, chatting and smiling with the queue of fans who had lined up to meet him in person. He listened to their stories and laughed along with their jokes, brushing off their compliments with as much modesty as he could muster.

An hour or more passed and the line began to dwindle. He was looking forward to leaving Florence and all its cares behind, but the practised smile he had ready for the next person in line froze on his face when he caught sight of who that person was.

Ryan.

"What the hell are you doing here?" Armstrong muttered, keeping his smile in place for the benefit of anybody who might see.

"Same as everyone else," Ryan said, cheerfully, and picked up one of the books stacked on the table.

He flipped it over and smiled.

"Nice cover," he remarked. "Very eye-catching."

"Thank you," Armstrong gritted out. "Now, if you've had your fun, I have a line of real fans waiting to meet me."

"Oh, but I *am* a real fan of the book," Ryan averred. "I thought it was a very good read. Quite different in style to some of your other works."

"A literary critic now, are you?" Armstrong drawled. "You must be exhausted, Ryan, with so many strings to your bow."

"Oh, not as exhausted as you must be," Ryan said softly. "There must have been quite a few late nights, over the past couple of months."

"That's to be expected, when one is travelling on an international book tour," Armstrong shot back.

Ryan smiled.

"Tell me, Nathan, how did you write *Il Mostro*? Was it on a computer, or on something more old-fashioned, like a typewriter?"

It was a rhetorical question, of course, and Ryan had already checked whether Armstrong had answered the question before. He had, numerous times over the years—on television, radio and in the press.

Each time, he confirmed a typewriter had been used.

"I used a typewriter," Armstrong bit out. "Now—"

"Not an Olivetti Ico Model 2, from the 1930s?"

Armstrong was silent.

"Strange that it should be an Italian brand, rather than an English one. They're very rare," Ryan continued. "Dealers tend to keep a record of their sale. But then, I'm sure you bought yours while you were in Italy…perhaps, even, when you were here researching."

Ryan let that sink in and then looked down at the book he still held in his hand.

"Well, look at that," Ryan exclaimed. "Here's a picture of you sitting right beside it."

Armstrong continued to stare at him, silently processing the implications of what had been, he now realised, a catastrophic oversight.

"I haven't used it in years," Armstrong managed. "Technology has moved on so much since the nineties. I have no idea where it is, now. Probably in a charity shop, somewhere."

Ryan shrugged.

"Pity," he said, then handed over the book for Armstrong to autograph. Who knew? It might be worth something, someday.

As soon as Ryan left, Armstrong leapt up from the table and scurried out of the bookshop, leaving a small crowd of disappointed readers behind him as he hurried directly to the airport, hailing a cab on the street outside.

They didn't matter, he thought. Nothing mattered except getting back to Kielder before Ryan could.

In the back of the taxi, he put a call through to the airline. He had his passport on him at all times—force of habit, he supposed—and his wallet. He didn't need anything else, for now; that could wait.

The first available flight from Florence to Newcastle left in two hours, with a changeover in Paris. In the meantime, he brought up the app on his smartphone and checked the

CCTV cameras and security system wired to his house, which he was able to monitor remotely.

No trespassers recorded.

No break in coverage since the last time he'd checked.

There was still time.

———

Ryan's flight from Pisa to Newcastle was a direct one and departed in ninety minutes. The journey from the Villa Lucia to Pisa Airport would take fifty minutes in good traffic—forty, since Ryan was driving. That left him around forty-five minutes to check in and get through security but, if he made it, Ryan would arrive in Newcastle an hour ahead of Armstrong. Inspector Ricci had already received a call from one of the airlines to say that their person of interest had just booked himself a flight to Newcastle and luck was on their side in that he hadn't thought to try Pisa Airport instead.

"So far, so good," Ryan muttered, shoving his passport into the small rucksack Anna had packed for him.

"Be careful," she said.

Ryan slung the rucksack over his shoulder and simply walked across the room to take her in his arms for a breathless kiss.

"I'll be back in time," he promised.

"You better be," she said. "I love you."

"Same goes, Doctor."

As he made for the front door, Phillips and MacKenzie joined him in the hallway, bags in hand.

"Ready," Phillips said. "Are we getting a taxi?"

"Sorry, Frank, there was only one seat left on the flight," Ryan lied. "Here, take these."

He chucked a set of keys to the villa towards his friend, who caught them one-handed.

"Look after things while I'm gone," he said.

"We could catch the next flight out," MacKenzie offered. "We'll only be a few hours behind."

"No need," Ryan told her, in the most authoritative tone he could muster. "I've got the team back at CID on standby, so everything's covered. Might as well enjoy yourselves until Morrison finds out."

And, with the flash of a smile, he was gone.

CHAPTER 47

As soon as they'd received confirmation that Armstrong was airborne and that his phone would not be connected to the internet, a team of CSIs led by Tom Faulkner entered Armstrong's house at Kielder, in Northumberland. Kielder Forest and Reservoir was a place they knew well, following a series of murders that had taken place a few months earlier that had been their first introduction to Nathan Armstrong.

Kielder lay to the west of the city of Newcastle upon Tyne, past rolling countryside, and consisted of a vast forest—not unlike the size and scale of those found in North America—with trees towering all around an enormous man-made reservoir. Armstrong owned a house on one of its southern banks, on a secluded bluff known as 'Scribe's End', in honour of its illustrious owner. The old stone hunting lodge was accessible only by a footpath from the road or by motorboat, affording total privacy from the rest of the world. It was also protected by a sophisticated alarm system and numerous CCTV cameras fixed to the tall trees which surrounded the house and were cleverly positioned to capture the entry points from every angle.

They chose to enter via one of the French windows to the rear of the property, which opened out from a large living space directly onto yards of decking with a sheer drop onto the water and the short jetty which moored Armstrong's small rowing boat.

"Quickly now," Faulkner said, as one of their police consultants—a former master thief turned security specialist—unlocked the door with a practised hand.

Immediately, the silent alarm was triggered and he hurried into the house to find the main control box. If all went to plan, he'd be able to reset the system and remove all trace of their intrusion so that Armstrong would never know they'd been there.

While their expert fiddled with the CCTV controls and alarm settings with nifty fingers, Faulkner gestured forward a team of CSIs.

"We have forty-five minutes to get this done," he said. "Let's make this short and sweet."

———

When Nathan Armstrong completed the last stage of his journey from Newcastle Airport to Kielder, night had fallen. The flight had been delayed, and a half-hour layover at the airport in Paris had only added to his rapidly increasing stress levels. As soon as he landed, he'd picked up a hire car, preferring that to the less discreet option of a taxi, and floored it all the way from the city until the dark outline of Kielder Forest appeared on the horizon.

The darkness at Kielder was complete, so black he might not have been able to see his own hand in front of his face, were it not for the moon and stars shining diamond bright in the heavens above. Armstrong hardly noticed them, so intent was he on completing this final task—disposing of the last possible link between himself and the man whose talent had lain there in the back of his mind for two decades, taunting him. Whispering to him in the still of the night.

Everything you have should be mine, the voice would say. *You would be nothing, if not for me.*

It was there each time he saw the book advertised on a railway station platform, each time he saw the movie replayed on television. Every time an interviewer or even an ordinary reader asked him about his influences or about the research he had done, the secret knowledge of his deceit would linger in the recesses of his mind. Nagging away at him, unresolved.

And there was nothing he hated more than unfinished business.

He parked the car off-road and made his way down a pathway that followed a gentle slope down through the trees until it reached the reservoir and one of his homes, 'Scribe's End'. He'd already checked his security app, in Paris and then as the plane had taxied along the runway at Newcastle, but there was no alert to show his system had been breached.

Armstrong emerged from the trees and into a small clearing where his house nestled, like a gingerbread cottage from a fairy tale, with the lake lapping gently in the background. He hurried to the front door and cleared himself for entry, watching the small security light switch from red to green before unlocking the door with his key.

He scented the air like an animal in case he caught the drift of forensic chemicals on the air, but the house was musty from disuse over the past few months and nothing more.

He wasted no more time, hurrying directly to his workspace in the impressive, Scandinavian-style living space which ran along the entire length of the house. He switched on the desk lamp and then let out a sigh of relief.

The typewriter was sitting neatly on the shelf next to his desk, just where he'd left it—beside a number of other trinkets of various shapes and sizes.

His little trophies.

It would be a pity to lose one of them, but needs must.

Armstrong gathered together the typewriter and retrieved Andrew's notebooks from the safe he kept beside his bed, then hurried out into the cold February night. The mist rolling across the water was so cold it sliced at his skin and he struggled to maintain his footing as he slipped and skidded along the icy deck towards the jetty. One or two loose papers escaped the stack he gripped in his hand and floated on the air, but he told himself he'd come back for them later.

He peeled back the boat's covering and then dumped the typewriter inside before easing himself down from the jetty and casting off the rope to begin rowing steadily out towards the centre of the lake, where the water was deepest.

It was a hard journey, since the water was choppy, and the blistering wind buffeted the boat in all directions, calling upon all his strength to keep her steady.

"That's far enough," he muttered, and without any pomp or ceremony, hurled the typewriter overboard where it landed with an almighty *splash* that seemed to reverberate around the silent lake. He remained perfectly still, listening for any other sign of life, but only a madman would be out on the water in conditions such as these.

A madman, a desperate man, or both.

Armstrong waited until the last of the notebooks had disappeared beneath the rippling water and then turned around to make the same tiring journey back, his spirits considerably lighter than before.

CHAPTER 48

Ryan waited until Armstrong had tethered his boat before stepping out from the shadows of the forest. Specialist firearms officers had taken up positions all around the clearing with orders to disable but Ryan had refused to allow permission for a critical shot to be fired, even if it turned out that Armstrong was armed. Unlike Tony Manetti, he did not believe that prison was too good for a man like Nathan Armstrong; he happened to believe it was the best place for him and he'd been waiting a long time to be the one to boot him in there.

"Out stargazing, Nathan?"

Armstrong's head whipped around at the sound of Ryan's voice and he abandoned the knot he'd been tying.

"You're trespassing," he called out, although he could barely see Ryan's outline in the surrounding darkness. "Leave, or I'll call one of your colleagues and have you removed."

Ryan ignored him completely.

"I thought you were heading to Naples," he said. "I had it on very good authority. Why the change of heart, Nathan?"

"I'm perfectly entitled to change my travel plans. Now, get off my property."

"It's interesting that you should change your plans so soon after our little chat at the bookshop in Florence," Ryan said, coming to stand at the other end of the jetty so they faced one another like two men in a duel. "But, it's my very good fortune that you did. I came along to see if you still had that old typewriter we were talking about."

"I already told you, I have no idea what happened to it," Armstrong lied. "And, even if I did, I would hardly tell you. Now, produce a search warrant, or go to hell."

Armstrong began to walk along the jetty, more confident now. Even if Ryan had a search warrant, it would only be to look for those specific items, none of which remained.

Just in the nick of time.

But, why was Ryan smiling at him? Why didn't he react?

"What were you doing out there on the water?" Ryan asked again. "Don't tell me you were destroying material evidence?"

Armstrong looked around the clearing but saw no sign of anybody else, no rustling in the bushes to suggest they were not alone.

"And, if I was? What would you do then, Ryan?" he asked, smugly. "Let's say, if I had—hypothetically, you understand—disposed of certain unwanted knick-knacks I had in my possession, what could you possibly do about it?

Any remaining trace evidence that may—or may not—have been preserved would now be destroyed beneath the water."

Ryan made a tutting sound and folded his arms across his chest. He'd grabbed a thick jumper belonging to his father before leaving the Villa Lucia, but even that wasn't enough to stop the air from working its way beneath the heavy wool to prick at the skin beneath.

His breath clouded on the air as he let out a long, thoughtful sigh.

"Well, let's say—*hypothetically, you understand*—that I suspected you had certain knick-knacks in your possession that may have valuable trace evidence incriminating you in the murder of Andrew Wharton in 1998. Let's say these knick-knacks were a typewriter and perhaps some notebooks containing detailed research he did to write the book and which you have passed off as your own for nigh-on twenty years. In those circumstances, I'd want to make sure a forensic team swabbed both the typewriter and the notebooks, and any other interesting evidence, before you had a chance to dispose of them for good."

"You'd have needed to catch an earlier flight," Armstrong said, stopping a few feet in front of him.

"Indeed, I would," Ryan said. "Such as the one I caught from Pisa Airport, an hour ahead of yours."

Armstrong searched Ryan's face for signs he was bluffing.

"I don't believe you."

"That's irrelevant," Ryan said. "The jury will believe me, when I show them the results from the DNA swabs we took over two hours ago. They'll believe me when I show them the recording of you hurrying through your house, rushing directly to the typewriter, gathering the specific items you needed, then stealing off into the night to dump them in a place you hoped nobody would find them. Those aren't the actions of an innocent man. But, you see, your dumping the typewriter in the lake doesn't matter now, Nathan. We took all the samples we needed from it long before your plane landed."

Armstrong's hands curled into tight fists as he felt his world begin to shatter, collapsing around him in an avalanche of sand.

"And, if they didn't believe me after all *that*, d'you know what they might be interested to see? The original manuscript of *Il Mostro*, the one you sent your UK publisher as a keepsake, after submitting the photocopied one Andrew had already given you. Both copies have already been seized by our colleagues in the Metropolitan Police Force and they're testing them for Low Copy Number DNA belonging to Andrew Wharton."

Ryan swept his eyes over the man who had hurt so many, for so long, and took great satisfaction in the words he was about to say.

"Nathan Armstrong, I am arresting you on suspicion of the murder of Andrew Wharton, of Duncan Gray and of Kate Robson," he said, remembering those who were murdered less than a mile from where they now stood. With the new evidence that had come to light, he hoped the CPS would reconsider their decision not to prosecute, especially since there may be more to come. "You do not have to say anything, but—"

"Damn you, Ryan."

"—it may harm your defence—"

Armstrong lunged at him, going directly for Ryan's throat and the sensitive flesh he knew lay hidden beneath the thick sweater. But Ryan had been prepared for this and met the force of Armstrong's body with a powerful jab to his stomach, followed swiftly by another fist to the face, which connected with the man's jaw with a satisfying *crack*.

As Armstrong fell to his knees, winded, Ryan shook off the mild pain in his knuckles and wondered if it made him petty to admit that it had felt bloody good.

The police took that as their cue to emerge from the woods and Armstrong watched them approaching like sentries on a battlefield.

"It may harm your defence," Ryan continued, "if you do not mention when questioned something which you later rely on in court. Anything you do say may be given in evidence."

"This isn't over," Armstrong gasped.

Ryan bent down to yank him upward and slap a pair of handcuffs around his wrists.

"Yes," Ryan said firmly. "It is."

With that, he took a firm hold of the man's arm and marched him back across the clearing and into the next stage of his life, without money or prestige, without accolades or acolytes. In prison, Armstrong would only have memories.

CHAPTER 49

Wednesday, 28ᵗʰ February

Villa Lucia, Florence

MacKenzie awakened to a shaft of wintry Mediterranean sunshine spilling over her face. She blinked sleep from her eyes and, yawning, focused on the window, watching the light filtering through one of the curtains that was hanging askew. As her mind cleared, she realised it was not a curtain but some sort of fabric hanging from the uppermost curtain pole; yards of ivory fabric that fell in beautiful folds from a velvet hanger.

A dress.

She pushed herself upright, then turned to look for Frank, whose gentle snores would usually be rumbling from the pillow beside her. Instead, she found the space on the bed empty except for a single red rose and a small notecard.

With trembling hands, she flipped open the envelope to find an invitation which read:

'*You are invited to attend the wedding of Denise MacKenzie and Frank Phillips at eleven o'clock at the basilica of San Miniato al Monte. All my love, Frank xx*'

Before she could fully comprehend what was happening, there came a tap on the door and Anna slipped inside the bedroom, armed with a breakfast tray stuffed full of Magda's finest offerings including a glass of something fruity to start the day with a bang.

"What's happening here?" MacKenzie demanded, in a voice that quivered with excitement and trepidation.

"What's happening is, Frank's giving you your dream," her friend replied, setting the tray down gently on the bed. "I've been instructed to tell you that he'll be waiting for you at the basilica at the top of the hill at eleven o'clock today and he hopes you'll join him, not just there at the church but for the rest of your lives. If you don't want to, he'll understand, but he also wanted me to tell you not to worry about the wedding breakfast because there'll be stottie cakes aplenty; Magda has it all in hand and is catering for an intimate party of loved ones and friends who've flown in especially. They've been hiding at hotels around Florence for the past couple of days, terrified they'd run into you and give the game away," Anna chuckled.

MacKenzie's mind boggled.

"But—the dress? The church? How did this happen?"

"With a little help from your friends," Anna murmured, and reached across to give her hand a bolstering squeeze. "Have a sip of that mimosa," she added. "You look as if you need it."

MacKenzie murmured something unintelligible and took a generous glug before absently nibbling on one of the pastries arranged on the tray in front of her.

"I don't know what to say."

Anna waited, a bit nervously, then watched MacKenzie's face crease into a smile.

"I never imagined anything like this would ever happen to me. I'm forty-four, for goodness' sake," she said, with a hint of embarrassment.

"It doesn't matter how old you are. What matters is how happy you are," Anna said firmly. "Now, do I have to force feed you those pastries, or what? I've got a schedule to keep. Next up is a bubble bath."

MacKenzie watched her friend head towards the en-suite bathroom and a moment later heard the taps running. Alone for a moment with her thoughts, she sat there in the beautiful bedroom and looked down at the engagement ring winking on her finger. It had been chosen with care, just as this surprise had been chosen with care; every detail planned with her in mind. There would be no awkward fanfare, no argumentative relatives she barely knew, no sense of obligation. There would only be the two of them, surrounded by love.

Anna called out that the bath was ready and MacKenzie flung back the covers, grabbing another pastry for the road.

"I'm coming!"

The basilica of *San Miniato al Monte* stood at one of the highest points in Florence, tucked against the hillside overlooking the *Piazzale Michelangelo* which held unrivalled views of the city. Like the Duomo, its façade was a triumph of colourful inlaid marble whilst the interior had been decorated with an iridescent mosaic which gleamed as the sunlight reflected against the tile. It was a beautiful place, infused with history without being overpowering and Phillips had loved it as soon as he'd seen it. There had been a bit of red tape and bureaucracy to wade through, and the priest had needed some convincing, but anything was worth the effort for the woman he loved. That included asking their good friends and limited family to fly out at a moment's notice, and that alone could not have been achieved without military precision and planning from Anna.

"She's late," he muttered, glancing again towards the open doorway.

"She's exactly on time," Ryan said. "Keep your hair on, Frank."

"Too bloody late for that," the other complained, patting down his thinning mane. "What if she doesn't like any of it?"

"She'll love it," another voice chimed in. "Especially when she finds out there's an Italian ceilidh band organised for later."

Phillips turned to Detective Constable Jack Lowerson, who was seated on the front pew next to Melanie Yates. It wouldn't have been the same without the young man who had been like a son to him these past few years, and it warmed his heart that Jack had set aside his own recent troubles to come and celebrate their happiness.

"All I need now is the bride," he joked, a bit nervously. "Here, d' you think she's had second thoughts?"

Ryan simply shook his head and nodded towards the entranceway.

"I don't think so," he murmured.

Phillips turned to see a vision in the doorway, with the sun framing her back like a halo. His throat burned with sudden emotion and he blinked furiously as the music began, the soft strains of *Ave Maria* guiding MacKenzie's footsteps as she walked down the aisle towards him. He'd been married before, he thought, to a good woman who'd passed away too soon. But this was something else. Something new and bright, like a new star having been born in the cosmos. It burned fiercely, his love for Denise, so strong that he struggled to remember all that had come before it.

When she reached him, he took her hand in his own and found himself overwhelmed by her radiance, her beauty, her strength.

"You sure?" he said, in a voice that wobbled slightly. To him, she was perfect and could have chosen anybody. He could hardly believe that she had chosen *him*.

MacKenzie smiled and reached up to brush an errant tear from his face.

"Silly," she whispered. "I've never been more sure of anything in my life."

He raised her hand to his lips to press a kiss to her skin and then grinned like a puppy.

"Howay then, let's get hitched."

EPILOGUE

Six months later

Ryan, Anna, Phillips, MacKenzie and Chief Constable Morrison, alongside representatives from the Independent Police Complaints Commission, the media, local government, LGBTQ rights groups and numerous professionals from across the publishing world had gathered at the Literary and Philosophical Society of Newcastle to honour the life and death of Andrew Wharton.

After a short speech from the CEO of Nathan Armstrong's UK publishing house—whose reputation had only just weathered the storm surrounding Armstrong's forthcoming trial for multiple murders—a new version of *Il Mostro* was unveiled to the crowd. On its cover, in bold type, was the name of its author, Andrew Wharton, whose original foreword and dedication to his beloved partner, Tony Manetti, had been included in the new print run.

Old copies printed under Armstrong's name had been pulped or recalled, not because they were under any legal obligation to do so, but because the publisher owed it to the family of Armstrong's victim to reduce their widespread circulation.

Armstrong had been stripped of his awards, which were attributed posthumously to Andrew Wharton and presented to his family, who were still coming to terms with everything.

"I know Andrew isn't around to see any of this, but it makes a difference," Anna said.

"His life was valuable," Ryan said. "His contribution deserves to be acknowledged."

They fell silent as Andrew's mother stepped forward to unveil a plaque which had been simply engraved:

ANDREW JOHN WHARTON
1970—1998
HIS MEMORY LIVES ON

AUTHOR'S NOTE

Warkworth Castle and Hermitage is truly a beautiful spot and it was a delight to rediscover its history and setting as I started to plan 'The Hermitage'. I remembered visiting several times during my childhood but, since moving back to Northumberland, it has been a treat having the castle and its pretty village almost on my doorstep. Indeed, when I imagined a place where a man might go to escape the world, Warkworth, with its ethereal, fairytale beauty seemed an obvious choice. For anybody who is inspired to visit the real hermitage after reading this book, I should warn you that I took a small liberty with its opening times for the purposes of my fictional story set in winter. I would therefore advise that you check it is open, before you plan your trip!

On the subject of taking liberties, it is also worth mentioning that the Palazzo Russo discussed in this story is entirely fictional. However, there are numerous palazzos in the city which have been converted into apartments and hotels, so its essence remains authentic.

Whilst the Vasari Corridor is very real—and hopefully re-opening soon for visitors to explore—the section running from the Uffizi to the Ponte Vecchio is suspended above a series of arches and therefore does not give direct access to any building along that part. This was chosen deliberately and altered for the purposes of my story, to preserve an important distinction between fact and fiction. However, if you ever find yourself in Florence, it is well worth taking a tour along the corridor to see how the Medici once got about!

The themes of this story are revenge, love, friendship and home. I wanted to uncover a bit more about Ryan's background and to illustrate that it doesn't matter where you are in the world; when you are with those you love, that place becomes home.

L J Ross
October 2018

ACKNOWLEDGMENTS

Once again, I have been overwhelmed by the generosity and kindness of my readers. Before it was even published, 'The Hermitage' reached Number One on the Amazon UK Kindle Chart on the strength of their enthusiasm alone! Thank you all very much—I hope you enjoy this instalment in DCI Ryan's adventures, which straddles Northumberland and Florence, Italy. It represents the first 'globe-trotting' experience for Ryan and the gang, which was a lot of fun to write and I hope you have enjoyed their little foray to warmer climes!

As always, there are numerous people to thank. First and always, my husband, James. He is a constant source of love and encouragement, which is invaluable whenever I step into the unknown and begin to write a new story. My son, Ethan, is now a great reader himself (although, not of his mother's books quite yet!) and there is no happier moment for me than when he crawls onto my knee and reads me a story he has written himself! My parents, Susan and Jim, and my sister, Rachael, are constant sources of love and inspiration and I thank them for their unstinting positivity. I thank Dr Alexandra Baker, who was able to advise me on various medical questions, and the numerous retired police officers who kindly shared their insights into life as a real detective, so I could add colour and depth to the fictional ones on the page. Finally, my thanks to English Heritage, who do such a marvellous job looking after Warkworth Castle and Hermitage for the generations to come.

ABOUT THE AUTHOR

LJ Ross is an international bestselling author, best known for creating atmospheric mystery and thriller novels, including the DCI Ryan series of Northumbrian murder mysteries which have sold over five million copies worldwide.

Her debut, *Holy Island*, was released in January 2015 and reached number one in the UK and Australian charts. Since then, she has released a further eighteen novels, all of which have been top three global bestsellers and fifteen of which have been UK #1 bestsellers. Louise has garnered an army of loyal readers through her storytelling and, thanks to them, several of her books reached the coveted #1 spot whilst only available to pre-order ahead of release.

Louise was born in Northumberland, England. She studied undergraduate and postgraduate Law at King's College, University of London and then abroad in Paris and Florence. She spent much of her working life in London, where she was a lawyer for a number of years until taking the decision to change career and pursue her dream to write. Now, she writes full time and lives with her husband and son in Northumberland. She enjoys reading all manner of books, travelling and spending time with family and friends.

If you enjoyed reading *The Heritage*, please consider leaving a review online.

DCI Ryan will return in
LONGSTONE: A DCI RYAN MYSTERY.
Keep reading to the end of this book for a sneak preview!

LONGSTONE

A DCI RYAN MYSTERY

LJ ROSS

PROLOGUE

Autumn, 1995

Seahouses, Northumberland

The man they called 'Hutch' watched a woman wind her way through the punters in the main bar. His heart quickened at the sight of Gemma, just like the very first time he'd seen her, when they were only kids in the school playground. She was a woman now, no doubt about that. Tall and slim, with long blonde hair that fell in shining waves down her back, and the kind of self-assurance beautiful women often had; the kind that came from knowing they had only to look a certain way to have men like him falling at their feet.

The Cockle Inn was surprisingly busy for a Thursday night off-season and he watched as she fought her way past a rowdy crowd of locals, like an exotic flower trying to pick its way through thorny undergrowth, her eyes searching the sea of familiar faces as she made her way towards the bar.

Towards him.

He continued to pull pints, keeping his eyes firmly on his task.

"Hiya, Hutch," she said. "Y' seen Kris anywhere?"

His lips twisted.

"I thought you two were taking the boat out, today?" he said, buying himself more time.

"He was supposed to meet me at the harbour twenty minutes ago," she muttered, casting a quick glance up at the old wooden clock on the wall.

"Only twenty minutes?" He smiled. "I've waited longer than that for Kris to turn up."

When she smiled back, it was like a knife in his gut.

"I know," she said. "He's never on time. Maybe I should just head back down to the harbour and see if he's there now—"

"Might as well stay inside, where it's warm," he said quickly. "How about a drink?"

He moved towards the shelf where he kept the white wine he knew she preferred, but Gemma shook her head.

"No, not today," she said. "I'll just have a coke, thanks."

He shrugged.

"So, how've you been?"

Gemma slid onto a stool and folded her arms on the bar, only half listening.

"What? Oh, fine, thanks. Just trying to get *Shell Seekers* up and running but it's the wrong time of year. Hardly anybody wants to go diving when the weather's like this."

He made a rumbling sound of agreement. Autumn in Northumberland was not the best time to start a new diving school; only the keenest amateur and professional divers would want to go down into the freezing depths of the North Sea and they already had their own diving gear—and probably their own boats, too.

But he didn't have the heart to tell her any of that.

"They found another wreck near Beadnell," he said instead. "That's bound to attract a bit of new interest."

The North-Eastern coastline boasted a high number of shipwrecks; unfortunate galleons and cargo ships, paddle steamers and military vessels having been lost to its rocky shoreline and tempestuous weather over the centuries. Whenever a new wreck was found, it attracted salvage divers and marine archaeologists from around the world.

"Hopefully," she murmured. "I—"

Whatever she'd been about to say was cut off as a pair of sinewy arms wrapped around her waist.

"Here you are!"

Kristopher Reid—'The Kraken', to his friends—smiled broadly and then lowered his dark head to nuzzle at Gemma's neck with an elaborate growl, which made her laugh. Hutch turned away to busy himself with the next order, trying to block out the image of her enraptured face, trying to forget the way it had come alive when she'd caught sight of his younger brother.

"I've been looking for you," Kris lied, as he lifted his head. "D' you still fancy a run out?"

Gemma's forehead crinkled in a frown.

"I was down at the harbour. I thought we agreed to meet there—?"

"No, babe, we decided to meet *here*, don't you remember?" He gave her a patient look, then brushed his lips against hers. "Oh well, it doesn't matter now, does it?"

Looking into his deep brown eyes, she might have believed anything.

"Sure, it doesn't matter," she agreed, all smiles again. "We can go now, if you like?"

With a wink for his brother, Kris helped her down from the stool and, a moment later, they were gone. Very carefully, Hutch set the glass of coke down on a bar mat, untouched. He watched his brother leave with the woman he loved, watched his hand trail down her back and further still, watched her pause and reach up to kiss him, lost in the moment.

Then he turned away, unable to watch any longer.

Three days later

He found Gemma on the beach at Bamburgh, a mile or so north of Seahouses. It was practically deserted at that hour of the morning and she was sitting amongst the sand dunes staring out to sea, lost in her own thoughts. It was a beautiful spot; a golden, sandy beach swept out for miles beneath a mighty castle fortress perched on a craggy hilltop where, once, early kings of England had reigned.

"Gemma?"

She turned distractedly.

"Hutch?"

His feet sank into the fine sand as he made his way over the dunes to join her, turning up his collar against the sharp wind rolling in with the tide.

"Mind if I join you?"

Close up, he could see the ravages of tears that had dried in salty tracks against her pale skin.

"He hasn't come back," she said brokenly. "Kris left, and he hasn't come back."

"It's only been a couple of days," he replied. "You know what Kris is like—"

She closed her eyes and another tear escaped.

"This is different," she said, raggedly. "He—I—"

Unable to stop himself, he reached across to grasp her hand, finding it limp and cold.

"I-I told him about the baby," she whispered. "I told him he was going to be a father and, the next morning, he was gone."

Hutch felt something inside him shatter, some hitherto untouched area of his heart breaking into tiny pieces. His eyes strayed down to her belly, hidden beneath the folds of her jacket. It was still flat but, somewhere within, life had blossomed.

"What did Kris say when you told him?" he asked quietly, working hard to keep his anger in check.

She raised shaking fingers to wipe away fresh tears.

"He was…surprised, at first. Then, he seemed happy. I thought he was happy," she repeated, her voice breaking on the last word. "But I know he's been worrying about money, about the business."

Hutch knew it too. Kris had already come to him twice for hand-outs, although she knew nothing about that.

"We went to bed and, when I woke up in the morning, he was gone."

"And you've heard nothing since?"

She sniffed and shook her head.

"I know—I know he's not ready to be a father," she said. "But that doesn't mean he would be a bad one. I tried to tell him it would be okay, that we'd be *fine*."

Hutch said nothing.

"He hasn't gone to your mum's house," she continued. "I already rang her. I don't have his dad's number, though—"

The two brothers shared a mother but had different fathers.

"I'll find it," he said.

"But, if—if he isn't there, I don't know what to do. I don't know what *we'll* do."

His hand tightened on hers and he opened his mouth to say all that he longed to say, all the words of love he carried like a weight against his chest, but she was not ready to hear them.

"If Kris isn't there, we'll call the police," he told her. "If they can't help, maybe he doesn't *want* to be found."

His jaw tightened, thinking of the man who was his brother, of the years of disappointment and frustration.

Kris had been blessed with a strong body and mind—and the kind of good looks that meant he would never be lonely. But he took them for granted, never thinking of the hurt and destruction he could wield.

He hated him.

Hutch sighed deeply, trying to expel the feeling, to cast it out, but it returned stronger, waves upon waves of hatred coursing through his body as he looked upon the devastation of the woman he loved.

"You'll never be alone," he promised her. "I'll look after you."

But Gemma wasn't listening; she was far away, watching the sea roll back and forth against the shore in a timeless dance. On the far horizon, a boat bobbed across the water, only a speck against the sky that was awash with colour as the day came alive.

After a moment, she turned and looked at the man sitting beside her. There was a slight family resemblance, she thought. But where Kris's eyes were dark brown, Paul Hutchison's were a bright, bold blue and swirling with emotion.

She looked away, brushing away tears with the heels of her hands.

"I-I should get back," she whispered.

He helped her to her feet.

"Thank you," she said softly. "I—"

But she merely shook her head and turned away, walking across the dunes; away from him, and the life he had offered.

LOVE READING?

JOIN THE CLUB...

Join the LJ Ross Book Club to connect with a thriving community of fellow book lovers! To receive a free monthly newsletter with exclusive author interviews and giveaways, sign up at www.ljrossauthor.com or follow the LJ Ross Book Club on social media:

 #LJBookClubTweet

 @LJRossAuthor

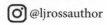 @ljrossauthor